9/22



*Harmony and High Heels*

# Other Books by Tracy Wolff

**A Hacked Novel**
*Every Move You Make*
*Every Breath You Take*

**The Hero Agenda Series**
*Relentless*

**The Ethan Frost Series**
*Flawed*
*Exposed*
*Addicted*
*Ruined*

**Shaken Dirty Book**
*Crash Into Me*
*Drive Me Crazy*
*Fade Into You*

**A Hotwired Novel**
*Accelerate*

**The Diamond Tycoons**
*Pursued*
*Claimed*

**An Extreme Risk Novel**
*Slashed*
*Shattered*
*Shredded*

**Other Books**
*Lovegame*

*Play Me: The Complete Story*
*Tie Me Down*
*Full Exposure*
*About the Baby*
*Healing Dr. Alexander*
*From the Beginning*
*Deserving of Luke*
*Unguarded*
*Beginning with Their Baby*
*Tease Me*
*The Christmas Present*
*From Friend to Father*
*A Christmas Wedding*
*No Apologies*

# Other Books By Katie Graykowski

The Marilyns Series
***Place Your Bets***
***Getting Lucky***

The Lone Stars Series
***Perfect Summer***
***Saving Grace***
***Changing Lanes***
***The Debra Dilemma***

PTO Murder Club Series
***Rest in Pieces***
***Blown to Pieces***

Texas Rose Ranch Series
***Texas Rose Forever***

# Harmony and High Heels

Tracy Wolff
&
Katie Graykowski

Formatting by Anessa Books

# Dedication

*For Andrea who almost got shanked by an Okinawa hooker*

# Chapter 1

Harmony Wright was bored, and that was never a good thing. The last time she'd been bored, there had been a fire... a very big one. She'd like to say it was accidental, but that would be a damn lie. And she never lied to herself. The rest of the world was a different story, though. She'd spent most of her thirty years making sure everyone believed exactly what she wanted them to believe, when she wanted them to believe it. She might not have inherited much from her mother, the queen bee of San Angelo society, but she'd definitely inherited the ability to keep up appearances... and to make those appearances look like reality.

For example, all of her mother's friends—and her enemies, for that matter—believed that Harmony was a perfect daughter. A chip off her mother's hard-as-diamonds block. And while Harmony herself viewed this as the truth too, it wasn't because she wore pastel sweater sets and pearls, just like Livinia Wright. It wasn't because she taught Sunday school or was secretary of the garden club and treasurer of the Junior League. And it certainly wasn't because she co-owned the Wright Way, which just happened to be the most successful bakery in San Angelo, Texas.

No, she wasn't a good daughter because of any of those reasons, Harmony mused as she picked up a custom-made cannoli shell. She was a good daughter because she co-owned this damned bakery with her mother and, despite numerous opportunities and even more provocations, had yet to smother the woman with one of their Wright Way frilly aprons or slip rat poison into her morning Southern Comfort coffee. For that she figured she deserved the Motherfucking Daughter of the Year Award. Maybe even a Nobel Prize. Did they make one of those for children who survived impossible mothers? She picked up another cannoli shell shaped like a Glock nine millimeter. If they didn't, they certainly should. In the very least she deserved some hazard pay.

She hummed a few bars of "Deep Six" by Marilyn Manson as she piped double-dark-chocolate ricotta filling into the barrel of the cannoli—which she called Take the Gun, Eat the Cannoli in honor of *The Godfather*—then set it down next to its fellow and picked up the next one. Gun cannoli might have seemed an unusual choice for a gentile, pearl-wearing baker, but this was Texas. Texans liked Jesus, guns, and football... not necessarily in that order.

Once she finished the cannoli, she moved on to a tray of her city-renowned donuts. It had taken years to perfect not only the recipe, but the various donut shapes as well. Each donut was a hand, with the fingers molded into a variety of different hand gestures, including the UT Hook 'em Horns and the Texas Aggie thumbs-up. She would have done a bear paw for Baylor, but come on, the bakery already had a bear claw, so it seemed redundant. Recently, she'd even designed a hand holding a lasso as an homage to her new brother-in-law, former quarterback and newly appointed offensive coordinator for the Fort Worth Wranglers. The fact that her personal favorite hand gesture—the stiff middle finger—was the only symbol she *didn't* sell was yet another example of what a fine, upstanding daughter she was.

It was with that thought in mind that she picked up the first donut hand and refashioned it so that the middle finger pointed skyward. Then she carried it to the fryer and with a practiced hand, gently set it in and fried it up. When it was golden and lovely, she fished it out, plopped it on a drying rack, and smothered it with sugary glaze.

She poured herself a cappuccino, leaned against the stainless-steel work table, and gave herself ten minutes to enjoy her bird and 'cino. It was all of 5:18 a.m. Anyone who was anyone was just now dragging their sorry ass home from a night out. But she was here playing the good girl and stuffing cannoli. She bit into the middle finger.

Yep, she was bored, and it was making her antsy. Very, very antsy.

Thank God her annual vacation with her twin sister, Lyric, was in less than two weeks. They traded off planning and booking the vacations, and this year it was all Harmony. She'd put together a fun-filled two weeks that involved both BASE jumping and heli-skiing in Chile. The fact that volcanic eruptions were at an all-time high in the Andes only made her vacation choice more exciting.

And God knew she needed a little excitement after spending last year's vacation in Williams Bay, Wisconsin. She and Lyric had spent two hellish weeks staring at stars through a telescope. While the place was beautiful, the fact that it was called "the birthplace of modern astrophysics" should have been a tip-off that the only person who'd be having fun was her astrophysicist sister. If Harmony hadn't talked a local hot air balloonist into letting her do a little bungee jumping from his balloon, and a local cowboy into letting her hog-tie him up, the trip would have been a total bust.

That so wasn't going to happen this year. With that thought in mind, Harmony finished up her donut, turned up the volume on her smartphone so that the walls shook with death metal, and got back to work.

An hour later, she turned off the death metal, zipped herself into a pink-and-black-striped sundress from Talbots, tied a starched, white lacy apron around her waist, and applied a respectable amount of respectable pink lipstick and just a hint of mascara.

As she checked herself out in the full-length mirror on the back of her office door—just to make sure that all remnants of early-morning Harmony were sublimated—the left corner of her mouth turned up in a crooked smile. She looked just like every other Livinia Wright disciple, which meant that no one but her twin—and a few one-night stands that all lived at least fifty miles outside of town—knew that underneath all of this Talbots Suburban Housewife were breast-to-thigh tattoos, nipple rings, a hood piercing, and a shit-ton of bad attitude.

Which was exactly how she wanted it.

Kenny G's saxophone hummed out of the bakery's speakers as she closed her office door, grabbed the last tray—cheesecake brownies—and went to open up for the day. She flicked on the light for the dining room and slipped the brownies into the glass refrigerated countertop display case.

Five of her "coffee club" stood waiting outside the door. Every single one of the men had fought in Vietnam, insisted on drinking rotgut Folgers, ate more sweets than they confessed to their wives, and downed bad coffee like it was water. Since she'd refused to buy them cheap coffee, they brought their own can, used their own Bunn coffeepot, and had their own table in the corner.

With a smile as sweet as her cream-cheese brownies, she unlocked the door and held it open for them. In seconds it was wrenched out of her hand. These men were real Texans, and they would rather eat nuclear waste direct from "Commie Russia" than have a door opened for them by a lady. It wasn't a slight against women's lib. Just a deep-seated fear that their mommas could see them from heaven and would know that they'd passed up an opportunity to be good Southern gentlemen.

"Good morning, Mr. Laramey." She stepped back and smiled. After Vietnam, Stan Laramey had moved to Hollywood and become a stuntman for Harrison Ford. After Stan had broken both of his legs shooting *The Fugitive*, he'd moved back to San Angelo to run his daddy's cattle ranch.

"Hey there, baby girl." His West Texas drawl held onto each word, making them slow as molasses and twice as thick. "Did you make them pecan sticky buns I like?"

"I made a whole two dozen, with extra orange zest just for you." She kissed his cheek.

"Today's his birthday, and I'd hate to hear him whine about not getting sticky buns on his birthday." It was Jeremiah Pearson. His polyester pants had swallowed a good two-thirds of his torso, and the tennis balls on his walker shushed on the tiled floor. "Nobody whines as much as Stan Laramey."

"I think you're right about that." John Horner, retired Texas Ranger turned cattle rancher filed in next. "Whiney little girls got nothin' on Stan."

"Now let's all just get along, gentlemen." Reverend J. Cooley Sadek was next. Since he was a man of the cloth, everyone looked to him as the peacemaker. Of course, they also looked to him to hold the bets for all sporting events, to run the Tuesday night poker game, and to drive the River Valley Baptist Church van when the coffee club took their monthly trips to the casino in Eagle Pass.

"We're getting along. No one's murdered anyone lately." Lucas McDonald, Civil War enthusiast and ex-history teacher at San Angelo High, hunched over his cane and shuffled into the bakery. He gave Jeremiah Pearson the stink eye. "Even though it ain't for lack of trying."

"What did I do?" Mr. Pearson was all innocence.

"Them trash cans of yours been down at the end of your driveway for going on a week." Mr. McDonald took neighborhood beautification to a whole new level. He'd been known to take a yardstick and measure the length of his neighbors' grass.

"I just had both of my knees replaced. Walking is kinda painful, especially if I'm dragging a trash can behind me." Mr. Pearson popped the top on the Folgers, stuffed a coffee filter into the Bunn, measured out the coffee, and hit the brew button.

"You're here, ain't ya?" According to the town in general, Mr. McDonald had always been an ass. The only reason anyone put up with him was because twice a year he ran the best Civil War reenactment in Texas—maybe even in the whole South.

Harmony mashed her lips together to keep from grinning. She kinda liked that about him. No one ran over Lucas McDonald, and God knew many had thought about it when they were behind the wheel and he was crossing the road.

"Life's too short for you to act like a snapping turtle." Reverend Sadek was a terminally cheerful person. More than once, Harmony had wanted to choke him with the chain holding the cross around his neck. It was only the fear of the wrath of Livinia Wright that had held her back.

She could see in his eyes that Mr. McDonald wanted to punch Reverend Sadek. The chocolate macadamia nut cookies he favored were totally on the house today.

She closed the door after them. "I'm guessing y'all are ordering the usual?"

Harmony didn't know why she even bothered to ask. They always ordered the same things.

They all "yes ma'am"-ed in unison.

"Are we really celebrating your birthday, Stan?" Mr. McDonald eased down into his chair at their table. "You're two hundred years old. Why are we celebrating your birthday?"

"You're seventeen days older than I am and we celebrated your birthday," Stan Laramey said around the toothpick that was always sticking out of the left side of his mouth.

"Yeah, but people like me. Nobody likes you." Besides harassing humanity at large, Mr. McDonald's favorite hobby was being cheap. He didn't want to have to pick up Laramey's tab because it was his birthday. Everyone knew not to use the bathroom at McDonald's house, because he actually divided the two-ply toilet paper into two rolls. Of course, he was living on a teacher's pension …

Harmony smiled to herself as she gathered their usual order. Cannoli for Reverend Sadek, eclairs for Pearson, sand tarts for Horner, and one pan of piping-hot sticky buns complete with a birthday candle for the table.

She walked through the doorway that led to the kitchen. She grabbed a pot holder and pulled the sticky buns out of the warm oven. Their orangey, cinnamon scent filled the air. Harmony picked up the blue birthday candle she'd set out on the counter, lit it, and carried the pan out front. She drew the line at singing.

"Happy Birthday, Mr. Laramey." She set the pan in front of him. "Make a wish."

"How come I didn't get no candle for my birthday?" McDonald folded his thin arms and stuck out his bottom lip.

These men might have the combined age of half a millennium, but they were still little boys. Men, no matter how old they grow, are all still little boys.

"She likes him more than she likes you." John Horner grinned. "She has great taste."

"That's not very nice." McDonald continued to pout.

Harmony set their favorites in front of each man as Laramey blew out his candle. When she got to Mr. McDonald, she set his plate of chocolate macadamia nut cookies down in front of him and leaned over and whispered, "You didn't get a candle because you're not as needy as Mr. Laramey. I hate to see a grown man cry, and we both know he's a crier."

"You're a good girl." McDonald patted her hand. "Must have gotten that from your daddy, 'cause your momma is a menace."

Mr. McDonald certainly knew how to hold a grudge. A million years ago, back when he'd taught her mother history in high school, something bad had happened in his class. He blamed Momma and had hated her ever since. Maybe that was why Harmony loved the old man.

"You're such a good girl." Reverend Sadek put his liver-spotted hand on her forearm.

"Thank you." She smiled. Every time he said it, it was a stroke to the old ego. If they only knew she regularly drove to the next county over to raise hell, they wouldn't be so quick to call her a good girl.

It wasn't that she was afraid of telling the world the truth, it was more that she enjoyed the dual life. San Angelo was a small town. Airing her dirty lingerie here wouldn't be nearly as much fun as secretly wearing it under all of this good girl. Or so she liked to tell herself …

Three hours later, just as she'd hit the late-morning lull before the lunch rush, Neil Diamond's "Cherry Cherry" buzzed out of her phone. Harmony rolled her eyes. It was her sister's new ringtone. God, she hated that damn song.

She pulled the phone out of her pocket and hit answer. "Are you packing your ski parka?"

"Ummm." Lyric took a deep breath and let it out slowly. "Harm, I... um, kind of can't go."

"What's wrong?" Harm leaned against the front counter and watched Clara Nutter, her assistant, wipe down tables. "Are you sick? Or pregnant?"

"Neither." Lyric sounded embarrassed, and rightly so, as she continued, "Heath won't let me go."

"Excuse me? Tell me I heard you wrong. Tell me you didn't just say that your husband forbade you from doing something. Gloria Steinem would be rolling in her grave if she heard you say that." God knew, subservience pissed Harmony off—well, unless she was the one demanding subservience.

"Gloria Steinem isn't dead."

"Not yet, but if she hears that you let your husband order you around she just might keel over." Harmony was pretty sure she was going to keel over herself. That or her head was going to spin around and she was going to spit pea soup all over everything. She ducked back into the kitchen for some privacy. "Women haven't fought for equality since the beginning of time so that you can wimp out on our vacation at the last minute. What the hell is wrong with your husband?"

Heath had just made the top of her shit list. Which wasn't exactly a change, since he'd been there since high school. But after seeing how happy he made Lyric these days, she'd been just about ready to forgive him for being such an ass when they were eighteen.

"Gloria Steinem doesn't care about me." Lyric sounded resigned, like her fate was always going to be at the hands of someone else.

That wasn't okay.

"Gloria Steinem cares about all womankind, no men, they can kiss her ass... Your husband forbidding you to go on vacation so he can keep you barefoot and pregnant in the kitchen—"

"I am not pregnant." Lyric enunciated every word like Harmony was hard of hearing. "He didn't forbid us from going on vacation. In fact, he wants to pay for us to go to Paris or London or the Caribbean. Whatever you want."

Paris, London, and the Caribbean were lame. "Where I want is to go is BASE jumping in—"

"That's what Heath isn't sure about."

"What?" Harmony all but spit the word out of her mouth. "Why?"

"When I mentioned how I broke my leg that time we were skiing in New Zealand—"

"That was a freak accident. Your ski got caught in the lift chair. If that tree hadn't broken your fall, it could have been a lot worse." She propped one fist on her hip as she contemplated the best way to murder a six-foot-five, nearly three-hundred-pound man. "Did you tell him that?"

"I don't think that would have helped our case." Lyric was always the voice of reason—a.k.a. a total pain in the ass.

"Heath Montgomery is *not* going to push us around. We are going on this vacation." She needed this vacation. Pretending to be her mother's younger clone was one thing, but doing it all the time—with only the occasional trip to the next county over to be herself—was not okay. She counted on these trips to let her hair down, to show the world—and herself—that she hadn't gotten lost no matter how many years she'd spent kissing Livinia Angleton Wright's pasty, white, upper-class ass.

"We are," Lyric agreed. "I swear. We just need to pick a different spot, someplace where there's a much lower chance of me dying."

"Your chance of dying is just as great at home, or have you forgotten about the planetarium bouncy house disaster?" Her sister had almost suffocated when a blow-up planetarium had collapsed at her neighbor's kid's birthday party.

"When they said they'd rented a planetarium for Billy's birthday, how was I supposed to know that it was a converted bouncy house? Who's ever heard of a bouncy house planetarium?" Lyric took a deep breath. "Anyway, that's exactly my point. If I can almost die just doing normal things, how can I be expected to survive BASE jumping?"

Lyric was in logical PhD mode. It really pissed Harmony off.

"Is that your point or Heath's point?" Harmony's annoyance was turning to anger—and to hurt—deep inside of her.

There was a long silence. "Heath's," Lyric reluctantly admitted.

"Wow. Married three months and already he's got you whipped." Harmony was never getting married. Marriage seemed to be a license for men to push women around.

"That's not fair, Harm, and you know it." Her sister sounded resigned. Another point against marriage.

"What I know is that you're my sister. My twin sister. You know more than anyone how much I need this trip—"

Call-waiting beeped, interrupting Harmony before she could work herself up to full steam. Which was probably a good thing, considering she didn't want to say anything she might regret. After all, it wasn't Lyric's fault she was married to an ass. Or, at least, not completely Lyric's fault.

Harmony knew what she needed to do. "I'm coming to visit. I'll be there this afternoon. Heath and I need to nail down some boundaries. He may be your husband, but I'm your sister. Sister's before misters."

She'd been blinded by his love for her sister, but this macho madness ended today. Men didn't dictate anything to the Wright sisters.

"Look, I've got to go. Someone is calling on the other line. It's probably a customer." Harmony was running a bakery. She didn't have time for her sister to be wimpy.

"Harm, wait—"

"I'll call you back when I'm done taking the order." More like when she finally had her mouth under control—which, come to think of it, might be never. Still, she had to give it a shot. The last thing she wanted to do was alienate her sister and best friend.

Clicking off without bothering to say good-bye, she moved right into her usual spiel on the other line. "Thank you for calling the Wright Way. This is Harmony speaking.

How may I make your day a little sweeter?" She tried not to gag as she said the last line—it was totally her mother's brainstorm, and though Livinia wasn't here, she had ways of finding out if Harmony was doing things her way. FBI interrogators could learn a thing or two from Livinia Wright.

"Is this Harmony Wright?" the slightly nasally voice on the other end said.

"It is." She narrowed her eyes, preparing to unload her bad mood on whatever unfortunate telemarketer had chosen the worst moment to call. Bitch-slapping telemarketers was so much fun.

"Please hold for Holly Braeburn."

Nasally woman was getting on Harm's nerves. "You called me. I'm not holding for anyone—" She broke off as the name registered. Holly was the woman who had run *Cupcake Cage Match*, the Las Vegas cupcake war competition she'd secretly participated in last fall. It was part mixed martial arts and part *Cupcake Wars*.

Harmony had won the competition—of course she had, her cupcake recipes and her cage-fighting skills were unparalleled in the baking world. The ten thousand in prize money she had won was what she was using to finance the trip to Chile.

She barely had time to wonder what Holly could possibly be calling about, when the woman herself came on the line. "Harmony, how are you?"

"I'm good, thanks." She knew she sounded cautious, but she really hoped Holly wasn't calling because she needed the money back. Then again, with the way her day was going... anything was possible.

"I'm so glad to hear that. We need you in tip-top shape for the show we want to do." Holly was all business. Harm really liked that about Holly.

"The show?" More cupcake MMA fighting sounded good to her.

"Yes. We're looking to liven things up over here at Food Network, and when I started thinking about a new baking show, you were the first person who came to mind." It sounded like Holly was shuffling paper on the other end of the phone.

"A new baking show?" Harmony knew she sounded like a parrot, but she was having a hard time keeping up.

"Yes, we want to call it *Badass Baker*, and we want you to be our resident badass. Kind of like *Ace of Cakes*, but with more sex appeal and more accessible recipes that the average baker can pull off. Kind of a Kat Von D meets Betty Crocker kind of thing."

# Chapter 2

"*Badass Baker*?" Harmony repeated. Damn it, she really had to stop repeating everything that came out of Holly's mouth. But seriously? "My own show?"

She loved Kat Von D. Personal hero and style inspiration.

But her own show? These things didn't happen in real life. TV producers didn't just call you up when you lived the most boring life possible in itty-bitty San Angelo and tell you they wanted to give you your own show.

"Absolutely your own show." There was a smile in Holly's voice. "This can't be that much of a surprise, can it? You dominated *Cupcake Cage Match*, and not just because of your baking and fighting skills. You have to know how much charisma you have. You're sexy and beautiful and have a wicked sense of humor. The camera loves you—and so does the audience."

Harmony glanced down at her pink-and-black Talbots dress and sensible pumps. Not much sex appeal or charisma in this getup, that was for sure. And absolutely no sense of humor. "I don't know that I fully understand the show concept."

"We want something edgy. All you have to do is just be your charmingly badass self." Holly sounded so sure.

She thought about the middle finger donut she'd eaten for breakfast that morning, and again looked down at her soccer mom dress. "I don't know about the charm, but I have plenty of bad attitude." A terrible thought struck. "I wouldn't have to go on *Chopped* as a judge, would I?"

Holly laughed. "Not unless you wanted to."

"Good. I'm not eating things made out of Skittles and lamb hearts." This was a dream that she hadn't even known she'd wanted coming true. "Will I have complete creative control? I refuse to bake complicated, weird things that no one has ingredients for and wouldn't want to eat anyway. And there will be *no* kale." There were some things a woman couldn't compromise on, and kale was one of them. Just because everyone in California thought it was manna from heaven didn't mean that the rest of the world wanted a thousand kale recipes. "And rose water. Where the hell do you even buy rose water. If you can't get the ingredients at your local IGA, I don't make it on my show."

Damn—her show? She was starting to sound like a diva.

The bitchy comments just kind of came out without her permission. Like being on the phone with someone who knew the real her—and liked her enough to offer Harmony her own show—had totally ruined the years and years she'd spent hiding her thoughts behind a mask.

Holly didn't seem to mind, though. She was laughing like Harmony was the funniest thing since cat videos. "That's the kind of comment we want on the show. We love that you don't take any shit from anyone and do things your way. Also, we love that you run a small-town bakery—it's one more dichotomy that the audience will just eat up."

Harmony loved the word dichotomy. More people should use it in conversation.

"In fact, we want to film in San Angelo—partly in your bakery and partly in a studio we set up for you. To your specifications, of course—although we do have some design ideas already. We want it to look as badass as you are, so we're thinking black and chrome with red accents.

Everything will be sleek and sexy—including your appliances and bakeware. If we do this right—and we will—we'll be able to launch a whole Badass Baker product line. Everything from baking pans to temporary tattoos."

"Temporary tattoos?" She wasn't sure why, but of everything Holly had just said, that was what Harmony's mind latched onto. How could the secretary of the San Angelo garden club get on TV and hock temporary tattoos? Livinia would have apoplexy.

Damn, that was reason enough to do it.

"Absolutely." Holly was very excited. "We'll design them to mimic your own tattoos, so women can feel as badass as you are when they put them on. I'm telling you, Harmony, this show is going to be big. Huge, even. Between the money you make from it and what it does to drive traffic to the Wright Way... you're going to be richer and more famous than you ever dreamed."

But she'd never dreamed of being rich or famous. All she'd ever wanted was to be herself... and to have her family love her anyway. But she'd never had that option. Lyric had taken up all the zany in the family, just like she'd taken up all the chances to make mistakes.

With her tranquilizers and her Southern Comfort and her miles upon miles of ridiculous rules for women, Momma was already close enough to the edge without both of her daughters going hog wild. Harmony had stepped in sometime in junior high and towed the Livinia Angleton Wright line. It had kept Momma happy, which had kept Daddy happy, which had kept the heat off of Lyric, with her too big brain and her too sensitive soul.

"Harmony? Are you still there?"

"I am. I need to think about this …" Yes, she wanted it, but how was she supposed to be a badass baker in a town that thought of her as the good girl?

"What's there to think about? We'll pay you ten thousand dollars an episode, we'll come to you so your life won't even be disrupted during the first season, we'll put your bakery on the map and turn you into a star. Just say yes. You know you want to." Holly knew she was handing Harmony the brass ring.

Of course she wanted this. Who wouldn't? She'd never thought about having her own show before, had only gone on *Cupcake Cage Match* because she'd wanted to blow off some steam and it had looked like a fun way to earn some traveling money. No more Talbots dresses and no more Junior League meetings—that was reason enough to say yes. But how would that work?

"I know that you're only co-owner of the bakery, so we'll have to get the other owner—your mother, isn't it?—to sign the filming waiver."

Harmony could practically hear all of the wind being sucked out of her sails. Momma would *never* sign off on *Badass Baker*. Maybe *Prim and Proper Baker*, but who wanted to watch that?

"Oh, and we're thinking of trademarking your catchphrase, 'the Wright Way,' so we'll need her to sign off on that too, since it's the name of the bakery. But that won't be a problem." Holly sounded so sure. If she only knew.

It was going to be a huge problem. A gigantic problem. One of infinite proportions. There was about as much of a chance of her mother signing off on *Badass Baker* as her mother joining an outlaw biker gang. The mental image was pretty funny, but hell wouldn't only have to freeze over, Jesus was going to have to change his forwarding address to 666 Satan Avenue for that to happen. Nope, Momma wouldn't be on board with this.

Not in a million years.

Even if Harmony decided she wanted to blow her whole family dynamic straight to hell—which she wasn't sure she did, no matter how she felt about Momma—there was no way in hell Livinia would ever agree to let a show like *Badass Baker* film in her bakery. And in her mother's mind, the Wright Way was very much *her* bakery, no matter that Harmony was the one who showed up there every morning at 3:00 a.m. to do the actual baking—and created all of the recipes and did all of the work.

Just the idea of her youngest daughter showing up on a TV show in leather hot pants, all tatted up, and with attitude to spare, would be enough to send her mother spiraling straight to the bottom of her bottle of Southern Comfort. Not to mention, the world's Xanax supply would take a huge hit. With Thanksgiving and Christmas just around the corner, Xanax was the one thing keeping in-laws around the country from serious bodily harm.

Holly had obviously taken her continued silence as encouragement, because she continued, "Why don't you let us come down there? We'll set up at the bakery, put together a mock show just so you can see what we're thinking of doing, let you see how much the camera loves you. Maybe film part of the pilot. Then, if you don't like what we're doing or the direction we're going, I promise I won't push you. You can stay a secret in San Angelo and we will look elsewhere for our Badass Baker."

"You're willing to do that?" Harmony massaged the tension at the back of her neck. She wanted this, but convincing her mother was going to be difficult. "Doesn't it cost a lot of money to come down here and film a show?"

Holly laughed. "Well, it isn't cheap, that's for sure. But that's how much I believe in you, Harmony. I'll set everything up, get my bosses to sign off on it, and see you in three weeks. All you have to do is say yes."

"Yes." It was out before she could stop it.

Butterflies started fluttering in her stomach... and she never got butterflies. She never got nervous. What the hell was there to get nervous about, after all, when you had nothing to lose—and nothing to look forward to beyond a two-week vacation every other year?

And that was the problem, wasn't it? It was why she felt so testy all the time—and why her stomach was flipping all over the place now. Because for the first time in longer than she could remember, she actually wanted something for herself. And it was within her reach—all she had to do was reach out and grab it.

But could she do it? Could she really throw away a lifetime of pretense and show the world—and her mother—who she really was?

Damn right she could. The Badass Baker wouldn't hesitate in a situation like this, and neither would Harmony. Livinia and her Xanax were just going to have to get on board. Because the Wright Way was about to become one Badass Bakery.

# Chapter 3

An hour later, Harmony wasn't so sure she was a badass anything. Dealing with her mother was like handing nitroglycerine. She was unstable, explosive, and went off for no good reason.

This must have been how Custer felt when he realized he wasn't getting out alive.

"*Badass Baker*?" Her mother actually choked on the words. Or maybe she was choking on her too-large sip of Southern Comfort. It was hard to tell, what with all of her pacing and drinking and coming as close to ranting as her ladylike Southern drawl would let her. "That's not acceptable, Harmony. That's just not acceptable. And where would they even get the idea that you would be interested in a show like that?" She made it sound like Harmony would be smoking crack and screwing johns on camera.

Her fingers went to twisting at the pearls around her neck, a sure sign of her agitation. And the glazed, somewhat frantic look in her mother's eye said it was real agitation, not the fake stuff she manufactured on a regular basis to keep her husband and her oldest daughter towing the company line.

"It's just a gimmick. Something to distinguish it from all the sweet-baking shows out there." Even Harmony didn't buy that one.

"What's wrong with sweet-baking shows? People love watching good old hometown shows with lovely Southern women showing off their cooking skills. Who do they think will actually watch a show with some woman dressed like a tramp and pretending to be a badass?" Her mother looked her up and down. "There's nothing badass about you, Harmony Marie Wright. A fact for which I am eternally grateful."

"I want this." The words slipped out before she knew she was going to say them. But once they were out, she didn't regret them. She'd spent her entire life hiding who she was—and what she wanted—from her family in order to keep the peace. She was tired of hiding, tired of pretending to be less than who she was. "I really want this."

If Livinia were really the loving mother she pretended to be, that would have been enough to persuade her, but Livinia's love had limits—great big ones.

"You don't know what you want, Harmony." Her mother turned away and poured another two fingers of Southern Comfort. It wasn't ladylike to swig directly from the bottle. "If you're seriously considering parading around a television set in leather and high heels, you definitely don't know what's good for you. Or for this family."

"Nobody said I was going to be parading around in leather." Leather was always a good choice. Black leather pants or shorts, depending on the season, could be her signature look for each show. Add different pairs of crazy-ass heels and sexy tops each time and she could totally show off her inner—and her outer—badass.

"I certainly hope not," her mother replied. "Every Southern lady worth her salt knows leather is only good for accessories."

Harmony wanted to scream. Or to beat her head against the wall. Or to grab her mother by the throat and beat her head against the wall. Was an overbearing parent why Lizzie Borden had picked up her ax and gone on a chopping spree?

Harmony would have liked nothing better than to shake those ridiculous Southern manners right out of her mother and replace them with some actual common sense. And compassion. And basic understanding for someone outside of her very rigid social circle.

Harmony had resigned herself to the life she led a long time ago, had accepted the secrets and the sneaking two towns over to let her hair down as just something she had to do to survive. Now she wanted more for herself. She wanted her own life. Was that too much to ask?

"I think we should try it." Harmony wasn't going to give up. This was too important to her. "Think of all the business the bakery could get from being in a national show on the Food Network. We could singlehandedly put San Angelo on the map."

Harmony might be the good daughter, but she knew how to work her mother.

Livinia stopped pacing. "What do you mean?"

"It will be just like what HGTV did with *Fixer Upper*. *Fixer Upper* has made Waco, Texas, a tourist destination. Wouldn't you like to be one-half of the reason tourists flock to San Angelo?" If Harmony knew anything, it was that her mother was the queen of vanity.

"I don't know …" Her mother looked like she was weighing the good with the bad.

"People would come from all over to watch us film." She had no idea if that was true or even possible, but she'd deal with that later. "Our business would grow. The online orders alone are going to be huge. Think about all of the marketing opportunities." Harmony was smart enough to leave out the temporary tattoo revenue stream. "If the show is successful enough, we would be TV stars." Well, not Momma. Holly didn't even know Momma existed. "Think of how much that increase in tourism could benefit the whole city. Restaurants, gas stations, small businesses. And it would all be because of the Wright Way."

Momma's eyes lit up.

She knew she was laying it on a little thick, but subtle wasn't going to get the job done here. Not when Livinia would love nothing more than to be San Angelo's biggest benefactor. If the Junior League and the garden club knew she was single-handedly—because in Livinia's head, this would all be about her—responsible for increasing tourism and city revenue, she would be even more revered than she already was.

Harmony could see her mother's mind working, could see her calculating the subsequent rise in her status that would come if she signed the stupid waiver. She was just starting to congratulate herself on finding the one thing that would make this palatable to Livinia when her mother slammed her cut-glass tumbler down.

"And what would happen when all these people showed up and found you looking like this?" She gestured to Harmony's matching lavender twinset, straight midi skirt, and string of pearls. "What happens when they find out there is nothing badass about you?" She said "badass" in the same whisper she used when talking about cancer or a fatal traffic accident or a debutante's teen pregnancy and subsequent fall from grace.

Harmony didn't know if it was the tone that did it or if it was the look on her mother's face. Maybe it was a combination of both. Or maybe it was the fact that she was sick of being underestimated, sick of hiding, sick of pretending to be something that she wasn't just to make her mother happy.

Whatever it was, it had adrenaline pumping through her. It had annoyance and frustration, and the desire to do something just for herself just because she wanted to, mixing with that adrenaline.

"Sign the waiver." She held her mother's gaze, and this time it wasn't a question.

Livinia's perfect salon-arched brows hit her forehead. "Don't be ridiculous. This is a terrible idea and there's no way I'm going to let you be a part of it. There's certainly no way I'm going to let my bakery be a part of it."

"It's my bakery too." This time, Harmony was doing what she wanted.

Her mother's eyes turned the size of macaroons. "Excuse me?"

"The Wright Way is my bakery too. I built it from nothing." If her mother wanted a fight, Harmony was all in.

"Don't you mean you built it from the seventy-five thousand dollars I gave you to build it?" Her mother's tone was all don't-sass-me-little-girl.

"I want to do the show." She was doing the show.

"Yes, well, I want a lot of things, Harmony Marie. Doesn't mean I'm going to get them." Her mother nodded her head like it was final.

Harmony gritted her teeth so hard it was a wonder she didn't grind them to dust. "I want this. This is *my* dream. Shouldn't that be enough for you? Don't you want me to be happy?"

Harmony's happiness was something her mother had probably never given any thought to.

Livinia sighed like she was tired of dealing with a petulant child. "If you want a show that badly, we can see about putting a proposal together for one. Something tasteful and sedate. Something that showcases our shop just the way it is." Her mother held her arms out like Julie Andrews in *The Sound of Music*.

The bakery was decorated in Early-American Snotty Debutante. It had crystal chandeliers, subdued lighting, and a shit-load of white. Harmony had always hated the décor but had tolerated it because changing it wasn't worth the fight.

Her mother poured another glass of Southern Comfort, then shuddered delicately as she raised the liqueur to her lips. "Just think of what a show like *Badass Baker* would do to your reputation. And more importantly, to the family's reputation. I won't have it, Harmony. I just won't have it."

"So, that's it, then? You won't have it, so I don't get a vote?" There wasn't a chance in hell Harmony was giving this up.

"Of course you get a vote, dear. But I own fifty-five percent of the bakery, so no matter how you vote, mine trumps yours. And I can assure you, there is absolutely no way I'm signing that waiver for them to use my name—my bakery—on that dirty little show."

Dirty little show? It wasn't like they were making bakery porn. Was that even a thing?

"*Your* name. *Your* bakery. *Your* reputation." Nothing ever changed. The world revolved around Livinia Angleton Wright, and the rest of the world was just there to serve her.

"Yes, Harmony. My reputation is—"

"All you care about. Is it really more important to you than my dream? Is it more important to you than my happiness?" She knew the answer even as she asked the questions.

She'd spent her entire adult life living a lie so that she could live within the narrow parameters her mother set. Hadn't she hidden everything she was away, everything she wanted to be, so that she wouldn't damage her mother's perception of herself and her family?

She'd done it all so that Lyric could have a life, so that her sister could stop beating herself up trying to fit into a cookie cutter mold that she never stood a chance of fitting into. But Lyric had a life now. She had a husband who adored her and a job she loved. She didn't need Harmony to protect her anymore, didn't need Harmony to keep being something she wasn't in a misguided attempt to please a woman who could never be pleased.

That stopped now. It stopped right this second. Because if the family reputation was so important to her mother, if it really was more important to her than her daughter's happiness and career success, then there was only one thing to do.

It was time to show her mother just how much of a Badass Baker she really was.

# Chapter 4

Dalton Mane kicked back in his chair and looked out his office window at the Wranglers' brand-new practice field. They'd moved into the new training complex just a few weeks ago, and he couldn't be happier. Lasso Stadium had been his brainchild when he'd first come to the Wranglers more than a decade ago, and it had taken nearly seven years to build. And it was glorious, worth every penny of its one-billion-dollar price tag. This was more than just a sports stadium, it was a real shot in the arm for the local economy. God knew the price of oil was putting a good bit of the state of Texas out of work. But this mixed-use complex was providing much-needed jobs. At least, the city council thought so, and that was why they were giving him the key to the city next week at the grand opening cocktail party and ribbon-cutting ceremony. No expense had been spared and nothing was too extravagant. Even the team owner, Barry Lamont, had convinced his wife to attend, and she hated her husband so much she lived in another country.

With the best practice field in the NFL, state of the art training, physical therapy, and even medical facilities for the players, luxurious offices for running the business side of the team, a hotel complete with a two-thousand-spot parking garage, a team library, a museum, and Wranglers shops open to the public, the complex was everything he could have asked for and more. It certainly showcased just how far the Super Bowl winning Wranglers had come from their humble beginnings.

Kind of like him.

Kicking his feet up on his desk—a luxury he rarely allowed himself—Dalton couldn't help thinking that in his time here, he'd come nearly as far as the Wranglers had. And nearly as quickly. Fifteen years ago, he'd been a rough-around-the-edges business major with a questionable background and zero experience. He'd also been full of ambition, football knowledge, and the ability to deal swiftly and capably with rooms filled with testosterone-fueled giants. All of which had led him to where he was right now—namely, sitting behind the general manager's desk in the offices of the reigning Super Bowl champions.

It was a good life, if you could get it.

He took one more minute to survey his domain, and to check out the report on Blake Johnson, the quarterback they'd picked up to replace Heath Montgomery when he'd been injured. Johnson had a bad attitude that was almost as impressive as his throwing arm. But bad attitudes were nothing new to Dalton, and he knew exactly how to handle this one.

With that thought in mind, he swung his feet off his desk. Enough with patting himself on the back. It was time to get to work.

But before he could do much more than log back into his computer, his desk phone buzzed and the efficient voice of Eleanor Sanchez, his overprotective personal assistant, came over the intercom. "Coach Montgomery is here to see you."

Eleanor ran the office and him with a French-manicured iron hand. He was pretty sure that given the chance, she could run the world with one hand tied behind her back. He counted it as plain good fortune that she wasn't power hungry. She'd been with him for years, and the last thing he wanted was to lose her to plans for world domination. Especially when he had his own plans to dominate his corner of the world. He'd be named NFL commissioner within the next decade, or die trying.

But those were plans for another day. He pushed the intercom button. "Send him in."

As he waited for the arrival of the quarterback turned offensive coordinator, Dalton straightened the two pens next to his legal pad and checked to make sure his nameplate was square. Appearances were important in this game, as was control. He'd spent years learning how to keep up both.

Pasting a guarded smile on his face, he watched as Heath strolled into his office in the royal-blue-colored shirt worn by most of the coaching staff, tailored khakis, and a pair of worn, brown cowboy boots. The grounds staff had been complaining about the boots ruining the playing field, but Heath had them in his contract and he wasn't relenting. All of which had led the groundskeeper, Jacob Bennet—who was usually the nicest, most pliant guy in the world—to declare war on Heath's cowboy boots.

But bigger wars than this had been fought—and settled—from Dalton's state-of-the-art office chair, and this one would be as well. Babysitting might be the most unpleasant task of his position, but he took it as seriously as he took all of his other roles. After all, he'd worked hard to make sure that nothing went on in the Wranglers organization that he wasn't aware of and in control of.

"Heath, have a seat." Dalton gestured toward the two overstuffed, gargantuan black leather chairs on the other side of his desk. He'd started with normal-sized chairs all those years ago, but pro football players didn't fit into normal-sized anything, and eventually he'd gotten tired of having to replace broken furniture.

"Hey, man, what's up?" Heath grinned as they shook hands. "If it's about the boots," he pointed to his feet, "they aren't leaving my feet." He put his hand over his heart. "I'm a Southern gentleman and I have principles. I take my hat off inside, open doors for ladies, use a knife and fork to eat, and I wear cowboy boots. It's the first Texas Commandment—Thou Shalt Wear Cowboy Boots. I don't expect you to understand it, as you were born across state lines, but it is a rule. I don't make the rules, but I do abide by them."

Dalton was born in Oklahoma but had lived in Texas his entire life. He mashed his lips together to keep from smiling. Heath was so damn likeable that most of the time it was damn hard to lay down the law—it had been that way even when he'd been a player. Not that Dalton had any plans—or any desire—to take away Heath's Texan civil liberties. Why would he do that when he could use them to his advantage instead?

"I have no intention of taking those boots away. Not when I know how much you love them. The groundskeepers can find a way around the mess they make."

Heath grinned. "You're a good man, Dalton. I appreciate your support with this matter."

"You've always got my support, Heath. You know that. Which is why we're cutting Shawntel Green. He's a hell of a running back, but I know you're fed up with his diva ways. The last thing I want is to make your job harder." Green was also too expensive and a total ass, but Dalton felt no need to share his opinion on the subject. Better to let Heath think he was making two concessions before he took something away—especially something Heath loved as much as his favorite wide receiver.

Looking the big Texan in the eye, he lowered the boom. "We also need to cut Marcus Dunbrook."

Heath looked like Dalton had just reached across the desk and slapped him in the face. "No way are we cutting Marcus."

"You know better than anyone that he rode the bench most of last season. And last month at training camp he couldn't keep up." He did his best to look unconcerned, even as he watched Heath for signs of how this fight was going to go. Dalton liked it when things ran smoothly, but he'd learned to brawl before he'd learned to walk, and he'd never run from a fight since.

Heath didn't say anything for long seconds, but when he finally spoke up, he sounded determined. "I agree that he's a little out of shape, but when he's on, he's got the best hands in the game. Certainly the best hands we've got—"

"He *had* the best hands. He fumbles more balls than he holds onto these days." Dalton slid the file folder in front of him to Heath. "And he failed his latest drug test... again. Opioids this time."

Heath's face fell. "Can't we suspend him for a few games and send him to rehab? He's got five kids." But the look on his face said he knew he'd already lost the battle.

"We're beyond game suspension here, Heath. We've sent him to rehab... twice. It didn't work. This time, the dosage was more than he could claim a medical exemption for. He has a problem. We've done more for him than he's done for himself. It's time to move on."

Finally, Heath shook his head. "I'll tell him. It should come from me."

Dalton nodded, pleased with how the whole thing had gone. Heath was turning out to be a stand-up guy.

"Have you given any thought to—" Heath broke off as his phone rang. Reaching into his pocket for it, he said, "I know it's unprofessional to pull out your phone during a meeting, but Lyric is flying home today from Hawaii and she's supposed to call me when she lands. Considering her bad luck when it comes to planes, I just want to make sure she's okay."

"Family first." Dalton smiled. He liked Lyric. She was smart as hell, and—despite being a bit of an absentminded professor—she managed to keep Heath in line. Little remained of the hell-raising ladies' man he used to be, and that was something Dalton could definitely get behind. Especially since it made his job so much easier.

"Hey, baby. How was your flight? Did you make it without duct tape this time?"

Dalton watched as Heath's smile turned to a scowl. "What the hell are you doing with my wife's phone?"

Dalton sat forward as threats of high-profile kidnappings bounced around in his head. "Is everything okay?"

"Yes." Heath rolled his eyes even as he covered the phone with the palm of his hand. "It's just my crazy sister-in-law giving me hell because I won't let Lyric go jump off a mountain in the middle of a South American hailstorm."

A series of pissed-off-sounding squawks came through the phone then, and Heath winced as he held the thing farther away from his ear. "I *know* you heard that, Harmony. It's not like I made any attempt to stop you from hearing it." It was a blatant lie, but it wasn't like Dalton was about to call him on it. "I was just explaining to my boss that you are my sweet Lyric's evil twin." His top lip was curled into a snarl.

More shrill yelling.

"Yes, I do know the definition of evil." Heath was trying to remain calm. "I'll even agree that your mother is the embodiment of it on earth. But in my considerable opinion, Harm, your poisoned apple doesn't fall far from the Livinia tree."

That set off a full-blown shriek on the other end of the phone, one that was loud enough to blow Dalton back in his chair. Was Heath's sister-in-law an actual banshee? Lyric was so lovely, he had trouble imagining her twin could be anything but lovely herself.

"You can scream at me all you want. There is no way I'm going to be okay with Lyric taking on the Andes, especially while volcanoes are erupting in the general area." Heath was final.

More screeching. Was she part hyena?

"Yes, I'm sure you do have a plan. Normally, I'd be thrilled to have Lyric be a part of whatever you want to do." His tone of voice was anything but enthusiastic. "But I'm putting my foot down on this one."

This time the screams were loud enough that Dalton could almost make out some of the words. Of course, they were all obscene, so maybe he was hearing wrong. Although he really doubted it.

"Look, I don't have time for this. I'm at work. We can talk about this more when I get home, but I'm telling you now that I'm not changing my mind... yeah, I love you too, Harm." The sarcasm that came with that last statement told Dalton that whatever this Harmony had had to say, it wasn't "I love you."

Heath shook his head, exasperated, as he shoved his phone back into his pocket. "Sorry about that. The Wright women tend to be a little high strung when they're angry."

Dalton grinned. "Yeah, I could, uh, hear that."

Heath grimaced. "I bet you could. Harmony isn't one for stony silence when she's mad. It takes a lot to wind her up, but once she's there ..." He moved his hands apart in an explosive gesture.

"I didn't even know Lyric had a twin." Dalton rarely mixed business with pleasure, so he knew little about the players' or coaches' personal lives. Blurring the lines of work and friendship was never a good idea.

"Identical. Growing up, I thought I was in love with Harmony and then I bumped into Lyric and came to my senses. They couldn't be more different if they tried." Heath shook his head. "Now Harm is convinced that if she yells at me enough, I'll bow to her and let Lyric go heli-skiing."

"You know, not to add fuel to the fire, but heli-skiing in Chile *is* pretty incredible. I just got back from spending two weeks down there. And I never even got close to a volcano." Dalton might be a lot of things, but boring wasn't one of them. He knew he seemed sedate on the outside, but inside he was an adrenaline junky.

"You went heli-skiing?" Heath looked so incredulous that Dalton wondered if he should be insulted. Then again, it wasn't like he advertised that adrenaline was his only major vice. Usually, he bent over backward to make sure that no one at work knew anything about his personal life. But damn it, he liked Heath, and if he could help him get around that screaming banshee on the phone, he figured he owed it to the guy. Besides, the team always ran better when the coaches were happy.

"Yes, I know it's hard to picture me as an actual human, but I do have a life outside of the stadium."

Heath went from incredulous to calculating in two seconds flat. "You should go with Harm. The last time she took Lyric skiing, my wife broke her leg... in two places. Like hell am I letting her jump out of anything, much less a helicopter onto a mountain." Heath propped his left ankle onto his right knee. "Here's the thing, Lyric is kind of... uncoordinated. And by kind of, I mean, if there's even slightly uneven ground, she's going to fall and probably take someone down with her. And there's a good chance she'll end up naked on the way down. Don't get me wrong. I love my wife more than anything, but the poor thing not only trips over her own two feet on a regular basis, but anything else that might be in the way too. It's a miracle she's lived this long but she has, and I'll be damned if she hurts herself on my watch."

Dalton knew exactly the kind of clumsy Heath was referring to. His little sister, Cat, had been that way. At five she'd been a whirlwind who never left a room in one piece. At seven, she'd been all elbows and knees and knocking things down. And at ten... at ten, she'd had so much promise. Unfortunately, she hadn't made it to her eleventh birthday. That was on him. The same old spot under his heart started to ache, but he stopped himself before he could rub it. He liked Heath, but he didn't show his vulnerabilities to anyone.

Missing Cat cut deep, and he preferred to do his suffering in private.

"I better get home to see Lyric and calm Harmony down." Heath stood up and headed for the door. "It's poker night at my place tonight. 8:00 p.m. I won't take no for an answer." He waved as he walked out of Dalton's office.

"Wait, poker night?" Dalton stood. He didn't fraternize with coworkers.

Heath was already gone.

He started to go after him, then decided what the hell. One night wouldn't hurt. It wasn't like he had anything else to do. One poker game wasn't going to kill him or undermine his authority. Besides, he kind of wanted to get a look at Heath's evil sister-in-law. Anyone who could screech like that had his attention, if not his respect.

With that thought in mind, he leaned over and hit the intercom. "Eleanor, can you get me Heath's home address?"

"He already had me text it to your phone." Eleanor was all business. Then again, she was always all business.

"Great, thanks. Also, do me a favor and order a case of those fancy Cuban cigars Jacob Bennet likes and have them delivered to him with my apologies about Heath's boots." Maintaining the peace was so much easier when you knew how to control people.

"Of course."

He glanced out at the new practice field again, thought of the havoc Heath's boot heels were going to wreak on it. "On second thought, make that two cases."

# Chapter 5

"Your husband is an asshole." Harmony had given up assholes as a New Year's resolution. If it weren't for her brother-in-law, she might actually be able to keep the resolution.

"My husband loves me," Lyric countered as she grabbed her suitcase out of Cherry Cherry's trunk. "He prefers it when I'm in one piece. It makes having sex so much easier, after all."

Cherry Cherry was a red, 1970s-era, pimped-out Cadillac with a major crush on Neil Diamond.

Harmony rolled her eyes as she picked up Lyric's briefcase and purse. "Don't even get me started. I can't imagine why you'd even want to have sex with him."

Lyric fanned herself like the thought of rolling around with Heath Montgomery made her burn-in-hell hot. "Have you met my husband? The whole world wants to have sex with him."

Harmony raised her hand as she followed Lyric into the house. "Not me."

She set Lyric's bags down on the nearest counter before throwing herself on one of the huge, oversized sofas that filled up her sister's family room/kitchen. "He's just so average.

"The whole world can't have tattoos and wear skin-tight black leather. No matter how much you want them to." Lyric set her purse on the kitchen counter.

"I'm not saying they can—or that they should. I'm just saying men are a little more interesting when they do."

"I don't know. Nipple piercings scare me a little. Like, what if one of your boyfriends is climbing a chain-link fence and the piercing gets caught and is torn from his nipple?" Lyric was all about the practical, even when it was impractical.

"Ouch." Harmony covered her own nipple rings with her palms. "That's terrible."

"Nipple rings are terrible." Lyric leaned against the kitchen counter.

Harmony dropped her hands. "That's because you don't know how fun they are."

Lyric rolled her eyes. "Your vote doesn't count. You think genital piercings are fun."

"Hey. Don't knock them 'til you try them." Harmony waggled her eyebrows. She rather enjoyed her hood piercing.

"That's what I'm saying about Heath." Lyric paused and looked like she was replaying that sentence in her head. "Not that I want you to try Heath or anything. Because that would be weird. I just meant—"

"Don't worry, Wonder Woman. I know what you meant." Harmony loved the nickname that had been given to her sister by Tre, a well-meaning flight attendant on the flight where Lyric had reconnected with Heath.

Lyric shot her a dirty look as she walked over to the fridge and pulled out a chilled bottle of wine. "I told you that story in confidence."

"I've kept that confidence. We're the only two people here." Besides, who would believe that a flight attendant had duct-taped a willing passenger?

Lyric got down two glasses, then started to open the wine bottle. Since she was wielding the corkscrew the same way Norman Bates's mother wielded a knife, Harmony felt honor bound to leave her comfortable spot on the sofa to help her twin. What had the poor cork ever done to Lyric?

"Give me that." Harmony finessed the cork out.

A few minutes later and they were both settled on the couch, glasses of wine in hand. Harmony planned on letting Lyric get a little alcohol in her before she started haranguing her about the whole BASE jumping trip again, but she should have known better. They might be totally different in everything but looks, but it was rare for the two of them to be on anything but the same wavelength.

"We could go to Hawaii on vacation." Lyric watched her as she took a drink.

"You lived there for years and just flew home from Hawaii. How is that a vacation? Besides, we've spent the last several months in Texas's version of weather hell. I want snow. I want adventure. I want—"

"To outrun your demons. Yeah, I know."

Harmony nearly choked on her wine. "That's not what I was going to say. It's not true. I don't have any demons."

Lyric shot her a yeah-right look.

"What?" There were some things she didn't even share with her sister.

Lyric continued the yeah-right look. "Why are you running so hard?"

"I'm not running." Harmony sprang off the couch and started to pace. "I have nothing to run from. Except our mother, who *is* a demon, but any sane person would run from her, so I don't think that counts." She finished her wine in one long swallow and poured a little more.

Make that a lot more. She filled up the whole glass. If this was the way this heart-to-heart was going to go, she needed as much wine as she could get. Maybe they should open a second bottle? Just to be on the safe side …

"Besides." She drained the second glass of wine. "If we don't go down to South America to heli-ski, how am I going to prove to Momma that I'm a total badass? Usually we hide our trips from her, but I want to rub this one in her face."

"If that's your main reason for choosing heli-skiing," Lyric took another drink, "I'm sure we can—"

"It's not. I've always wanted to ski the Andes." She sounded whiny and like it wasn't true, but it was. And if Momma hated it, well, more the better. "If not heli-skiing, then what do you suggest? I'm not spending two more weeks in some remote place looking at the stars. You got last year, and this year it's my turn to pick."

Had Harmony complained when Lyric had taken them bird-watching in South Texas? No. Well, not too much.

"Oh God, you're not going to bring up the bird-watching thing again?" Lyric rolled her eyes. "In case you forgot, I got hurt there too. Who knew wood decks could be so slippery after a light rain?"

"See, you hurt yourself bird-watching. Could there be a safer sport?" They might be twins, but Harmony hadn't inherited her sister's clumsiness.

"Look, why don't we stay here in Fort Worth and see what we can come up with to prove you're a badass? Just think, if you're badass enough, you'll make the news. You can ruin that reputation that Momma is so proud of. That's something you can't do in Chile." Lyric was always the logical one... damn it.

Harmony stared at her twin for long seconds as Lyric's words slowly sunk in. "That's not half bad."

The only downside Harm could think of was that she wouldn't be in San Angelo to see her mother's face when her perfect daughter turned to the dark side.

"That's downright diabolical." Harmony nodded. "I like that about you."

"I have my moments." Lyric grabbed another bottle and the corkscrew. Harmony didn't have the heart to watch her murder another cork, so she opened the wine herself.

She poured her sister another glass and one for herself. Her head was spinning, but at least she had an idea of how to get her mother in line.

Lyric saluted her twin. "Let's figure out how to lose your reputation in ten days or less."

Harmony pulled out her phone to take notes. "Momma won't even know what hit her."

Three hours later, the two of them were dressed to kill as Harmony pushed open the door to Dead Shot, the worst biker bar she could find on the Internet. As she did, the scents of stale beer and unwashed humans wafted out.

Lyric stopped dead in the doorway. "Are you sure about this?"

"Shut up and come on." She pulled Lyric inside the dark room. "We are so doing this."

They stood in the bar's entryway for long seconds, waiting for their eyes to adjust.

"I don't know why we couldn't have just gotten a drink at one of the hotel bars downtown," Lyric muttered under her breath. "There's a nice new Chili's right around the corner from my house. You could get into trouble there too you know. Maybe dance on the bar or something."

"It wouldn't be the same." Harmony needed a badass place to be a badass in. Bar dancing at Chili's would have gotten some laughs, but that was it.

"No kidding." Lyric looked around like she was trying to recall the date of her last tetanus shot. "Your chances of catching hepatitis would be so much lower at Chili's. But really, who wants that?"

"Exactly," Harmony said with satisfaction.

"Seriously, though …" Lyric scooted a little closer to her sister as she looked around. "This place is really dirty, Harm. And dark. Did I mention dirty?"

"You did," Harmony growled. "Keep your voice down."

It was too late. Lyric's voice tended to carry, and her last comment was perfectly timed with the ending of whatever biker bar song had just been playing. Everyone stopped and stared at them.

Pissing off the entire clientele wasn't the best idea in the world, but Harmony wasn't into backing down. Not anymore. What better way to make the news than to cause a riot in a place like this?

She rolled her shoulders back and tried to take up as much room as possible. She glanced over at Lyric, who was smiling manically at the largest man in the room.

"Stop smiling," Harmony said without moving her lips. "And don't make eye contact."

Lyric kept on smiling.

"Statistics show it's harder to kill someone who's smiling at you," Lyric said behind her creepy smile. "You should probably smile too."

"I don't smile." Sometimes a person had to draw a line in the sand, and this was one of those times.

The mountain of a man—who was about seven feet tall and four feet wide—stepped directly in front of Lyric. "You ladies lost?"

He was wearing a battered, black motorcycle jacket with a large patch pronouncing him vice president of the Bastards of Hell.

Shouldn't it be the Bastards from Hell? God, she hoped Lyric wouldn't point that out.

This was exactly what she needed to give Momma an aneurism. "Not lost at all. We're looking for a good time."

Screw not smiling. She plastered on her biggest, brightest smile. But it was a little bit hard to maintain, considering her new thigh-high black leather boots were rubbing a patch of skin raw on her right inner thigh and their pointy toes were crushing her pinky-toes—but her mother needed to suffer, so she was willing to put up with a lot.

"In that case ..." He offered Harmony his left arm and Lyric his right. "Fun is my middle name. Let me buy you beautiful ladies a drink."

"Southern hospitality... I like that in a man," Harmony cooed as she batted her eyelashes.

She glanced over at Lyric, who was looking about as out of place as a Democrat at a Tea Party rally. Her big sister had on a "Nerds Do It in Space" T-shirt, baggy jeans, and sparkly pink Birks. Harmony had been hoping for something a little less virgin-geek, but in the end, she took what she could get. At least she'd managed to pry Lyric out of the house, even if it had taken half an hour of fast-talking to convince her that she should be mad at Heath for forbidding her to go to Chile.

Harmony smoothed down her midriff-baring tank top and black leather micromini in a manner she knew would attract more than a few pairs of eyes. Tonight *was* about women's liberation. It was for women everywhere. The fact that it was also a shot at their controlling mother and Lyric's suddenly boring husband only made it better.

"My name's Rooster on account of my red hair," Mountain Man said in a voice that was one pack away from lung cancer.

Harmony glanced up at his bald head. "Nice to meet you, Rooster. I'm Harm and this is my twin sister, Lyric."

"Tiny, this here is Harm and Lyric. Give them whatever they'd like." Rooster nodded at the bartender. "Ladies, I'll be right over there playing pool if you need anything else."

Tiny grinned and a set of huge, blinding-white dentures sparkled in the fluorescent light. "Is Harm your name or your state of mind?"

"Both." Lyric plopped down on a red pleather barstool. "I'll have a white wine spritzer."

Tiny, who was in fact tiny, looked at Lyric like she was from Mars. "We're fresh out of white wine spritzers."

"Okay, I'll have a piña colada." Lyric reached for a bowl of peanuts, but the woman sitting next to her grabbed the peanuts and pushed them out of Lyric's reach.

"Lady, this ain't the country club. We have beer and we got booze. Most days we even have ice, but that's as close as we get to a piña colada." Tiny had a big attitude.

"Well, what kind of beer do you have?" Lyric glanced around like she was looking for a menu. She leaned over, as if to reach for the peanuts, but Tiny shot her a warning look.

"You don't want to mess with Yoko. Since her old man left with her sister, she's been in a bad mood." He pulled out two bottles of Shiner, opened them, and set one in front of Lyric and the other in front of Harmony. "We have the kind of beer that comes in a bottle."

Lyric turned to Yoko. "I'm so sorry about your boyfriend. Was it recent?"

"Twenty year ago, bitch, but he coming back to me." Yoko's English was accented.

She was wearing so much makeup that Harmony hadn't realized she was Asian until now.

"*Konnichiwa*." Lyric clasped her hands together and bowed respectfully.

"Just 'cause I Asian, you think I Japanese?" Yoko pulled out a switchblade and stabbed it directly into the bar top. "I kill you, bitch."

"You are Japanese." Tiny pulled the knife out and stowed it behind the bar. "You're from Okinawa."

"That not the point. Not all Asian Japanese." She pulled a Buck knife out of her purse, unfolded it, and stabbed the bar. "My pimp say I no take shit from nobody."

Harmony stepped in between Lyric and Yoko. If things turned ugly, Harmony wanted to throw the first punch. God knew Lyric fought like a girl.

"I agree." Harmony took a sip of beer. "You shouldn't ever take shit from anyone."

"That what he say." Yoko pulled the knife out of the bar and used it to clean the dirt from under her fingernails. "I like you." She leaned forward to look around Harm. "I don't like her. She go... you stay."

"What did I do?" Lyric threw her hands up.

Harm ignored her sister—she had to save womankind.

"You shouldn't take shit from your pimp either." Harmony hip-pushed Lyric off the stool and sat down. "You should work for yourself. Why give him a cut of your hard-earned money?"

Tonight Harmony was standing up for women everywhere and from everywhere.

The whole bar went silent.

Yoko turned careful black eyes on Harmony. "I don't think that good idea."

"It's a great idea. Think about it. You get to keep all of your money." And stick it to the man. After her run-in with Heath, Harmony was in the mood to stick it to the man... any man.

Yoko refused to make eye contact.

Harmony looked around. "Your overhead is low and if you got to keep all of your... um... salary, you could afford to lower your prices."

Yoko's eyes snapped up and she leveled a defiant glare at Harm.

Harm threw her hands up. "Not that you need to, I'm only saying that you could. To drum up business." She couldn't help but notice that business was down, as Yoko was sitting alone.

Lyric peeked her head over Harmony's shoulder. "Have you ever heard of Groupon? I hear that's a great way to build up your small business."

Harmony elbowed her sister and sent her a shut-up glare. "I don't think they have Groupon for hookers."

"Well, they should. It makes sound business sense, really. Just think about—"

Lyric had never been able to read body language or simple shut-up glares. How had Harmony forgotten that?

"It's time for you two to stop talking now," a dark-haired man said as he leaned over a pool table, lining up a shot. He kept his eye on the ball.

Lyric turned around on her barstool. "Are you her pimp?"

"I prefer business manager." He made the shot, stood, and checked her out. "You seem familiar. Have we met?"

Lyric analyzed his face. "I don't think so."

"She's married to Heath Montgomery." Harm rolled her eyes. Not only was this guy poor Yoko's oppressor, but he was a freakin' football fan too. Fucker.

He shook his head. "No, that's not it." He studied Lyric. "I know you from somewhere."

"She's that lady from SETI who does the podcasts." It was Rooster. "You know that podcast I was talking about on the Crab Nebula? It was her."

Jesus. Seriously? Harmony felt like she'd fallen into some cheesy straight-to-video movie where geniuses had disguised themselves as bikers while they hid from the men in black.

"I'm doing one on the water plumes on Jupiter's moon Europa next week." Lyric looked excited for the first time since they'd gotten there.

"Fascinating." The dark-haired man lined up another shot. "You and your sister need to leave."

"We're not going anywhere." Harmony didn't take shit from anyone, especially a man on tonight of all nights.

"You know, I think we left the stove on." Lyric grabbed Harmony's arm and tried to tug her off the barstool.

"No we didn't." Harmony batted her sister's hand away. "Sit down and finish your beer. I've got this."

"You should listen to your sister." The dark-haired man finally looked over at them. "This is no place for a couple of soft women."

What the hell did that even mean?

"What is she?" Harm waggled her thumb at Yoko.

"An employee." He stood. "Unless you want to take her place, you need to move on."

"You don't scare me. This is a public bar and we're not going anywhere." Harm was a level-four black belt in Krav Maga. Her ass was staying put.

# Chapter 6

Dalton was having a good time playing poker, which surprised him. Once everyone had gotten over him being the boss and started treating him more like one of the guys, it was just poker and laughs and really good chocolate chip cookies.

Speaking of which—he grabbed the last one off of the plate in the middle of the poker table.

"These are really good." He bit into the cookie, which somehow managed to be crunchy on the outside and gooey on the inside. "Where did you get them?"

Usually he didn't allow himself junk food. Then again, he didn't usually allow himself to hang out with coworkers, so tonight was a new experience all around.

"I know... right?" Head coach Bobby Golden sat on his right. "My wife needs the recipe or the name of the bakery where she can pick them up. She would love them."

"Harm made them." Heath shuffled the cards and doled them out like a Vegas dealer.

"Lyric's twin?" The screamer from Heath's phone call earlier? Dalton grabbed his cards and peeked at his hand. A king and a couple of queens. Good. Five-card draw was his game and he was winning. He'd never understood people who just played for fun. In his opinion, only winning was fun.

"Your wife has a twin?" Bum Collins, the team's defensive coordinator, cocked an eyebrow as he checked out his cards.

Heath nodded. "Unfortunately. Her name is Harmony, but Harm fits her way better. Remember that psycho chick from *Suicide Squad*?"

Everyone yes-ed.

"That's Harm, only she has less social skills and even more attitude." Heath fanned out his cards and then laid them face down in front of him. "I fold." He stood. "She made cannoli too. I'll get it."

He left the room and returned a few moments later with a plate of cannoli filled with dark-chocolate cream.

For long seconds, they all just kind of stared at the plate.

"She makes cannoli shaped like guns? I'm raising." Dalton shook his head as he tossed some chips into the pot. Now he had to meet her. She was a badass.

"I told you. Harley Quinn with more attitude." Heath passed the plate around, and Dalton was the first to take one. Figuring it couldn't be as good as the cookies, he bit into it then whistled. "That's really good."

"She's talented, I'll give her that... crazy but talented." Heath bit into his own cannoli. "She calls these Take the Gun, Eat the Cannoli."

Bum grinned as he counted out enough chips to match Dalton's raise. "I'll call. Crazy or not, you gotta love a woman who loves *The Godfather*."

"The good twin and the bad twin. Is it like that old movie, *Twins*?" Coach Golden tossed his own matching bet into the pot and then reached for a cannoli. "They're twins but Danny DeVito got all of the ugly genes while Arnold Schwarzenegger got all of the good genes?"

Heath picked up the deck, ready to deal the draw. "Well, Lyric and Harm are indentical-ish. Except Lyric got all of the good, sane genes and Harm got all of the evil genes. Does that count? In fact—" Heath's phone buzzed on the table.

He set down the cards and picked it up, glancing at the screen. Then he swiped his hand across it and put the phone to his ear. "Hey, babe."

Dalton liked the way Heath treated his wife, how she always took priority over whatever he was doing. A settled coach was good for business.

Coach Golden took a bite of his cannoli. "These are better than the cookies."

Heath sat up and covered the ear that was minus the phone so he could hear better. "What? Wait... slow down. You almost got knifed by an Okinawan hooker?" Five horizontal lines popped out on his brow.

The sudden silence sucked all of the air out of the room.

"I don't understand. Harm's trying to talk who into leaving her pimp?" Heath leaned forward as if that would give him better cell reception. "Since when do they have hookers at Chili's?"

A minute passed and Heath's expression turned angry. "What do you mean you're not at Chili's? Where the hell are you that Harm is giving hookers vocational advice?" Heath stood and his chair rocked backward and crashed to the floor. "Dead Shot? What the hell is that... it's a bar? A biker bar? What the hell has your sister gotten you into now?"

Holy shit. Lyric and her sister were at Dead Shot? It was a rough place, which was the nice way of saying that murder was more commonplace there than in Washington, DC, and the Twin Peaks restaurant in Waco combined.

Normally Dalton tried to stay out of employee affairs, but he couldn't leave two women in that place alone. He'd never be able to live with himself if he did.

He dropped the cannoli, then stood up so fast his chair crashed to the floor. "Heath, we need to get them out of there. That place is really bad news."

The Wrangers' offensive coach took one look at his face and turned white under his tan.

"Okay, honey. I need you to go to the bathroom and lock yourself in." He shook his head while he listened to his wife. "Yes, right now. Who cares about Harm? She started this, let her finish it. I'll be there as soon as I can. I love you. Bye." Heath felt around his pockets, presumably looking for his keys. "Sorry guys, but we need to cut this short. Feel free to keep playing or let yourselves out."

"I'll go with you." Dalton caught up with him. He wasn't big on digging up old wounds, but he wasn't about to let something happen to Lyric. Heath would be useless for the rest of the season if his wife was hurt. "I'll drive. I know Dead Shot all too well."

"I didn't figure you as one for biker bars."

Dalton followed Heath through the kitchen and out to the garage. "Yeah, well, it's a long story."

"One I look forward to hearing once my wife is safe." Heath grabbed the first key ring on the holder nailed to the wall next to the garage door. "Looks like we're taking Cherry Cherry. You tell me how to get there."

He didn't look like a man who was willing to take no for an answer.

"Sounds good. But what's a Cherry Cherry?" Dalton stepped into the garage and one look answered his question. A red Cadillac circa a long time ago sat proudly between a black Porsche Spyder and a black Cadillac Escalade.

Heath nodded to the red car. "Jump in." He clicked the garage opener button on the wall next to the kitchen door.

Dalton slid into the passenger's seat and sniffed. "Do I need to remind you of the league's policy on marijuana use?"

The car reeked of reefer.

"I'm clean, but I'm pretty sure Cherry Cherry tokes up every once in a while." Heath slammed the key into the ignition, and Neil Diamond boomed out of the speakers.

"Your car smokes weed?" Now, he liked Neil Diamond as much as the next guy, but this was loud—really loud. "Can we turn it down?"

"No, Cherry Cherry is in love with Neil Diamond." Heath leaned into Dalton and whispered, "She doesn't like anyone who disses Neil."

"I don't understand. How can a car have a crush on anyone?" Dalton tried to appear nonchalant, but he made a mental note to review the team's health insurance to see if it covered mental health issues. How did he discreetly ask Heath to seek counseling? He was worried that all of those concussions through the years had added up to some serious head trauma.

Clearing his throat, he said, "You know cars aren't actually sentient beings... right?"

The car coughed and then backfired.

Heath patted the dashboard. "He didn't mean it. He likes you. And he's not going to say anything else bad about you, Cherry Cherry, because we have to go save Lyric from Harm."

The check engine light dinged and they sped up.

"Cherry Cherry likes Lyric." Heath was completely serious. "She hates Harm."

Cherry backfired again.

"Your sister-in-law can't be that bad, her cannoli were as close to a religious experience as I've had in a very long time." Dalton glanced around the car, looking for signs of intelligence.

Cherry Cherry backfired for a third time.

"Maybe we shouldn't mention my sister-in-law's name," Heath said as the check engine light dinged again. "Cherry Cherry is very protective of Lyric."

It wasn't possible. Heath was obviously insane—there was no way this car was alive.

Neil Diamond's song "Cherry Cherry" finished and then started up again. "You have it on repeat?"

"I don't." Heath glanced at Dalton. "It's her favorite song. She likes to play it over and over."

"Okay." Dalton drew out the word. He peeled his hand from the seat. "Why are the seats sticky? You know, there are people who can clean them for you."

The engine revved high.

"That's another sensitive subject. Maybe we should talk about something else?" He coughed, then shot Dalton a this-subject-is-closed look. "So... hang out at biker bars often?"

If he only knew. Dalton's past was his own business. He'd worked too hard at leaving it behind to unearth it now.

"Not anymore." He tried to roll down the window, but the button seemed to not work. "Can you roll down my window? My head's spinning from the contact high."

"Come on, Cherry Cherry, don't pout. Dalton's a good guy. Let him roll down the window." Heath sounded like he was reasoning with a toddler. "I promise I'll get you hand-waxed tomorrow."

The passenger's-side window rolled down. Dalton hadn't touched the button, and he couldn't help but notice that both of Heath's hands were still on the wheel.

Was he being punked or was this car actually alive?

"So, um, how exactly did you and Cherry Cherry meet?" He couldn't help thinking about the first *Transformers* movie, when Sam bought Bumblebee at a used-car dealer. Maybe the same thing had happened to Heath, and this old Caddy was an Autobot. What kind of robot would she turn into... some sort of bitchy, buxom bombshell with a Neil Diamond obsession?

Jesus, now *he* was doing it. Were mental health issues contagious?

He tried to be open-minded, told himself that Heath naming Cherry Cherry wasn't so different from when his father had named his motorcycle Loretta. Only, Dalton was pretty sure his dad hadn't thought Loretta was alive. Then again, even if she had been, she was truly dead now after his dad had tried to wrap her around a tree almost fifteen years ago.

"I bought her off a baggage handler at the Austin airport. They were out of rental cars." Heath kept his eyes on the road. "Lyric needed to get home. Her father was sick."

"Sounds like an adventure." As they hit the freeway, the wind got to be too much and Dalton tried to roll his window up. Apparently, Cherry Cherry approved of him enough to give him button privileges, because the window slid closed.

"The biggest of my life. We ended up married." The corners of Heath's mouth curled up in a smile that Dalton was quickly becoming familiar with.

It was definitely his Lyric smile, and it looked good on him.

# Chapter 7

Thirty minutes later, they pulled into Dead Shot's dirt parking lot. Dalton's first glimpse of the bar told him it hadn't changed one bit in the last fifteen years. It was still a windowless, gray, cinder-block box with a saggy, brown, shingle roof.

Then again, what else could he expect from the bar that the Bastards of Hell owned? At one time they'd owned him too—and he hadn't been much different than this place.

Fifteen years changed a lot. Instead of being just another biker, he was now just another suit... albeit a perfectly tailored Armani one.

He'd be lying if he said he didn't like the changes he'd made in the last decade and a half. Just like he'd be lying if he said there wasn't a small part of him that also missed being on the back of a Harley.

BA, short for badass, the leader, was either going to hug him or shoot him—there had never been any middle ground when it came to the Bastards of Hell. You were either in or out; they didn't deal in gray area. At one time he'd been grateful for the black and white of it all. Paradoxically, it was what had finally given him the strength to walk away.

Taking a deep breath, he told Heath, "You should know... I have history with the gang that owns the bar." He really wasn't prepared to give any more than that.

"Good history or bad history?" Heath turned off Cherry Cherry and pocketed the keys.

"Depends on who you ask." He opened the door and stepped out onto the dirt parking lot of the last place on earth he wanted to be.

"I don't have a weapon. Do I need one?" Heath pulled out his phone. "I can call the defensive line. They're intimidating as hell, but I kinda need them to not get hurt."

Dalton buttoned his navy suit jacket. His tie was in his suit jacket pocket. Should he put it on so his armor/disguise was complete? He took a deep breath and let it out slowly and tried not to show just how badly this little trip down memory lane was messing with his head.

"You're the offensive coordinator. Shouldn't you be calling the offensive line?" Dalton hoped rather than believed they wouldn't recognize him. He was the spitting image of his old man.

"Come on? Really? Everyone knows the defensive line is expendable." Heath grinned. "Don't tell them I said that."

"So your sister-in-law... does she normally get into this much trouble?" Dalton rolled his shoulders because his knots of tension had knots of tension of their own.

"Yes, only Lyric is usually blamed for all of the messes that Harm starts." He shook his head. "No idea why."

Dalton had been cleaning up his father's disasters ever since his mother tapped out when he was ten and Cat was two. Life wasn't fair, God knew. He'd committed that mantra to memory about five minutes after he'd learned the word Da-Da.

"Well, if I hadn't seen it with my own eyes, I wouldn't have believed it." The voice came from a large figure smoking a cigarette next to the double glass front doors.

Dalton walked toward the voice he knew instantly, even if it had been fifteen years since he'd last heard it.

"Hey, Rooster." The huge man pulled him in for a hug, and Dalton clapped him on the back. In all the important ways, Rooster had been more of a father to him than his own.

"The prodigal son returns." Rooster stepped back and beamed down at him. "Buff, look who it is. D-Boy's back. And he's all fancied up too."

Buffalo, the treasurer and Dalton's godfather, walked up to Dalton. "In case you forgot, we don't gotta dress code here." He pulled Dalton in for a rib-cracking hug.

"Been a long time. Guess I forgot." Dalton hated that his eyes burned just a little bit as he hugged Buffalo back. Hated even more how much this felt like a homecoming.

But how could it feel like anything else when he'd grown up in this bar? How many years had he and Cat spent living out of the back room on a blow-up mattress while their father was off doing God knows what to God knows who? Too many to count.

"BA's gonna shit himself when he gets a load of you." Rooster pulled him in for another hug, then glanced back at Heath. "Aren't you the Deuce?"

Heath shot him an affable grin, even as his eyes remained focused on the door to the bar. "Sure am."

Rooster nodded in the general direction of the front door. "I hope you're here for your sister-in-law. She's a firecracker. She broke BA's nose. He can't decide if he wants to kill her or marry her."

Holy shit. Who the hell was this woman, and how the hell had she managed to break BA's nose? Furthermore, how the hell was she still alive? BA had killed men for doing much less.

Dalton threw open the door with a renewed sense of urgency. No way in hell was he letting Heath's wife or sister-in-law die in this piece-of-shit bar. The place had already seen more than enough of its share of death.

But as his eyes adjusted to the dim light and smoky haze, he couldn't quite believe what he saw. A woman—Lyric, or possibly Harmony—was standing on the pool table in a black leather mini and bitch boots, waving around the leg of a broken barstool like a club. Surrounding her were all of the members of Bastards of Hell, except Rooster and Buff. Each one looked half like they wanted to tear her limb from limb and half like they wanted to run for the hills.

"Christ, Harm, what the hell?" Heath yelled at the woman on the table. "Where's my wife?"

"Lyric pussed out and locked herself in the bathroom." She pointed her club and shot a death glare at a bleeding BA. "Bring it, big guy."

BA growled, but he didn't move. Still, he was tracking her every move, and that made Dalton extremely uncomfortable. He, more than anyone, knew that BA was fast and mean and deadly.

Determined to avoid bloodshed—at least of the Wright sister variety—Dalton walked up behind BA and asked, "What's going on?"

BA turned around, and the anger in his face turned to suspicion. "Well, hello, little brother. Long time no see."

"Who the hell are you?" Harm demanded, waving her club at him like she thought it would actually protect her.

"Dalton Mane, I'm a friend of your brother-in-law." He didn't say any more. There'd be time for explanations later, when he wasn't terrified BA was going to murder this woman. But now that he had Harmony's attention, he continued, "I'd hold out my hand for you to shake, but you look a little busy at the moment."

Heath's sister-in-law was really something else. Dalton tried not to notice how sexy she was, but it was difficult to notice anything else, even as she waved that club around. She was built. Really, really built. Large, full breasts, a tiny waist, and legs that would have made a supermodel jealous—especially when encased in those black leather bitch boots.

And her tattoos—he'd spent years dating women with pale, perfect skin, years telling himself that tattoos didn't do it for him. Looking at Harmony Wright, he couldn't help thinking that he'd been lying to himself all those years. Because her tattoos were gorgeous. Vibrant, exotic, and dangerous, they added a whole lot to her already prodigious sex appeal.

Then again, he'd always had a thing for dangerous.

"And why are you here?" Harmony's eyes darted from man to man, clocking everyone's movements, even as she spoke directly to him.

"Stay out of this, little brother." BA's voice was slow and even, which Dalton knew from experience was a very bad thing. It meant that he was about to lose his shit. "She broke my goddamn nose. She has to pay."

"Don't you think you'd be better off taking care of it than standing here hassling a frightened woman?"

"I'm not frightened," Harmony squawked. "I'm pissed. If he comes any closer he's going to see just how pissed I am."

Goddammit. Didn't this woman see what kind of danger she was in? Dalton shot her a look that told her to keep her mouth shut so he could get her out of this. He could tell the look had been received—and rejected—by the fact that she got even more pissed off. And when she opened her mouth to say God only knew what, he decided to hell with it. There was only one way to stop this, and it was time to take matters into his own hands.

"I'm not your brother. I never was." Dalton waited until BA was looking straight at him, then he punched his stepbrother in the kidneys, grabbed his hair, and smashed his face into the pool table. Quick as lightning, he wrenched the club from Harmony's grasp, scooped her up, and threw her over his shoulder in a fireman's carry.

"Put me down." Harm wriggled and tried to kick her way free, but he held on tight.

He headed out the front door. Once in the parking lot, he yelled back to Rooster, "Tell them not to come after me. I don't want to hurt anyone else."

He might not be in a biker gang, but fifteen years of Krav Maga had taught him the most efficient way to hurt someone. And for some reason, seeing his old family circling Harmony like a bunch of hyenas definitely put him in the mood to hurt a lot of someones.

"Put me down. *Now*." Harm punched and kicked.

"Not until you settle down." He carried her over to Cherry Cherry. "You need to learn not to pick fights you can't win, little girl."

"What the fuck did you just call me?" Harm demanded, redoubling her efforts to beat the hell out of his back and kick him in the balls.

"Stop it," he ordered again, delivering a swift smack to her leather-clad ass. The sound made a nice *pop* in the night air.

It must have done the trick, because Harm stopped kicking and punching. He was just about to congratulate himself when a burning pinch came from his lower back. The burn quickly turned into flaming pain.

"What the hell?" He dropped Harm on her ass. "Did you just bite me?" He looked over his shoulder, trying to see if she'd drawn blood.

"You're lucky I didn't kill you." With that proclamation, Harm popped up onto her feet and nailed him with a mean right cross.

Jesus. She wasn't a firecracker, she was a hellcat.

He grabbed her, went to put her in a restraining hold, and she easily twisted out of it.

"Krav?" Dalton choked out as she twisted his arm behind his back. If she didn't stop, she'd break his wrist.

"Level-four black belt." Harm released his arm. "You?"

"Level two." Dalton stood, ears ringing as it registered that she could kick his ass.

"You shouldn't bite people." He rolled his shoulder—she'd damn near dislocated it.

"You shouldn't pick up strangers in a bar." Harm crossed her arms and smirked at him.

But before he could say anything else, Heath ran out of the bar, pulling Lyric behind him. "Time to go."

Dalton tried to open the passenger door, but it was locked. "Unlock it."

"It is unlocked." Heath didn't slow down until he was next to Cherry Cherry. He hit a button on the remote, but the doors didn't unlock. "Come on, Cherry Cherry. This is an emergency. We need to get out of here *now*."

Nothing happened.

"Come on, baby. Harmony needs a ride, just his once." Lyric was cajoling. "I promise I won't let her hurt you."

Cherry Cherry's trunk popped open.

"I'm not riding in the trunk of that possessed car." Harm rolled her eyes when the doors remained firmly locked. "Screw it. I'm going back inside."

"That's not a good idea." Heath leaned over and whispered something close to the car window and the doors unlocked. "We gotta go now. I set a little fire in the bathroom to distract them so we could get away."

"How big of a fire?" Dalton wrenched open the back passenger's door and practically threw Harm inside before he jumped into the front seat. Then he pulled out his phone to call 9-1-1. He might have walked away from them, but the Bastards were the closest thing he had to family. The last thing he wanted was for one of them to get hurt. Well, except BA. A little smoke inhalation could only improve his attitude.

Cherry Cherry peeled out of the parking lot and onto the road.

"I'd say a solid two alarm, but since the building is cinder block, the damage should be contained to just the bathroom." Heath drove like the devil was on his ass—or like the Bastards of Hell were.

That made Dalton feel a little better. As long as he didn't think about the fact that BA was going to be pissed as hell. Because all Dalton needed was his father's biker gang trying to kill his brand new offensive coordinator and his family.

Damn it. He was going to have to find a way to make peace with the Bastards. It wasn't like they wouldn't know where to look for Heath. Tomorrow morning, he fully expected his stepbrother to be waiting outside of Lasso Stadium with guns drawn and an extra bad attitude. It was how he'd gotten his nickname, after all.

"How exactly do you know those guys so well?" Heath didn't spare him a glance as he kept his eyes on the road and his foot down hard on the gas pedal.

"I grew up in the Bastards. My dad founded the club." Yep, Dalton was biker royalty. He didn't feel the need to go into his life with the gang any further.

"Wow. And I thought my dad was an asshole. He was only a drunk." Heath turned into the gated community where he lived.

"You have no idea." Dalton turned around to glare at Harmony. "You have no idea just how dangerous those men are."

"I can take care of myself." She cocked her head to the left. "We both know I can kick your ass."

"Yes, Krav is wonderful for taking people down. But you can't take down twenty angry and armed men at once. It's reckless. You put your sister's and Heath's and my lives in danger. If you want to die, there are easier and faster ways to do it."

"Nobody asked you to come save me, biker boy. I sure as hell didn't ask you to manhandle me and throw me around."

"Manhandle?" Lyric piped up for the first time.

"Don't worry about it," Harmony told her with yet another roll of her eyes.

Jesus, it looked like eye rolling was her favorite form of communication. Which might explain why she had the self-preservation sense of a thirteen-year-old girl. Maybe that was why he had the nearly overwhelming urge to spank her again.

He'd never met anyone who needed a spanking more than Harm. "Do you always cause this much trouble?"

"Yes," Heath and Lyric said in unison.

"All I did was try and help a fellow oppressed female by giving her some valuable vocational and financial advice. How was I supposed to know that her pimp was in earshot?" She truly sounded like she was in the right and was insulted that anyone could think otherwise.

"You're a five-alarm fire in high heels."

"Five-Alarm Harm," Heath said with a laugh. "That's a good one."

"Before you call me that again, I suggest you reflect on the fact that I know a dozen ways to kill a man while he's asleep and two dozen while he's awake."

Dalton loved the naked rage on her face and in her voice.

Harmony was definitely a hellcat, he decided, as Heath pulled into his driveway and pressed the button on garage door opener. Too bad he'd sworn off hellcats a long time ago.

# Chapter 8

Soooooo... last night hadn't gone well. Harmony was woman enough to admit that... to herself, even if the rest of the world could kiss her ass. Heath had spent an hour lecturing her after they got home, a lecture that ended up with him forbidding her to take Lyric anywhere ever again.

As if. Lyric was her twin sister and her best friend. No way was she giving that up just because her husband had a serious stick up his ass.

So did his very attractive friend.

She tried not to think of Dalton Mane as she poured canola oil into the commercial fryer in Lyric and Heath's kitchen. Right now they were both at work, which was fine with her since things had been a little tense around the coffeepot this morning. It just gave her a chance to make her donuts uninterrupted.

Not that they were a peace offering or anything. It was just that she needed donuts and latte and more donuts. And maybe some cookies too. And a cake. And maybe some more cannoli—

She made a list of the necessary ingredients in her head as she pinched off a piece of dough and started to shape it. She always baked when she was mad. Or sad or glad or bored or horny, and right now she was a little bit of all of those things.

How could she not be when, looking back on last night, she was willing to admit that possibly, in some itty-bitty tiny way, she was to blame for how everything went bad?

Dalton *might* have had a small point when he'd called her reckless. Maybe. In some teeny-tiny way.

It nearly killed her to admit it. Almost as much as it killed her to admit that Dalton Mane was Hot with a capital *H*. He might wear an Armani suit like he was born in it, but there was a chained-panther quality about him that really revved her engine. Something that said that once he broke free, whoever was in his path was going to have to deal with a whole lot of raw power and lethal animal. In his tailored designer suit and fancy-dancy loafers he'd looked so civilized, but underneath was an alpha male ready to tie her to the headboard and take what he wanted.

It was an enticing thought, one that had her nipples peaking and a shiver sliding seductively down her spine. At least, until she remembered that two alphas couldn't coexist in the same relationship. It was the way of the world, and there was no way in hell she was ever riding bitch behind him. She did enough of that when she bent over backward trying to please her mother.

She took the donut dough out of the proofing bowl, punched it down, sprinkled flour on the marble kitchen island, and rolled out the dough. Using a paring knife, she cut out her handprint over and over before setting the shapes out on a baking sheet to rise.

All of this silence was getting to her, so she pulled out her smartphone and cranked up Marilyn Manson before moving on to the oatmeal cookies.

She mixed the ingredients from memory, minus the raisins everyone seemed to love in this damn cookie. She hated raisins. On the whole, grapes were fine, but only *before* they dried up into shriveled raisins. Seriously, who in their right mind wanted to eat desiccated fruit?

With a cookie scoop, she plopped down mountains of oatmeal cookie dough into rows on a parchment-covered baking sheet, then popped them into the oven and went back to her donuts.

She flipped up the dish towel she'd used to cover them. After the finger test showed that the dough had risen just the right amount, she picked up the baking sheet and took it to the fryer. The oil was at a perfect three-fifty.

Abruptly, her music stopped, and a male voice said from behind her, "Do you always bake in a bikini and high heels?"

She jumped a foot in the air and nearly dropped the baking sheet into the hot oil. Damn it, she hated being sneaked up on.

She knew what she was going to find before she turned, and sure enough, she was right. Dalton was standing there in a perfectly tailored charcoal-gray suit that made his black hair and green eyes pop even more than they had yesterday. It also made him even more panther-like.

She felt that tug deep inside of herself again, the one that told her she wanted this man every way she could have him. The fact that she couldn't have him only made her voice bitchier as she countered, "Do you always walk into other people's houses without knocking?" She fashioned the first hand into a stiff middle finger and placed it in the oil before stepping back and leaning against the counter.

"I did knock, but you couldn't hear it." He pointed to her smartphone. "Always listen to your music so loud? At that decibel level, you're looking at another two years before the hearing loss kicks in."

"Thanks, Dr. Oz, I'll keep that in mind." She pulled the first batch of cookies out of the oven.

"Are those oatmeal raisin cookies?" He sounded hopeful, but she wasn't in the mood for company. Especially not company she was tempted to spread whipped cream all over before slowly licking it off.

"No." Technically, they were oatmeal raisinless cookies.

"They smell like oatmeal raisin cookies." He popped one in his mouth. "Taste like oatmeal raisinless cookies."

And damn it, it didn't help her little problem that he had the same damn sense of humor that she did. The bastard. Not that she had any intention of showing him how much he turned her on. She might be reckless, but she didn't do suicide missions, and the tiny voice at the back of her mind, which she usually ignored, told her that tangling with Dalton was going to fuck her up way more than she already was.

She was determined not to ignore it today, especially after last night's close call.

"So, not only do you break and enter, but now you're stealing food?" Too bad she'd left her guns by the pool. She could nip this thing—whatever it was—in the bud. "You Fort Worthers are weird. In San Angelo we have better manners."

His eyes roamed down her body. "Do y'all bake in bikinis? I've never been to San Angelo, but I just might move there so I can watch the bikini baking team."

"Pervert." As she turned back to the frying donut, she mashed her lips together to hide her smile. Apparently he liked the way she looked in her bikini—maybe as much as she liked him in that suit.

A quick test told her the donut was ready. Using a metal spider, she fished it out and covered it with a lemon glaze.

"Is that what I think it is?" Dalton's dark-green eyes turned huge.

"Depends on what you think it is." She arranged the donut on a plate so that the middle finger was the focal point, then aimed it straight at him. "If you think it's a donut flipping you off, you'd be correct."

"Can I have it?" He stepped into her personal space. He was so close she could smell him—sandalwood and something underneath it that was all male.

"No, this one's mine." She didn't back away or back down. Instead, she sucked in the middle finger and bit it off at the root. The smoldering look he gave her conjured images of her mouth swallowing something else entirely. So much for the voice in the back of her head.

Of course, she nearly choked on the mouthful of dough, but the look on his face made it almost worth it.

"Fine." He shrugged out of his suit jacket, folded it, and hung it on a kitchen chair back. "I'll make my own."

Clearly, he wasn't one to throw his clothes down. It appeared that he liked order. Which made her wonder, if she ripped his clothes off, would he put the groping on hold long enough to pick them all up and fold them?

Not that she was going to find out, but it was a question to ponder. Especially as he rolled his sleeves up and picked up a dough hand. "You want to give me a hand with this?"

His attempt at a joke was lame at best.

She figured the only way to counter was to go lame right back. She handed him another hand. "There you go."

"Very funny." He held the dough hand gingerly by the thumb. "Do I just toss it in or what?"

"You need a little more finesse than that." She couldn't help herself. She took the dough and with a practiced hand molded it until the fingers met the thumb in the age-old gesture for jerking someone off. Then she dropped it in the oil. "Wait until it turns golden brown and then take it out."

She flipped her sunglasses down from the top of her head onto her eyes. "Now if you'll excuse me. The latest *Cosmo* is waiting for me by the pool."

"Wait, shouldn't you stay here and make sure I don't burn down the house?" He grabbed the spider and tucked his tie over his shoulder.

"Nope, not my house." She turned and headed back out to the pool.

He whistled his approval of her backside. "Nice."

Normally, that would piss her off, but it was a free country. He could appreciate her ass just as much as she could appreciate his. There was equality in mutual ogling.

"Not too bad yourself." She didn't look back.

It was time to enjoy her one and only vacation this year. When Dalton left, she'd go back in and finish up the donuts. All that caged sex appeal was too much to handle in the confines of her sister's kitchen.

After setting her plate on the table between two of the six chaises, she folded her chaise flat, laid down on her belly, and propped herself up on her elbows. Then she grabbed her plate and her *Cosmo*.

"This is really good." Dalton sat on the chair next to her. "Is that lemon zest in the frosting?"

"It's a glaze and yes there's lemon zest." She flipped through ad after ad.

"You should go on that donut competition baking show," he said between bites.

"No way. They give the bakers weird ingredients. No one but a paid judge wants to eat a donut made out of ketchup and lemon pepper." She could go for a chocolate glaze right now. When Dalton finally left, she'd whip up some and dip the donuts in it.

"Mind if I have another one?"

Out of the corner of her eye, she saw him lick his fingers.

"Don't you have a job?" She continued to flip pages. "It's the preseason. Don't you need to go micromanage something?"

"Yes, but I'm hungry." He winked at her. "And I'm the boss, so I can do what I want... within reason."

"It seems to me that reason figures a lot into your personal life." She continued flipping.

"What's that supposed to mean?" He reached over and used the towel she was lying on to dry his hands.

"I don't think this is going to come as a shock to you, but you're dull." She flipped the page to find "Kuma Sutra—The Good, the Bad, and the Ugly."

"I'm not dull." His tone suggested that he didn't believe it either.

"If you say so." She scanned the article and was a little disappointed—but not surprised—that there was nothing new.

"I happen to live a very full and fulfilling life." Now he sounded like he was trying to justify his life choices to her. Or, more likely, to himself.

"Of course you do." She flipped more pages.

He stood. "I'm going to make myself another donut."

"Good luck with that." She didn't bother to look up.

He stood there waiting for something—probably for her to get up and help him. "Don't you want to make sure I don't burn myself?"

"Nope, I'm good." She handed him her empty plate. "Can you put that in the sink for me?"

He glanced down at the plate, and she could tell he was trying to decide how to play this. It was almost cute, the way he thought he had a shot of one-upping her. But she'd been trained by Livinia Angleton Wright on how to put—and keep—men in their place. He was going to have to work a lot harder than this to shake her up.

Eventually, he took the plate, but he didn't head back inside. "Do your tatts have meaning or are they just random things you picked out?" He moved closer, until he was standing over her blocking her sun.

Geez. This guy was harder to get rid of than chlamydia.

"They represent places I've been." She tossed the magazine on the table and flipped over. Obviously, he was in no hurry to leave. She pointed to an ornately dressed geisha. "That represents my trip to Japan." She pointed to a volcano. "This is Popocatépetl in central Mexico."

"Popocatépetl—good hiking when the ash isn't too thick." He sat on the edge of her chaise.

"How would you know?" There was no way that Mr. Folds His Jacket had hiked Popocatépetl.

"Hiked it during the off-season. About three months ago." He shrugged like it was no big deal.

"You're lying. It's been closed since January because the eruptions are so violent." She'd caught him in a lie—he was so busted. The only thing she hated more than a starched-collar guy was a faker. Which said something, considering her whole life was fake, apart from the three weeks she spent with Lyric every year.

"There's a back way onto the national park." He worked his phone out of his front pocket. He tapped on the screen several times and pulled up a picture. It was a selfie of him standing on the rim with the lava exploding in the background.

She took the phone from him and analyzed the photo, making sure it was real... not that she'd know if it wasn't. It looked like he really had hiked the closed volcano.

"Now who's dull?" He took the phone back from her.

"You made it all the way to the rim?" It was hard to refute with photographic evidence, but he just didn't seem the type to risk life and limb, not to mention time in a Mexican prison.

"You don't have to sound so surprised." He slid the phone back in his pocket. "There's more to me than meets the eye."

She really didn't like the fact that she wanted to know what that more was.

"So, where exactly is the back entrance to the park?" She wasn't testing him exactly, more like trying to satisfy her curiosity.

"Before I tell you, I want you to make me two donuts. One with chocolate glaze." He stood and offered his hand.

"Extortion... really? I didn't know you had it in you." It was one more thing she kind of liked about him. "Well played."

"Extortion is such an ugly word. I prefer to call it an exchange of goods for information." He put his hand at the small of her back and led her back to the house.

If another man had tried to touch her like that, she probably would have punched him. But with Dalton, it felt... nice. She didn't know how she felt about that.

"You never did tell me why you're baking in a bikini and heels."

"I'm inclined to make up this elaborate lie that involves spies and nuclear weapons and saving lives, but really, I just got hungry while I was out by the pool. And I always wear heels. It's my thing. Except when I'm hiking a Mexican volcano, of course."

She still couldn't believe that Dalton had snuck into a Mexican national park and hiked the freaking rim.

He sighed long and hard. "Yes, I really did hike the rim."

She threw her hands up. "What? I didn't say anything."

"It's written all over your face." He pulled out his phone again. "Feel free to check out all of the photos yourself."

"No, no, I believe you." Still, she totally took the phone and hit the photos icon. Not that she was looking for any women in his life, but if she did see one, she absolutely was not going to ask if he was in a relationship. Just because he appreciated the sight of her in a bikini, and just because he currently had his hand on the small of her back... nope. Didn't matter. She didn't care at all.

She totally scrolled through the photos looking for any photographic evidence of a girlfriend. Instead, she found several selfies of him just about to BASE jump. "You're into BASE jumping?"

She didn't mean for it to sound so improbable, but it did.

"Yes, I just got back from Chile." His eyes stayed on her. "Heath told me you and your sister were supposed to go next week. Sorry you had to cancel."

"Yeah, well, he's an ass. And the trip isn't cancelled. I'm going to change his mind. Lyric and I *will* be going on the trip." Especially since her plan to be a badass here in Fort Worth was currently foundering.

"Sure, I get it. I don't like people telling me what to do either."

She tried not to be impressed—and turned on—by the fact that he got her so well. It was hard, though, considering no one ever did—not even Lyric, who knew her better than anyone. But knowing and understanding were two different things, something Dalton was proving with every word that came out of his mouth.

Not that she wanted him to know that, of course. A woman had to have some secrets, and Harmony had spent her life guarding hers.

# Chapter 9

Dalton had a million things to do, but he just wanted to spend a little more time with Harm. He'd forgotten his phone last night and had meant to just pick it up and leave, but he'd smelled oatmeal cookies baking, and knowing who was behind them had forced him to check it out.

The oatmeal cookies were fantastic, but catching Harm in a bikini was even better than winning the lottery. He'd have loved nothing more than to spend the rest of the day exploring her lush body. She had fuck-me eyes, miles of hair, and legs that went on forever. Legs that he'd love to have wrapped around his waist as he ran is tongue over every single one of her tattoos. And then there were her natural Double D's. He could spend the rest of the day just on those. He tried not to stare at them, but he was most definitely a boob guy. Then again, around Harmony he was a boob guy, a tattoo guy, a leg guy... or maybe he was just a Harmony guy.

He wasn't sure how he felt about that. But he was pretty sure he'd like the chance to find out.

"Hey, eyes up here." Harm dropped the first of this latest batch of donuts into the oil.

"Sorry, they're just well... so uncovered and so spectacular." Fuck. That had made so much more sense in his head. "That really sounded bad."

"Yes, but at least you noticed and acknowledged it. So we'll just pretend you were talking about the donuts." She unwrapped two bars of some fancy chocolate that he'd never heard of, crumbled them into a glass bowl, and stuck the bowl in the microwave. "Easy ganache."

"That's a lot of ganache just for me." He wouldn't mind sharing, especially if sharing meant dunking every part of her in it and then licking it off. Slowly. His gaze went back to her chest before he could help himself, but he caught himself before she busted him again and made sure to look her in the eye.

His phone buzzed with yet another new text. It had been going crazy all morning, and as he pulled it out to check it, he already knew who it was from.

It was from Eleanor, just as the other five billion texts had been. She wanted to know where he was and if he was planning on coming into the office today. He pulled up his calendar. Budget meeting followed by a couple of advertising conference calls, and then there were the hundreds of emails he needed to go through.

He just didn't feel like messing with it today. He'd never played hooky—not from school and certainly not from work—but this morning, he wanted to hang with Five-Alarm Harm just a little bit longer. He shot off a quick text telling Eleanor he'd be in by eleven, then he did something else he'd never done. He turned off his phone.

Harmony noticed. "Wow. Should I be flattered?"

"By my gentlemanly behavior?"

"Yeah, because staring at a woman's tits is soooo gentlemanly." She nodded to his phone. "I get the impression you aren't a guy who ignores work very often."

"You know what they say about all work and no play."

"I don't." She leaned against the counter and arched her back in a way that somehow displayed her magnificent breasts to even better advantage. "Maybe you should come over here and fill me in."

He would love to fill her in, and fill her up. But that wasn't going to happen, not here and not now. Because he really did have to be at work in a couple of hours, and he had a feeling that once he got Harmony into bed he was going to keep her there for days.

"I think I'll just go ahead and let you work it out for yourself." He couldn't resist stepping closer, couldn't resist running a finger along the top edge of her bikini bottoms.

He liked how soft her skin was, how warm and silky she felt. But he liked even more the way she shivered and the way her breath caught in her throat.

He leaned in a little, close enough that his lips were almost brushing against hers. Her eyes sparked at him just a little, but she didn't push him away. Just shifted a little so that her stance was even more inviting.

Which, in the end, was why he pulled away when he really wanted nothing more than to feel her mouth beneath his. But Harm thought she was in control here, and that so wasn't going to fly with him. He liked control too much to give it up, even to her.

Especially to her.

Which was why, when the microwave dinged, he very casually reached past her and pulled out the melted chocolate. "So, got any plans for today?" he asked as he put the bowl on the counter and stepped away.

Harmony stared at him for several long seconds, eyes narrowed and mouth pursed in what he was quickly coming to recognize as her plotting look. Good. He liked that she felt the need to plot around him. It meant she was invested... and that she didn't quite know what to do with him. Master manipulator that she was, he had a feeling Harmony didn't meet very many people she couldn't handle or figure out. He liked that he was one of them.

Not that she was going to let him know he'd gotten her goat. Harmony didn't have any back-down in her. It was another thing he liked about her.

Which was why he wasn't surprised when she said, "The only pressing matter I have besides frying up the rest of these donuts is coming up with new and fantastically horrible ways to ruin my mother's reputation and torment my brother-in-law into letting my sister come on vacation with me next week." She poured cream into the melted chocolate as she spoke, then whisked everything together so vigorously that her Double D's bounced.

Dalton had to work really hard not to groan. And to keep his eyes above her neck.

"Any ideas on how you're going to do that?"

"No. But the day is young." She turned then and ran one hand straight up the row of buttons in the center of his custom-made dress shirt. "Do you have any ideas on what I can do?" She paused for a second, let her voice go breathy. "On what we can do?"

It was as amusing as it was arousing, and he had to tell himself to cool it as his dick twitched in his pants. He wasn't going to fuck Harmony yet, no matter how much she wanted him to. If he did, she'd think she had the upper hand, and that so wasn't how this was going to go down.

"I don't know about you, but I've got to get to work."

"Work is so boring," she said, leaning forward until the tips of those magnificent breasts of hers were pressed against his chest. He nearly caved when he felt how hard her nipples were—and the rings she had pierced through them. Fuck, she was a wild one. "Wanna know what I think we should do?"

He had a feeling he knew exactly what she thought they should do, and any other time—with any other woman—he would have already had her ass on the counter and her legs over his shoulders. But Harmony Wright wasn't any other woman. She was a five-alarm fire, and he was damned if he was going to be the one who got burned.

"I don't have a clue." He quirked his brow in a way he knew would set her on edge. "Why don't you fill me in."

Sure enough, her eyes narrowed even more, the smile on her face turning downright nasty as she answered, "I think we should have sex."

"Do you now?"

"I really, really do."

She stepped even closer, went so far as to hook a hand around the back of his neck and pull his head down to her. Heat sizzled between them, and for a second his mind went blank and his body took over. It would be so easy to say yes, so easy to take her a thousand different ways and make her beg for more.

But she wasn't ready for that yet, and he wasn't about to give into it. So instead of bending her over the counter as they both so desperately wanted, he brought a hand up to her cheek. Stroked his thumb over her mouth and whispered, "If only it were that simple." She slipped her arms around his neck. "What could be simpler than sex?"

"Not having sex." Although, now that he thought about it, that wasn't very simple either.

"That's not simple," she purred as she rubbed herself against him. "That's just boring."

Finally, something they agreed on. But right now, he was pretty sure boring was the way to go. No matter what his dick was telling him.

"So, what …" He nodded to the island. "We just go at it right here?"

"Absolutely. But I get to be on top. Marble can get pretty cold."

Oh, he knew she wanted to be on top, just like he knew it had nothing to do with the marble being cold. What a disappointment she was in for when they finally hit the sheets, because he didn't bottom for anyone.

Rolling up onto the balls of her feet, she pressed her mouth to the sensitive spot right beneath his ear. "Now would be an ideal time for you to kiss me."

"And here I was thinking it would be an ideal time for you to ice my donuts."

It was her turn to quirk a brow. "Is that what the kids are calling it these days?"

He grinned. "Something like that."

"So why don't you show me?" She pressed her hips into his, and when her eyes widened he knew the game was up. Playing it cool was one thing. Hiding his erection was something else entirely.

"There's something you should know about me," he told her as he unlatched her arms and set her a foot away from him. "I don't take orders well."

"Ooooh, playing hard to get." Her royal blue eyes were hooded and sexy. "I like it. But you should know, I like to be in charge."

And to prove it, she reached behind her neck and untied her bikini. The straps fell down to her waist, taking the two triangles of red fabric covering her nipples with them.

They were every bit as extraordinary as he'd imaged they would be. Full D-cups with perfect pink nipples—and he'd been right about the piercings. Both nipples were decorated with tiny silver rings.

He looked his fill even as his hands went to her waist. Then he leaned down, close to her ear, and whispered, "Nice. Very nice."

Gently he gathered up the straps and slid his hands up her back. "Thanks for the invitation," he said as he nipped at her ear, "but I've really got to get to work.

"We'll see about that." He'd tried to be gentle, but he could see the insult and the challenge in her eyes, even before her hands slid up the front of his blue silk shirt and then back down to his waist. And fuck, did it feel good. He loved the way her hands felt on him and couldn't wait until there was nothing between her skin and his own.

For a second he gave himself over to the fantasy, and she took full advantage of his distraction. The next thing he knew, she had popped the buckle of his belt and was working on the button of his trousers. And that's when he knew he'd hit his breaking point, when he knew he had to put a stop to this or he was going to end up fucking Harmony on every surface in this kitchen.

Gently, he took her hands in his, kissed each palm, and set them at her sides. "I'm not a fuck-you to Heath, sweetheart. I'm not going to let you use me to piss him off. When we make love—"

"Make love?" she sneered. " What are you, a teenaged girl? I don't want to be made love to, I want to be fucked."

"Too bad. Because by the time I'm done with you, you'll be begging me to make love to you again."

"That sounds like a challenge." She stood back.

His attempt to retie her top hadn't done much to cover her up. The bikini top drooped around her waist. "No, just a promise."

"You think so?"

"I know so."

"Hmm." Her look said she wasn't so sure. "Well then. Let the games begin."

Her thumbs snaked under her bikini bottoms, and the next thing he knew, that tiny piece of cloth was slipping right down her legs. Next, the top fell to the floor and she stood before him wearing nothing but red high-heeled shoes and a smile. "I need a shower. Are you going to join me or just watch?"

When he didn't respond—too busy trying to get a little blood flow back to his brain—she grabbed his tie and pulled him after her. "I guess you're going to watch."

Fuck that. He was no watcher.

His hands went to her waist and he spun her around. Then his lips were on hers and at that moment, he didn't give a shit about the consequences. Didn't give a shit about who topped or who bottomed or who was in control of what. All he cared about was the way she tasted. The way she felt. The way her breath hitched in her chest as he kissed her.

Picking her up, he wrapped her legs around his waist, and backed her up against the refrigerator. Her hands fisted in his hair and he let them, concentrating instead on cupping her round, heart-shaped ass. Fuck, he wanted her. Wanted all of her, right here and right now. Had never wanted anyone or anything as badly as he wanted her right then.

Which was why he pulled away.

Why he gave her one last, tender kiss before tucking his hands in his pockets.

Why he whispered a hoarse, "I've got to go," before turning and walking out of the house.

Because he might keep himself under rigid control, but every man had his breaking point. And he was pretty sure Harmony was going to be his.

# Chapter 10

The next morning, Harmony parked her vintage 1950s bakery delivery van in a parking spot close to the front gate of Wranglers Stadium. She was still fuming—and a little bamboozled—over the way Dalton had left her in the kitchen yesterday morning, and the man was going to pay for it. And she was going to enjoy every second of it.

After all, she was an instant-gratification kind of girl. When she was five and couldn't wait any longer for Santa Claus to show up, she'd gone to the garage, found some spare wood, and started building the table and chairs she'd wanted for her tea parties. True, the table was lopsided and the chairs only had three legs, but she'd gotten her instant gratification. Her parents still had the table and chairs in their house in San Angelo.

Which was why this whole business of waiting around for him to decide they'd known each other long enough to "make love" so wasn't cutting it for her.

###

She was a go-getter and not a wait-arounder, which was why it was bugging her so much that trying to get Dalton naked and between her thighs was proving so difficult. And she was done with that. She was here to take Dalton to lunch and then take him to bed.

Clearly he was as attracted to her as she was to him, and she was going to do what her daddy had always told her to do in difficult situations—take the bull by the horns. The fact that she was really looking forward to getting her hands on Dalton's horn was neither here nor there. She was a woman on a mission, and she didn't mean Mission Impossible.

Picking up the handcuffs she'd just bought at the Velvet Box, she slipped them into her perfectly respectable Coach purse. Then she grabbed the bakery box holding a bag of chocolate chip cookies and the chocolate pecan bourbon pie she'd made. It had been a lot of work, but it was totally worth it, as in her experience, chocolate pecan bourbon pie was almost always the dessert of choice for the overly efficient, pit bull assistant types who guarded their bosses like they would the fine china they'd inherited from their great-aunt Agatha. And since she was pretty sure Dalton had one of those, she had come prepared.

After sliding out of the driver's seat and locking the door, Harmony straightened her perfectly respectable royal-blue Ann Taylor wrap dress and strutted across the parking lot in a pair of black lace-up Christian Louboutin Megavamps. She had handcuffs, fuck-me shoes, and no underwear—what else could a man want?

With her black Coach hobo on her shoulder and the pie in hand, she used the shiny new building directory to locate Dalton's office. She took the elevator to the top floor—of course he had a top-floor office—and stepped out into a lobby of sorts. A woman with gray hair artfully scraped back into a bun sat at a desk in front of a set of double doors. Her nameplate proclaimed her to be Eleanor Sanchez, and she was a pit bull assistant if Harmony had ever seen one.

The only problem?

Harmony hadn't taken her age into consideration. Efficient females over fifty tended to be lemon meringue fans. Still, the chocolate bourbon should do the trick... unless she was Baptist, in which case Harmony's whole plan was up shit creek.

Eleanor's eyes snapped up from the computer she was sitting behind and she stood up, a huge smile dawning on her otherwise serious face. "Lyric, so good to see you again."

Harmony wasn't about to look a gift horse in the mouth. "So good to see you too, Eleanor. You work so hard for Dalton and this whole organization that I just wanted to thank you. So I brought you a chocolate pecan bourbon pie."

"Well thank you. That sounds... interesting. I'm usually more of a lemon meringue fan, but I'm up for trying something new." Eleanor's face screwed up. "Those stupid tabloids. Don't listen to them. It's a free country and you can go wherever you please."

Lyric had never been one to read tabloids, but Harmony would pass the reminder along just in case things had changed.

"Thanks." Harmony smiled and hoped that was all she needed to say. God willing, the woman wasn't a fan of Lyric's Crab Nebula podcast, because Harmony could only fake being a good girl for so long, and she sure as shit couldn't fake being an astrophysicist at all. "Can I have a minute of his time?" She pointed to the double doors.

"Yes, just a minute though... lots going on today." Eleanor put the pie down on her desk and opened the door for Harmony. "Go right in."

This Lyric thing was even better than she thought—no warning from Eleanor meant she had a clear shot to ambush Dalton. Yippee.

Harmony couldn't help admiring the expansive view as she stepped into Dalton's office. The entire back wall of the office was windows, and he had an amazing view of downtown Fort Worth.

Dalton was on the phone and typing on the computer, and he hadn't noticed her standing there, so she shut the door quietly behind her. Then turned the lock just as quietly.

"What morality clause? This is the NFL. If they required us to have a morality clause, we'd have no players left." He gritted his teeth. "I know, Barry. I'll have a talk with him. I understand that we don't need the bad press." There was a pause during which Barry was no doubt yelling at Dalton. "I'll take care of it. That's right. Thanks." Another pause. "I'll see you in five." He slammed the phone down.

"Bad day at the office, honey?" Harmony placed the handcuffs and the white sack filled with chocolate chip cookies on the desk. "I guess you don't have time for either of those." She sat on the corner of his desk, letting the front of her wrap dress fall open. "Or for this, either."

Dalton's eyes roamed up her legs, lingered on her upper thighs and then breasts and finally made it all the way to her face. "You're a sight for sore eyes."

"I guess playing hooky for the afternoon is out?" She dangled her left leg off the desk, which made the dress open further. "Since you're such a busy boss man?"

His eyes went to her thighs again, and he licked his lips. "Right now, I really wish I wasn't."

"Yeah, me too." What was wrong with him? He wanted her and she wanted him. They were adults. "Do you have a girlfriend or something?"

She sat forward, waiting for the answer. He hadn't said anything yesterday, but he was a guy and they were funny about honesty. God knew she'd been burned more than once.

"No. And before you ask, I'm not married either." His eyes stayed on her thighs as he leaned back. "I guess we should have sorted that out yesterday. Are you in a relationship?"

"No. Do you think I'd be nearly naked on your desk right now if I was?" Still, he got points for asking and being a decent human being. "Then why aren't we naked right now?"

"What is it with you and sex? Seems like you've got a one-track mind." He grinned, and damn it, both of his dimples popped out. Handsome men shouldn't be allowed to have dimples. It was overkill, especially since she couldn't help thinking about how much she wanted to lick them. "Don't you want to get to know me? I have layers."

"Yes, and you're wearing way too many of them." She leaned forward, and her boobs nearly fell out of her dress. "I, on the other hand, am only wearing one."

She had on a bra, but that was beside the point.

He shook his head. "I'm beginning to think you only want me for my body."

"Wow, it took you two whole days to figure that out?" She looked around. "I guess common sense didn't come with that MBA."

"You've been checking up on me." His smile widened.

"The Internet is very handy." She picked up the handcuffs and twirled one bracelet around her finger.

Like she weighed nothing, he reached out, picked her up, and settled her onto his lap.

"I wanted to do this the first night I met you, but I think Heath would have gotten out the large-caliber weapons if we'd made out on his couch." He kissed her cheek and worked his way over to the corner of her mouth. He sucked on her bottom lip.

Her arms snaked around his neck as her fingers raked through his hair. His tongue plunged inside her mouth and slowly explored. She couldn't help it, she felt herself melt into him. All she wanted was more. More of him and more of the feelings he brought to life inside of her.

Dalton must have read her mind, because his hand slid under her dress, inside her bra, and found her nipple. He rolled it between his index finger and thumb, tugging on her nipple ring just hard enough to make heat slide through her.

But what she really wanted was for his mouth to take the place of his hands. As she arched her back and urged his head down, he finally got the message. He licked his way down her neck, pushed her bra down and devoured her. She found his hand and slid it between her legs and inside of her. Then had to bite her lip to keep from letting him know how good he felt.

Dalton had no such issues. "Fuck, baby, you're so wet," he said, his voice low and dark and gravelly. "You feel so good."

She started to tell him that he did too, but a buzzing noise came from the general direction of his desk, followed by a female voice saying, "You're five minutes late for the meeting, Dalton. Mr. Lamont is looking for you."

Dalton froze and withdrew his hand and his mouth. "Sorry, duty calls."

"I seriously hate that woman." Turning her nose up at a chocolate bourbon pecan pie was one thing. But interrupting just when things were getting interesting... Harmony wasn't about to forgive her for that. Not when she was about to be left high and dry and sexually frustrated.

Still, she stood up. Dalton had work to do, and the last thing she wanted was for him to actually kick her out of his office. She wasn't sure her ego—or her feminine wiles—would recover.

"Sorry, Harm. Big meeting. The tabloids are killing us." He stood and buttoned his suit jacket.

"Eleanor said something about the tabloids too. What's going on?" She shoved her boobs back into her bra and retied her dress.

His eyes stayed on her breasts. "I don't suppose you'd do that again?"

His hair was mussed.

"I'd love to, but you don't have the time." She finger-combed his hair. "We didn't even have sex, but somehow you have after-sex hair." Which just pissed her off more. It really sucked getting caught *before* they did the deed.

He let her straighten him up, then bent to press a quick kiss to her lips. "Be careful when you're leaving here, Harm. The tabs think they're onto a story. Someone at Dead Shot took a picture of you dancing on the table and another one of Heath punching the bartender. The world is getting an eyeful of football's cutest couple acting out. Not only are the tabloids claiming that you're Lyric, they're all going on about how Heath and Lyric are meth addicts who frequent biker bars. One even suggested that you—Lyric—have turned to prostitution to pay for your drug habit." Dalton sighed like the weight of the world was on his shoulders.

Oh, shit. Why hadn't Heath or Lyric said anything? Ruining her reputation was one thing. Messing with Lyric's was something else all together.

But worry wasn't productive, so Harm did what she always did—went from concerned to pissed off in six seconds flat.

"Double standard much? You run an NFL football team not the Boy Scouts. Your players break more laws in an evening than Lyric and I do in a lifetime. But one small bar brawl makes headlines? Why don't y'all tell them to fuck off and mind their own goddamn business?"

She was pissed as hell. How dare people judge her sister and make up lies about her? Screw Heath, she didn't care what happened to him, but Lyric deserved better than that.

She smoothed out the wrinkles in her dress. "Let me talk to your boss. I'll straighten things out." By the time she was done with him, he'd regret ever meeting the Wright girls.

"Yeah, I don't think that's going to happen. I like my job and Heath likes his." He kissed her cheek. "I would like to finish what we started, though. Say, after we have dinner?"

"You can't stop me from talking to your boss or the press." She wasn't backing down.

"What exactly would you tell them?" He nuzzled her ear.

"To fuck off and mind their own goddamn business." Hello, that was enough... wasn't it?

"Yeah, I'm still gonna have to go with no."

"You can't stop me."

"Wanna bet?" He sucked on her earlobe.

"Stop that. I'm not about to be distracted from this." Still, she tilted her head back and let him nuzzle at her throat a little. Just because it was calming and she needed a little bit of—

She froze as something cold clamped around her left wrist and tightened.

"What the hell are you doing?" she demanded, pulling against the handcuff.

But Dalton tugged her forward and locked the other handcuff to a metal rail under the window behind his desk. "You need to cool off a little. You aren't going to talk to the press or to my boss or to anyone right now. You've caused enough trouble."

"Son of a bitch! You haven't even seen how much trouble I can cause." She grabbed for his jacket, but he stepped out of the way. She was going to scratch his eyes out. He could *not* do this to her. He could *not*. "Unlock these right now. This isn't funny."

He grinned. "It's a little funny."

Screw him, she had the key in her purse. She dove for it, but he was there a millisecond sooner. He snatched it up and set it on a chair well out of her reach.

"If you leave me locked in here, I swear I'll scream so loud even the Dallas Cowboys will hear me." She was going to kill him in some particularly horrible way. Maybe acid or boll weevils or flesh-eating bacteria. Whatever it was, it was going to be painful. She would make sure of it.

"Go right ahead. The walls are made of concrete. The only one who will hear you is you." He blew her a kiss. "I'll be back in an hour or so. By then you should have calmed down enough to face the world in a civil manner."

Civil manner? Was he British? Who talked like that?

"You really think that's how this is going to go down?" she demanded. "Because I promise, you're going to pay for this... big time." It was a wonder her teeth didn't grind to dust, she was so pissed.

"I'm counting on it." He raised the hand that she'd slid between her thighs not two minutes ago and licked his index and middle fingers. "Believe me, baby. I am so looking forward to you making me pay."

"Don't call me baby."

He just blew her a kiss and then disappeared.

"Bastard. You no-good, rotten son of a bitch. Get back here and unlock me!"

She got no response at all. Not even Eleanor peeked her head in the door. Damn it, maybe this office really was soundproofed after all.

Just the thought sent her from seriously pissed off straight into a towering rage. She kicked the desk and jerked at the cuffs, even pounded on the window, and still no one came to her rescue.

She tossed his desk, looking for a letter opener or screwdriver or something she could use to get the damn cuffs off. In the movies, all you needed was a paper clip, but she couldn't even find one of those. What kind of office was he running here?

Bastard. He'd better believe she was going to make him pay.

She sat down hard in his chair and tried to think through the fury.

Her eyes landed on his computer. It was a very powerful tool, and he'd left it in the hands of a sexually frustrated, angry-as-hell woman. That was his second mistake, right after locking her in these damn handcuffs to begin with.

At least now she knew how she was going to make him pay. He'd made a serious tactical mistake, and she was totally going to take advantage of it.

She hit the space bar and a screen popped up asking for his password. Of course he'd have it password protected. Bastard. So what were the chances he'd be one of the thirty percent of people who actually wrote down their password and left it on their desks? She didn't think the odds were great, but she checked anyway. She started by looking around the monitor for a password written on a sticky note, then pulled out all of his drawers and dumped the contents on the floor.

She kind of hoped she'd find something kinky, but the only weird thing was the alarming amount of pencils he had. How could she possibly be thinking about having sex with a man who had that many pencils?

She forced herself to stop counting the things at sixty-five, and finally, written on a sticky note taped to the underside of the bottom left drawer, she found what looked like a password.

She typed it in and bam, she was in.

So much power... so much time alone. Clearly, Dalton wasn't half as smart as he thought he was.

She could email the police and tell them that she was being held against her will, but that really wasn't painful enough.

She pulled up his contacts and smiled. Starting with Hank Alfred, she cut his cell number and pasted it into Cory Almoni's cell. For the next thirty minutes she played musical cell numbers so that when he linked his phone and his contacts updated, he'd try to call Marco Heinz and get Julie Jetter. There were three groups in his contacts, groundskeeping, support staff, and catering. Harmony pulled up his email and created a new message to groundskeeping, support staff, and catering. They were all getting a pay raise effective immediately of a thousand... no, five thousand dollars a year. Manual labor was hard work—they deserved every penny.

After pulling up his web browser, she signed him up for several prison dating websites, turned on the parental controls so that he could only surf the web from midnight to four thirty in the morning, and turned on Windows Narrator and set it to "echo user's keystrokes" so it would read along as he typed. Then she took a screenshot of his desktop, hid his icons, and put the screenshot up so it looked like his desktop. And finally, she changed his password.

But that only took fifteen minutes, and once it was done, she was bored again. She was sifting through the pile of junk she'd dumped out onto the floor, contemplating what she could do to all those pencils to really make him hurt, and that was when she found the dime. Her eyes went to the screws holding the pole she was handcuffed to to the wall and then back to the dime. It was almost too easy.

Slowly, she used the dime to work the screws loose and popped them out. Then she slid the cuff off the pole and she was a free woman again. She grabbed the key off the chair where Dalton had left it and unlocked the cuffs, letting them fall onto his desktop. A parting gift for him. She should slash his tires, but he probably drove a Maserati, and she really liked Maseratis. Plus that poor car hadn't done anything to her. The same couldn't be said for its owner.

It was time for Dalton to learn his lesson the hard way—no one handcuffed her unless she wanted to be handcuffed. On her way out the door, she gathered up all those sharpened pencils and stabbed them—one after another—into last year's Super Bowl winning football. Or at least that was what was engraved on the tag outside of the clear plastic box it was displayed in.

Dalton Mane deserved everything she'd done to him and more. She hoped he was man enough to come after her and get what was coming to him.

# Chapter 11

Dalton threw open the double doors to his office expecting the worst. He and Heath had just had their asses chewed out by the team owner, and returning to find Harmony in his office might have taken the sting out. But of course, he was right. She wasn't there. Not that he'd expected her to be. She wouldn't be the woman he thought she was if she'd just sat idly by and waited for him to return.

But good God, what a mess she'd made.

He walked to his desk, shaking his head as he saw the disaster that was his floor. Then again, he figured he'd had it coming. Locking Harmony up had been a big risk, but one he hadn't felt like he'd had a choice about. An angry Harmony was a liability. Having a coach involved in a bar fight really wasn't that big of a deal, but if Harmony had burst into Dalton's meeting with the team owner and Commissioner Goodell, things would have gone downhill in a big damn hurry.

Barry Lamont thought women were put on this earth to decorate it and should be seen but never heard, and, well, Dalton didn't know Commissioner Goodell's stance on women, but he was pretty sure that a pissed-off Harmony could have turned Gloria Steinem against her own kind.

He picked up the drawers and fit them back into his desk and then knelt down and scooped up all of the junk he'd collected over the years. He pulled the trash can over.

Now was as good a time as any to spring-clean the hell out of his office.

An hour later, he couldn't get Harmony out of his head. He didn't feel the need to apologize to her so much as he just wanted to see what horrible things she had planned in retaliation. Besides the pencil-stabbed football, which—he wasn't going to lie—hurt a lot.

Figuring the least he could do was send her a balloon bouquet—or maybe some high-end jewelry—he hit the space bar to bring his computer screen to life. Flowers seemed a little too cliché, and no baked goods on earth could compare to what Harmony whipped up with ease. But he wasn't really sure where to look for biker chic in balloons or jewelry—he'd been too broke to afford either when he was a member of the Bastards, so he figured he'd mess around on the Internet, see what he could find.

When he clicked the icon for his web browser, it didn't come up. So he clicked it again. And again. And again. Still nothing.

He clicked the icon for his monthly financial reports.

Nothing.

He clicked the icon for the team roster.

Nothing.

He clicked on the Apple icon to restart the computer, but no Apple menu dropped down.

What in the hell had Harmony done to his computer?

Pranks were one thing, but now she was messing with his job.

He grabbed his cell to call IT, but it was dead, so he grabbed the charging cable hooked to his computer and plugged in the phone. He hit the intercom button on his desk phone.

"Yes?" Eleanor answered.

"Can you have IT come up here? My computer isn't working." Shit. He'd known Harm was smart, but he hadn't taken her for a computer genius. Maybe he should have, considering who her sister was.

"Absolutely. And thank you so much for that raise. I feel very appreciated, and so does the entire support staff. You're very generous." Eleanor sounded extraordinarily happy.

What raise?

"Yes, well, you deserve it." He let go of the intercom button as his mind whirled with possibilities.

The *entire* support staff? Harmony had given a raise to the entire support staff? Jesus. Just how generous had she been? He banged his head on the keyboard, but all he got was a headache. He reached for his phone, but it still wasn't charged enough to check email. Damn it. Five-Alarm Harm had struck again.

An hour later, IT still hadn't fixed his computer.

"No way," Jess Carlyle, head IT tech, said under his breath. "Whoever did this is a diabolical genius."

Yeah, Dalton had already figured that out. But he wasn't feeling nearly as warm and fuzzy about it as Jess seemed to be. "What do you mean?"

"The reason you couldn't click on the icons is because your desktop is a picture of your desktop. Your actual desktop is underneath it. See?" He hit escape and the picture minimized. "I'm going to restart your computer and it should go back to normal." He hit a series of buttons and then the log-in box came up. "Enter your password."

Dalton leaned forward to type it in. Instead of opening to the desktop, the screen flickered for a second before saying he'd entered the wrong password. He entered it again and still nothing. She'd reset his password too. He'd give her points for creativity—right after he turned her over his knee and spanked that luscious bottom of hers.

"Can you reset my password?"

"Sure." Jess typed and a series of screens came up. He typed and typed. "Enter your new password."

Dalton typed in a new password and made a mental note to add it to the password list in his phone as opposed to the sticky note under his desk. He had no doubt he'd do something to piss Harmony off again soon, and he was a man who learned from his mistakes.

"What in the holy hell is going on here?" Barry Lamont boomed from the doorway. He stabbed the air in front of him with his tablet. He touched the screen, pulled something up, and waved it like Dalton could see it from fifty feet away. "You gave everyone a raise?"

"Jess, can you please excuse us?" Dalton shoved his hands in his pockets and tried not to think of all of the ways he was going to kill Harmony.

"You bet." The computer guy left his laptop on the desk and strolled out of the office. "I'll just see if Eleanor has any of that pie left."

Wait a minute. Harmony had brought his assistant a pie? All he'd gotten were chocolate chip cookies, and Harm had taken those with her before he'd even gotten one. Which, come to think of it, didn't seem fair considering all the havoc she had wrought.

"A raise ...?" Barry was a domineering control freak who liked to think that he ran the world. "Son, what were you thinkin'?"

"My computer was hacked and an email was sent out without my knowledge or consent." He'd gotten and kept this job by not backing down. "I'll fix it."

He couldn't exactly say that he'd handcuffed Lyric Montgomery's evil twin in his office and it was payback. Especially not after the meeting they'd just had with the commissioner.

"You'd better, or start looking for a new job." Barry stormed out just like he'd stormed in.

Dalton took a couple of deep breaths and pulled up his sent emails. Harm had given everyone except the players, coaches, and cheerleaders a five-thousand-dollar-a-year raise. He scrubbed his face with his hands. With a few keystrokes, she'd added six hundred and twenty-five thousand dollars to his annual budget. How exactly did he revoke an almost company-wide raise without angering his employees?

Yes, he could send out another email explaining the situation, but people were funny about their money. They wouldn't care that it had all been a joke.

What a big fuckin' mess.

It looked like he'd be spending the rest of the afternoon finding a way to squeeze an additional six hundred and twenty-five thousand dollars out of the budget—which was not at all what he'd had planned.

Then again, nothing had gone as he'd planned since Five-Alarm Harm had walked into his life. The woman was a force of nature, and trying to control her was proving was fruitless.

What surprised him the most was that he didn't want to control her. Even after everything she'd done, he wanted to sit back and watch her in action.

# Chapter 12

"I still don't understand why didn't you tell me about the tabloids running with the bar fight?" Harmony was having a hard time making eye contact with her twin because Lyric had her eyes trained on her laptop. When Lyric was working, the world around her stopped spinning.

It was high school all over again. Harmony raised hell and Lyric got blamed for it. What did a girl have to do to lose her good reputation?

"Because it's stupid. Everyone is making a big deal out of nothing."

Lyric was super smart, like genius smart. Because her brain was too busy solving the mysteries of the universe, she tended not to notice or care about things like pop culture, tabloids, and social interaction. Sometimes it was hard to impress upon her that other things besides astrophysics actually mattered.

"Are you sure?" Harm watched Lyric for any sign that her twin was taking fallout because of her. The last thing she wanted was to hurt Lyric in any way. They might be as different as two twins could be, but she would do anything for Lyric.

"Yes, I'm sure. It's dumb and I don't acknowledge dumb."

It was a familiar refrain, one Lyric had been spouting ever since they were sophomores in high school and Brent

Neuhaus had spread rumors that he'd slept with Lyric. It had made no sense to Lyric what the big deal was. She knew she hadn't slept with him, so what did it matter what the rest of the world thought? She hadn't realized what people were saying about her behind her back and what was getting back to Momma. But Harm had. She'd cornered Brent outside of the band hall and kneed him in the nuts hard enough to raise his voice three octaves.

He'd stopped talking about her sister.

In Harmony's opinion, that was the trouble with adulthood. You couldn't just knee someone in the balls to make them shut up when they were being an asshole. And there had to be women working at the tabloids too, so a knee to the southern region would be awkward and not very satisfying. She supposed she could knee women in the boobs, but the physics involved seemed overly complicated. Which meant she was going to have to find another way to shut this thing down. It might not bother Lyric, but Harm had been fighting battles her sister didn't know about their whole lives. She wasn't about to stop now.

Lyric finally stopped typing and looked up. "So, what's the deal with you and Dalton?"

Harm cringed at the name. "I hate him. He's an asshole. End of story."

Lyric studied her like she was trying to use X-ray vision to map the inside of Harmony's brain. "Here's the thing... I'm not sure I buy that, because you only get this mad when you're interested in someone. Remember Lance Smith?"

"How could I forget my first love?" Harm sing-songed as she fanned herself. "I just knew we were destined to end up married with four kids. Soul mates whose eyes met across the wide expanse of the cafeteria on the first day of sixth grade. It was fate."

"Until his eyes latched onto Brianna Winsor." Lyric closed her laptop.

"The slut." There wasn't much heat to the insult, since Brianna Winsor-Smith had been one of her best friends to this day. "He only wanted her because of her early-developing C-cups." She pointed to her own D-cups. "My boobs are so much better. And so are yours." She thought about it for a second. "Now that I think about it, Brianna and Lance are married with four kids and did fall in love in middle school and never looked back. Now he's an out-of-work mechanic who hangs Christmas lights for a living, drinks too much, and talks about his glory days in high school. Dodged a bullet there."

The "great" thing about San Angelo was it was small enough that you got to keep tabs on all your old classmates—whether you wanted to or not.

"The point is, you were hurt and sad and glued his locker shut. When Sam Ellinger broke up with you, you started laughing because you didn't care." Lyric leaned back and crossed her arms. "And all I'm saying is, you were pretty mad when you got home this morning."

"Dalton handcuffed me to a pole in his freakin' office. Who does that?" Bastard—she could feel herself getting mad all over again.

"I gotta tell you, I didn't think he had it in him. Where did he even get the handcuffs?" Lyric's brow scrunched up. "Did he just pull them out of a drawer or something? I can't see him just having handcuffs lying around."

"Never mind where he got the handcuffs. That's not the important part. The point is that he handcuffed me against my will and then left me there while he went off to some important meeting." Harmony sighed. Sometimes Lyric just couldn't see the big picture through the forest of minutiae.

"For no reason? I don't know Dalton that well, but he doesn't seem like the type who does anything for no reason." Lyric thought about it for a minute. "Is there a type of person who handcuffs people for no reason?"

"I hope not." Harm shook her head. "Anyway, he's on my shit list. I doubt I'll ever see him again." The thought made her sad. She liked hanging out with Dalton. He wasn't boring like most men.

"Wanna bet?" Lyric's eyes gleamed in the overhead fluorescent lighting of the kitchen.

"No." Harm had a feeling something was up. Lyric only wanted to bet when she knew she could win.

"Too bad for me." Her sister reached for an apple from the fruit dish in the middle of the table. "He's coming over for dinner tonight."

Harm told herself the pitter-pat of her heart was just indigestion from the Taco Bell mad feast she'd eaten on her way back to Lyric's house.

"Oh no he isn't. He isn't that brave. Or that stupid."

"Oh yes he is. Brave, I mean. Not stupid. He seems like a pretty smart guy. Or at least he did, until he got on your shit list."

"Exactly what I'm saying." She'd get her chance to kill him after all. And it wouldn't even have to be a messy affair. Poison was completely undetectable if you hid it in from-scratch brownies and then covered those brownies with strawberries and whipped cream. Or so she'd heard …

Now all she had to figure out was where to hide the body. She didn't know Fort Worth that well, and a body-dump search wasn't exactly what she wanted on her Google search history when Dalton went missing. Then again, Heath and Lyric had a huge backyard. They probably wouldn't even notice if she dug up a corner.

"Wait, why is he coming to dinner? Are he and Heath best buddies now or something?" If they were, it would complicate her plan. People tended to get upset when their sisters-in-law killed their BFFs. Harmony had never really understood why, but that was the way of the world.

Maybe she'd misjudged Dalton's relationship with Heath?

"No, this is the first time. He called Heath and invited himself over. I think he wants to apologize to you. He's bringing dinner." Lyric clamped a hand over her mouth. "Crap, I wasn't supposed to tell you. Dalton wanted to surprise you."

Harm had a feeling it was less about surprising her and more about making sure she was here for dinner. That was the kind of tricky thing he would pull. Of course, since her first thought was to disappear before he got here, it proved he knew her a little better than she wanted him to. Better than she wanted anyone to, if she was being honest.

But now that she knew what he was up to—and what he expected her to do—she couldn't run. Partly because she wasn't a coward and partly because there was no way she was going to give him the satisfaction of knowing he'd won this round. Because he hadn't. And he wasn't going to. Since he was bringing dinner, she'd put herself in charge of making dessert. And just to prove she was a lady, she would leave the rat poison in the garage.

That didn't mean she was taking this whole thing lying down. No freaking way. If Dalton didn't want to have sex with her, she'd find someone who did. And she'd bring him to dinner.

Maybe all Dalton needed was a little healthy competition. Once he realized he wasn't the only guy she was interested in, he'd step up to the plate. And she'd exact her revenge by hitting him in the balls with a hundred-mile-an-hour fastball. Metaphorically speaking, of course.

Now the only problem was figuring out where she could get a date on short notice. She didn't know anyone in the Fort Worth area except her sister and her new husband and, well, Yoko the Okinawan hooker. Plus Rooster and BA, but she figured sometimes it was better to let sleeping dogs lie. Besides, she'd already been there and done that, and Dalton had come out on top. But how could she have known—how could anyone have known—that Heath's general manager would be stepbrother to the head of one of the most dangerous biker gangs in Texas? The whole thing was absurd.

Which meant that this time she was going old school. If she was lucky, she could not only land a date that would make Dalton fume, she'd also get herself on the cover of the tabloids—taking Lyric's place, once and for all, as the evil twin. Once that was complete, her reputation would be in tatters and Momma would—hopefully—wash her hands of the bakery once and for all.

Speaking of which …

"Has Heath come around about our vacation next week?" Harm still hadn't cancelled their trip to Chile, because she really wanted to go. And because she was certain her powers of persuasion would be able to change Heath's mind eventually.

"Nope. Heath is convinced I'll break my legs, and he likes my legs just the way they are." Lyric bit into the apple.

"That's right." Heath walked in with a football in one hand and a phone in the other. "If Lyric breaks her legs, she can't put her ankles on my shoulders." His grin practically swallowed his face. "And I really like having her ankles on my shoulders."

"Apparently. I heard y'all last night *and* this morning. You two make a lot of noise." Harmony looked around the room. "You'd think a house this nice would have soundproofing. It's not like my room is anywhere close to yours."

"Oh no, you didn't hear us. You heard him." Lyric pointed to Heath. "He's so loud, I'm not sure soundproofing would do much good."

"It's not that I'm loud, darlin'." Heath put his hand over his heart. "It's just that I'm enthusiastic. It's your fault for being so bendy. It gives a guy ideas."

Lyric's smile was a little sultry as she eyed her husband. "I like it when you have ideas."

"Believe me, the feeling is mutual. Especially when you get an idea like you had last night." He turned back to Harmony. "Lyric was playing the part of very expensive call girl and well... I really got into it."

"You sure did. I made two grand and had a whole lot of fun doing it." Lyric grinned. It was obvious that she loved her husband and the life they were making together.

"Speaking of hookers, can Lyric borrow your thigh-high boots from the other night? It's so cool y'all wear the same size. She would look spectacular in those boots." His eyes glazed over like he was already imagining his wife in them.

"Cool down, lover boy. Remember, Dalton's coming to dinner and—"

"We have a couple of hours." Heath kissed Lyric and then turned to Harm. "Boots."

"My room in the closet. I'll be here in the kitchen with my music turned up extra loud. Feel free to defile my sister. At least one of us is getting laid. God knows my lady parts haven't played with any boy parts in a very long time."

"Don't say things like that." Heath gagged and spit into the trash. "Sorry, I just threw up a little bit in my mouth. Don't you know sisters-in-law aren't supposed to have lady parts?"

Before she could answer, he scooped Lyric up Rhett Butler style and headed for their room. She could hear Lyric giggling the whole way.

"I would lend you my handcuffs but Dalton stole them," Harm called after him. She loved making Heath uncomfortable.

"Something else I didn't want to know about you," Heath called back, right before a door slammed.

Harm grabbed her smartphone and stuck it on the charging dock/speaker on the expansive gray marble bar top. She scrolled until she found her baking playlist number five—for when she was feeling really mean—and

Megadeath blasted out. Then she closed the door to the kitchen and turned up the sound to drown out whatever noise might come from the other side of the house.

As she started on the triple-chocolate-chunk brownies—without arsenic—she started plotting how she could get a date in the next two hours.

She put butter, sugar, and a bit of water in a saucepan and set it to boil. In a small mixing bowl, she combined the flour, baking soda, espresso powder, and just a hint of cayenne pepper. While she waited for the butter and sugar mixture to boil, she made a mental list of any male she knew who lived close enough to play her dinner date.

JJ Meuler had moved to Plano last year, but he'd moved in with his boyfriend.

Eric Peterson lived in Arlington, but his personal hygiene left a lot to be desired.

Terrence Shuck had moved to Dallas, but his wife Arlene probably wouldn't like him going out on a date with Harmony. She'd always been the jealous sort.

The butter mixture was bubbling, so Harm took it off the heat and added two cups of sixty percent Callebaut chocolate chips, then set the mixture aside to cool.

So what the hell was she going to do? She needed to find a date and fast. She thought about a Tinder hookup, but she didn't even have a profile yet. She was pretty sure two and a half hours wasn't enough time to make a profile, get a date, and also get him over here to rub in Dalton's face. Fort Worth traffic *was* a bitch, after all.

It was definitely time to go old school... like lemonade-stand old school. All she needed was a gold-lamé bikini, some poster board, a chaise lounge, and a can-do attitude. And lucky for her, she had all of the above except for the poster board. Which she figured could be remedied easily enough.

The chocolate mixture had finally cooled, so she stirred in a couple of eggs and then added the dry ingredients. She poured the batter into a baking pan, added more chocolate chips, and put it in the oven to bake for half an hour.

With that taken care of, she headed to her room to dress for Operation Quick Date. Or undress, as the case may be.

Thirty minutes later, the brownies were cooling on the stove top and she was out in the front yard wearing her favorite gold-lamé bikini and holding a sign that read, "I NEED A DATE for dinner tonight, are you in?"

She'd dragged one of the chaise lounges and a side table from around the pool to the front yard so she could be comfortable while she panhandled for a date. She didn't think it would take that long, but she'd brought a big glass of lemonade out with her, just in case.

This was Texas, and it was always good to stay hydrated.

Ten minutes went by and there were no takers. Then again, nobody had even driven by. Stupid gated golf course community.

Maybe if she walked around and strutted her stuff a little the neighbors would call all of their single friends and she'd be set. Figuring it couldn't hurt to test the plan out, Harm stood on her six-inch Christian Louboutin gold spiked platforms and took a lap around the front yard.

As she did, she twirled her white poster board like she was standing on the corner of a busy highway holding a furniture store going-out-of-business sign. At this point, subtlety wasn't an option. She was going for as much attention as possible as quickly as possible.

About two minutes later, a pimply-faced teenaged boy rolled up on a dark-blue Schwinn. "You really need a date?"

"Depends." Maybe she should have put a minimum age on her sign. "Are you legal?"

"Had my bar mitzvah last week. My dad says I'm a man now." He pulled out his smartphone and snapped several pictures of her.

Harmony didn't want to know what he planned on doing with them.

"I don't think the cops accept Jewish law as proof of age." She shook her head. "Move along, I'm on a tight schedule."

"Can I take a selfie with you?" He hopped off the bike, leaving it in the middle of the road, and ran over to her. "Or, I could take a video of you running around the front yard and post it on YouTube with your address. You could probably drum up business that way."

It was a good idea and she almost went with it, but Lyric and Heath would kill her if she broadcasted their address over the Internet.

So instead she pointed in the direction bar mitzvah boy had come from. "Kid, get back on your bicycle and go home. I don't have time for this."

"Just trying to help you out." He shoved his phone in the back pocket of his jeans. "I live four doors down on the left if you change your mind."

Harmony grabbed the black Sharpie she'd used to make the sign from the table and added an asterisk at the bottom of her sign, along with, "Must be over twenty-one."

Five minutes later, a golf cart pulled up in front of the house.

The man driving the golf cart waved. "Still need a date?" Slowly, he turned around and pulled a walker out of the backseat. It took him three tries, but he finally stood and climbed out of the golf cart. Then he shuffled up the sidewalk toward her at a rate of one millimeter per minute. He looked like a sweet old guy and she didn't want him to trip on the curb and break something, so she went to him.

She opened her mouth to tell him that yes, she still needed a date, but closed it when he started talking.

"I'm Elroy McTavish." He grinned and stuck out his hand for her to shake. She shook his hand and tried to pull her hand away, but he held it. "The pharmacy just delivered my new prescription," his furry eyebrows waggled up and down, "if you know what I mean. Which means, if you give me an hour, I can rock your world, Cutie Pie. Only—if we're going out, you have to drive. I lost my license on account of that liquor store I accidentally drove through."

She really hadn't thought this out.

"I'm going to have to pass." She tried to think of a reason that didn't make her sound ageist but couldn't come up with anything. "Do you have a heart condition?"

"Just a little one." He puckered up. "Give me a kiss."

She twisted her hand free and stepped back. "Sorry, I'm like those roller coaster rides at Six Flags. You have to be at least this tall," she held her hand just over his hunched shoulders, "and can't have a heart condition to ride this ride."

"I'm willing to risk it if you are."

"Elroy McTavish, you get in this house right now." It was a mad female voice from across the street.

"Damn, I'm busted. That's my wife. Quick, pretend you're choking." He waved at his wife. "Gloria, this young woman was choking and I stopped to help her."

Gloria, wearing a pale-pink tracksuit, garish orange hair, and an excessive amount of blue eye shadow, stomped down the front walkway wielding a cast-iron frying pan. "Hussy, you better stay away from my husband. Elroy, you stay away from her. She's a fallen woman. Jesus hasn't forgotten about that liquor store you wrecked. You've got a heart condition, high cholesterol, high blood pressure, and constipation. Your days are numbered. I'd hate for Jesus to kick you out of heaven on account of being around a loose woman. I told you there'd be trouble when those sports people moved in across the street. Now get in this house right now."

"I'm coming, dear." Elroy hightailed it back to the golf cart, threw his walker into the passenger's seat, and hit the gas. He pulled into the driveway, rolled over some bushes on the side, and then bounced back into the driveway. It was like watching live-action pinball.

Gloria pointed to her eyes and then to Harm in the universal "I'm watching you" gesture.

This just might be the low point of her day. And considering she'd spent an hour handcuffed in a nonsexual manner earlier, that was saying something.

She added another asterisk to her sign, along with, "Must be under fifty and healthy."

Seconds later, a fairly new model black Mustang screeched to a stop in the middle of the road. Which was a problem, considering the red Mazda behind it hadn't anticipated the stop and ended up plowing into the Mustang's rear bumper. The whole back of it crumbled, and a hubcap popped off and rolled down the street, barely missing another kid on a bicycle.

Rush hour had obviously started.

The driver of the Mustang stepped out of the car, smoothed down his stringy black hair, and headed her way without so much as a glance at the semi-totaled Mazda behind him. Or even his own crumpled bumper.

"I'm Max and I'm your date." His black pencil mustache didn't go with his full hipster hillbilly beard, but she had to admit she admired his confidence.

"What the hell?" An angry man in a gray business suit jumped out of the Mazda. "You stopped in the middle of the damn street for no reason."

He started to stay more, but then he caught sight of Harmony and read her sign. Seconds later, he was straightening his tie and smiling directly at her. If he hadn't been missing some pretty important front teeth, it might have been a fairly good smile. "I'm Chester and I'm your date."

"Man, I was here first." Max glared at Chester.

"You wrecked my damn car." Chester's eyes turned mean.

"Accident, bro. You're the one who crashed into me." Max pulled out his wallet, retrieved a card, and flicked it in Chester's direction. "Here's my contact info. I have full coverage with USAA. Call me later. You can go."

"I'm not going anywhere." Chester reared back a fist and landed a decent right hook to Max's jaw. Chester pulled his punches, so Max should have seen it coming—God knew she had—but now didn't seem like the best time to point that out.

Max shook his head as he recovered, then tackled Chester with a roar. Harmony stepped back to give them a little more room as they rolled around on the lawn.

This so wasn't turning out how she'd thought it would.

Seconds later, a blue Dodge truck pulled up and the passenger's-side window rolled down. The driver called, "I'm here about the hot girl who needs a date."

A white Ford truck pulled in right behind him, followed by a dark-green Chevy. The Chevy's driver laid on the horn and looked around like he was trying to figure out why all the vehicles were stopped. At least until he caught sight of Harmony and her sign—then his eyes nearly dropped out of his head.

He was out of the truck and making his way to her before the other guys had even turned off their ignitions.

Yeah, she really hadn't thought this one through.

Thirty minutes later, the front yard looked like a war zone. Bloody men dotted the lawn, some of the bushes had been crushed by flying bodies, and the police were questioning witnesses.

Harmony, who'd put on a swimsuit cover-up, much to the dismay of the two police officers who'd questioned her, sat on the front steps next to Lyric.

"I'm willing to admit that this wasn't my best plan." She put her head on her sister's shoulder. "Sorry about the mess."

"No problem." Lyric patted her leg. "Don't feel bad. This isn't nearly as bad as the time I posted an ad on Craigslist for a conference I was giving on self-pubbing research papers. Spell-check changed it to self-rubbing... freakin' spell-check. Every pervert within a two-hundred-mile radius showed up to my conference."

"Damn, I bet that was fun. Sorry I missed it." Heath stepped out the front door with a heaping bowl of popcorn. He sat down on the other side of Lyric. "Eat up, darlin'. Dalton's going to be late. Apparently SWAT has locked down the neighborhood and won't let anyone in or out. Some inmate saw Harm on social media, escaped from the county jail, and is headed here. Good news is he was in for a white-collar crime—no history of violence."

"Damn social media. I bet it was that kid who snapped all those pictures of me." She should have confiscated his damn phone.

Heath held out the bowl of popcorn to her. "Butter makes everything better."

"Words to live by." Lyric wrapped a comforting arm around her shoulders.

Harmony let herself sink into her twin's hug for just a minute. She'd bounce back with a new plan—she knew that. After all, this wasn't anywhere near the worst day of her life. It probably wasn't even in the top ten.

But right now—right this second, as the police sorted out the carnage on the front lawn and Dalton waited with dinner on the other side of the neighborhood's gates—she really needed a hug.

# Chapter 13

Two hours later, Dalton finally pulled into Heath's driveway. The front of the house looked like the morning after a biker rally. Numerous pieces of clothing lay scattered around the torn-up lawn. A few liquor bottles and a half-eaten bowl of popcorn littered the porch. He squinted—was that *blood* on the driveway?

Part of him was afraid to ask what had happened here, but the other half already knew. Five-Alarm Harm had struck again.

Grabbing the four giant brown paper sacks from the backseat, he headed to the house. Was it safe to eat two-hour-old fajitas and fixin's? Botulism probably wasn't the best way to say, "I'm kinda, but not really, sorry."

Hoping for the best, he knocked and then rang the bell. Not that he was anxious to see Harmony or anything. He just wanted to stave off the botulism as best he could. Or at least that was his story and he was sticking to it... especially since Harmony was sure to be pissed as hell.

The fact that that only made him more anxious to see her probably wasn't the healthiest thing. Then again, people looking in would probably say there wasn't much about their relationship that *was* healthy. But that was because they'd be missing one crucial detail. Being with Harmony made him happy. It also frustrated him, turned him on, and drove him downright crazy at least fifty percent of the time, but that didn't matter when she made everything inside of him light up like Lasso Stadium during a championship game.

Was it the damage she wrought that captivated him so completely? Or the badassed attitude she wore like some women wore diamonds? Or maybe it was the fact that no matter what, she gave as good as she got. He had no idea. All he knew was that he couldn't get her out of his head. No matter what he was doing, she was always there wearing a wicked smile, killer high heels, and absolutely nothing else.

But she was trouble... all kinds of trouble. Just the type of girl he'd left behind when he'd turned his life around. Growing up—and even coming of age—as a Bastard from Hell had taught him all he needed to know about women like Harmony. Mainly that the hotter they were, the bigger the mess they made.

When he'd broken with his family, he'd sworn off women like her. Had promised himself that one day he'd find a nice, sweet lady who would never think about running off with the leader of a rival gang—or football team—and leaving her children behind.

And yet here he was, all but chomping at the bit to see Harmony again. To get his hands and lips and numerous other body parts all over her hands and lips and numerous other body parts.

It was only dinner, he reminded himself as he waited impatiently for someone to open the door. It wasn't like he was signing over his soul—or even his Maserati—to the woman. The fact that he was looking forward to whatever terrible vengeance she had planned for him was neither here nor there.

Finally, the front door opened and Heath leaned against the door looking like he'd been through a war. "Sure you want to enter Harmony's Hell House?"

"Got nowhere else to be." Dalton found himself grinning wide enough to make his cheeks ache. He'd known Heath for years and had never bothered to get to know him. Which had obviously been his mistake, since the quarterback turned offensive coordinator was turning out to be a hell of a guy. One Dalton wouldn't mind counting among his very small circle of friends.

"It's your funeral." Heath stepped back and let him in.

"I don't know if the fajitas are still good. They've been sitting in my car for well over two hours. The SWAT team was... thorough."

"Don't we know it."

Heath led the way back to the kitchen, and Dalton realized he already felt at home here. Unlike most of the players' showrooms posing as houses, Heath and Lyric's place was a cozy mix of clean, modern lines and laid-back, lived-in spaces.

"No worries, Harm's made a feast. She may be a pain in the ass, but she cooks when she's plotting to take over the world." Heath led him to the kitchen.

The tangy scents of garlic, onions, tomatoes, and ground beef made the air smell like heaven.

"Taking over the world seems overly ambitious." Dalton could picture her taking over the world. It would be both better and fucked up as hell.

"True. Then again, she's just as likely to burn it all down." Heath stepped into the dining nook area and grabbed a seat next to his wife. He gestured to the large ice bucket filled with beer sitting at the edge of the table. "Grab a drink."

"I still vote for sex scandal," Lyric commented from out of the blue. She didn't bother to look up from the open laptop in front of her. "That would certainly do the trick."

Dalton put the sacks down on the kitchen table. Harmony was at the stove stirring a pot and glaring daggers at him. She was dressed in skinny jeans with lots of rips and holes and a plain red T-shirt. Her hair was back in a ponytail and she looked good enough to eat.

"That's a slippery slope. In order for it not to scare off Food Network, the video would have to be pretty tame. If it's too tame, it makes you look like a prude." Heath looked like he was weighing the options in his head. He turned to Dalton. "What do you think?"

"What do I think about what?" He'd walked into one of the strangest conversations ever. Then again, looking at whom he was keeping company with, he shouldn't be surprised.

"We're trying to come up with the best way for Harmony to ruin her 'good girl' reputation so Livinia, my mother-in-law, will let Harm buy out her half of the bakery they own together." Heath made it sound so normal.

"Why does she have to ruin her reputation to do that?" He'd forgotten that Harm owned a bakery.

Both Lyric and Heath looked at Harm for explanation.

Harmony slammed down the whisk she'd been using to stir whatever was in the pot on the stove. "Why are you even here?"

"I brought dinner." He pointed to the bags.

She checked her watch. "The meat's been out too long. I made meatloaf."

"I love meatloaf. My favorite." His mouth was beginning to water.

"Who said you were getting any?" She leaned against the counter and crossed her arms. "I need to ruin my reputation because my mother is a pretentious bitch who only worries about how things look and not how things are."

"Think wicked witch meets Jackie O." Heath put his arm around his wife.

"With just a little Margaret Thatcher thrown in," Lyric added.

Harm nodded. "That is a perfect description of Momma."

"I can't even picture what that would look like," Dalton admitted. "But why exactly do you want to buy out your mother? And why won't she let you?"

As he talked, he pulled out the bottle of red wine he'd brought to go with the beef fajitas. Then he shrugged out of his suit jacket, loosened his tie, and went to help Harm make dinner. "Where's the bottle opener?"

"Top drawer on the left." Heath pointed to the set of drawers next to the double ovens.

"So all of this is because you want to destroy your reputation." Dalton found the opener and screwed it into the cork. "Why now?"

Harmony just glared at him, but he knew exactly how to handle her. "Really? Not talking to me? That's the best you've got?"

Harm picked up a wooden spoon and fired it off at him like a pitcher during the softball world championship. He ducked. "Come on. You're better than that."

If looks really could kill, the one she was giving him right now would have burned him from the inside out.

He pulled her into his arms. To her credit, she didn't try to scratch his eyes out or punch him, and he easily blocked her knee to the nuts, which just proved she wasn't trying that hard. "Come on, let's hug it out."

Harm went as rigid as a cedar plank and kept her arms firmly at her sides.

"Do I need to be worried that she poisoned my food?" He continued to hold her as he glanced at Heath.

"Is that why she made individual servings of meatloaf?" Heath wondered. "Now it makes sense. Just make sure you don't mix his up with mine."

"You're assuming I didn't poison two of them." She smiled broadly. This time when her knee came up, he knew enough to let her go. It was a bit early to push his luck.

Careful not to turn his back on her, he stepped back and started opening cabinets until he found the wineglasses. Since Heath was the only one drinking beer, he poured three glasses and set one in front of Harm. "I feel like you could use this today."

He brought the third glass to Lyric, then took a long drink from his before facing off with Harm again. "What can I do to help?"

Harm ignored him, but picked up the wine he'd poured her. He counted it as a win. "What about an accidental boob pic on Twitter?" she wondered, returning to the topic they'd been discussing when he arrived.

"I'm not sure I'm okay with that." He'd spend hours looking at her breasts if she let him, but the idea of anyone else gawking at her didn't make him happy.

"You don't get a vote." Her tone said he was an idiot for thinking he might. But she took a small step closer to him.

Lyric shrugged. "Maybe, but it could be brushed off as accidental."

Heath pointed at her with his glass. "I'm telling you, your best bet is a sex tape. And not your average run-of-the-mill sex tape either. Something wild. I mean, no farm animals because that's just wrong, but I say you push the limits of what two consenting adults can get up to. Maybe three, if you really want to push the boundaries."

Lyric cocked her head to the side and looked at her husband. "Have you ever pushed those boundaries?"

Heath shot her a deliberately lascivious look. "Baby, we push those boundaries every day."

"I meant the three people boundary."

"Oh. Umm—"

Dalton's brows rose as Heath squirmed a little. Quarterbacks, man. Quarterbacks.

"Honestly, darlin', I can't remember what I got up to before you came back into my life—"

Harmony snorted. "Take that as a big fat yes."

"I didn't say that." Heath's face was turning red.

"But you didn't not say it either." Harmony grinned. Clearly she loved making her brother-in-law uncomfortable.

"No need to get so freaked out. I figured you had." Lyric went back to her computer screen.

"You figured I had?" Heath's voice was so high it was squeaky.

"Of course. Statistics say—"

"Oh no." Harmony shook her head. "You are not going to start spouting statistics. We'll be here all night and I'll be no closer to ruination. I can't afford that. I need to shake my good girl reputation once and for all."

Dalton nearly choked on his wine. "Good girl reputation? You?"

The look she gave him was cold enough for him to feel like he had frostbite on his ass. "There's a lot about me you don't know."

"Obviously." He was about to ask about all those things he didn't know, but Heath rolled right over him.

"I'm telling you, nothing will get Livinia's panties in a wad faster than a sex tape. And if you do it with a Democrat or a vegetarian, she'll drop you even faster."

"Okay, that's it." Dalton threw up his hands. "What is really going on here?" Because none of this made any sense to him at all, and the only thing he was sure of right now was that Harmony was *not* doing a sex tape. And she sure as hell wasn't doing one with someone other than him.

Heath looked at him like he was an idiot who needed to get with the conversation. "Livinia won't sign off on Harm's new TV show being filmed in their bakery in San Angelo. Food Network came knocking and wants Harm to do a show called *Badass Baker*, but they want the Harmony who won *Cupcake Cage Match* and not the innocent little baker from San Angelo." He sounded so nonchalant.

"Wait a minute, Food Network wants to give you your own cooking show?" He one-arm-hugged Harm, who still didn't respond. "That's awesome."

"I know, right?" Lyric beamed with pride. "Only now, she has to get our mother to sign off on it, and the only way Harm thinks we can get her to sell her half of the bakery to Harm is if Harm no longer is the good girl the town thinks she is."

"Wait, the town thinks Harm is a good girl? And what's *Cupcake Cage Match*?" He'd never heard of it. Not that he watched all that much TV, but when he did, he usually at least cruised past Food Network.

Harm still wasn't speaking to him. That was starting to get on his nerves.

"It's some sort of underground baking competition turned fight club. Sounds weird to me." Heath's shrug said, *what can you do*?

Dalton could think of a whole hell of a lot to do, most of which included him turning Harmony over his knee and spanking her—and doing other things—until she came. A cupcake fight club? What the hell?

"It's not as weird as it sounds. It's a great honor and obviously one that the network execs are paying attention to." Harm downed her wine in one long swallow. "And it's not a fight club. It's a mixed martial arts baking competition. Sort of like *Cupcake Wars*, only instead of sending competitors home if they don't win the round, they have to cage fight to move on."

"Like MMA cage fighting to knockout?" Now he was intrigued. He could totally see Harm winning that—and looking like a million bucks in some tiny bathing suit as she did.

"Yes. And before you ask, I've only had to fight a couple times. But I was always ready." It looked like she was talking to him again.

"I have no doubt." He grinned at her. "You're totally going to be the next Food Network star. I can see it now."

"I will be if my mom gets the hell out of the way." Harm emptied the bottle into her glass and then tossed it into the recycling bin.

"Not that my mom was the best mother ..." Or the most reliable, or even the most sober. "But wouldn't most moms want their daughter to have this opportunity?"

Harm's face went flat. "You don't know Livinia. Wicked witch, remember?"

"She can't be that bad."

"She is," the three of them said in unison.

"So, we're back to sex tape or accidental boob pic?" Lyric turned to Heath. "I don't think tonight's going to be enough, though it should get the ball rolling. What do you think?"

"What happened tonight?" Dalton could barely keep up. It was like watching a ping-pong match where everyone was playing in shorthand.

"Well, Harmony?" Heath looked at her expectantly. "You want to fill Dalton in on what happened?"

"There's nothing to fill him in about."

"I'm not so sure I would agree. It was a hell of a three-ring circus for a little while." Heath bit his top lip to keep from laughing.

"Two hours to be exact." Lyric nodded, but one look from Harm had her diving back behind her computer to hide.

And that's when he got it. "Wait a minute, are you the hot girl looking for a date tonight?" It had been all over his news feed when he'd been searching for the root of the SWAT problem. He'd even seen an aerial pic of a curvy girl in a gold bikini. He just hadn't put it together. But now that he had, he couldn't help grinning. "Looking for a date to make me jealous, huh?"

"No." It was way too fast and high pitched to be true.

"Aww, that's so sweet." He pulled her in for another hug and felt her thaw ever so slightly, even as she dug her heel into the top of his foot. But he'd worn his steel-toed hiking boots for a reason. When trying to woo a woman like Five-Alarm Harm, a guy could never be too careful. "I like you too."

He kissed her hard on the mouth. He took the fact that she didn't bite his tongue off as a good sign.

"They're not about to have sex in our kitchen are they?" Heath made gagging noises. "We might have to move if they do."

"Hopefully they'll wait until after dinner. I'm hungry. That popcorn didn't fill me up the way it usually does." Lyric put a hand on her stomach. "Besides, there's not a square inch of that countertop we haven't already done it on."

Harm stepped back and made her own gagging noises. "I cook here, people."

"Babe, remember, what we do in private is private." Heath's face was turning a nice shade of red.

"This from a man who just last year actually did have a sex tape that hit the tabloids." Dalton couldn't believe the man Heath had become since getting married. Lyric seemed to level him out.

"Really?" Lyric turned to Heath. "Can I watch it?"

"No, you can't watch it." Heath's face was full-on maraschino.

"Why not? It would be good to get a third-party look at your technique. I'm going to Google it." She turned back to her laptop.

Heath closed it. "I don't need constructive criticism."

"Sure you do. There's always room for improvement." Lyric was dead serious.

Heath looked at Dalton. "My wife is an astrophysicist and processes everything analytically. So when she says that everyone has room for improvement, she means—"

"What's the big deal?" Lyric looked around. "If I had a sex tape I'd let you see it and give me constructive criticism."

"Honey, if you have a sex tape, I'd better be in it with you." Heath stood and gently pulled Lyric up with him. "We're going out for dinner."

"What?" Harm practically vaulted the island to get to them.

"We think it's best." Lyric put her arm around her sister's shoulder. "Those individual meatloaves have put the fear of God into Heath. He still remembers the Ex-Lax chocolate chip cookie episode."

"He'd just broken your heart. Like I was gonna let that slide." Harm tossed a dish towel over her left shoulder. "It's not my fault Ex-Lax makes chocolate chews."

Dalton couldn't help but wonder what they were having for dessert.

"Have fun, you two." Heath put his arm around Lyric as they walked toward the front door. "If you do get freaky in my kitchen, please use bleach and lots of it."

Harmony took a deep breath and let it out slowly as she watched them go. "Don't think we'll need the bleach."

"Why do you say that?" Dalton wasn't playing hard to get so much as I'm-not-easy.

"I know you're into me, but I don't know why you're... oh." Her voice fell away as her eyes fastened onto the front of his slacks. "I get it."

"Get what?" He was baffled.

"I don't know how to bring this up." She never took her eyes from his zipper.

"Bring what up?" He didn't know how to react. He'd never had a woman stare at him like that when he was fully clothed before. It was disconcerting.

"You know... your little problem." She nodded at the front of his pants. "Want me to run across the street and borrow some of Elroy McTavish's Viagra?"

He felt himself blanche as things finally sunk in. "Oh, God no. No, no, no. I don't have …" He couldn't even get the word to come out of his mouth. "All of my parts are in perfect working order."

"Whew, thank God." Harm fanned herself. "I was getting worried." Her eyes scrunched up. "So what's the problem then?"

# Chapter 14

He was still trying to answer that question half an hour later, as they worked their way through meatloaf, mashed potatoes, green beans, and a really delicious spinach salad. Because now that he'd gotten to know her better, now that he knew what made her tick, there really wasn't a problem. In fact, if things went according to plan, he'd have her handcuffed to her bed in under an hour. Especially if they skipped the dessert she'd taken to calling Brownie Surprise.

He didn't mind the brownie part, but the surprise part made him wary as hell.

Not wary enough to leave, though. Not now that she was finally letting him in a little. Normally, that was the last thing he wanted in a woman he was dating. He liked to keep things neat and compartmentalized—it helped him keep his eye on the ball, so to speak, when it came to the Wranglers.

For his entire adult life, work had come first. Sure, he liked to play hard, and he definitely liked the rush of adrenaline that came with extreme sports. But when he was working, he was working. He gave it the same single-minded attention that he gave BASE jumping, where his life depended on his focus.

But ever since Harmony had come along, that focus had eroded some. He thought about her when he was at work—even when she wasn't handcuffed in his office. He wondered what she was up to, what she was thinking. What she would look like spread eagled on his bed. Oh, and of course, what diabolically evil thing she was going to do next to keep him on his toes.

"I'd think all of this silence was you lost in your thoughts, but based on the way you inhaled your food, I'd say you were too busy chewing to make polite dinner conversation." Her smile of satisfaction was a thing of beauty. She was a feeder, and it was obvious, despite whatever bad attitude she projected, that she liked watching other people enjoy her labor of love.

"First time I've had homemade food in a very long time." The last time must have been when his mother was around. She'd always made Thanksgiving dinner, even though drive-thrus provided his meals the rest of the year. Now he could afford to eat at the finest restaurants instead of off the value menu, but he still loved the taste of homemade mashed potatoes.

Harmony brought over dessert—the pan of brownies, along with some fresh-cut strawberries and homemade whipped cream. "Can I get you some dessert? I didn't think about the fact that you're twice my size and eat like a football player when I dished up your meal."

"I eat like a football player when you're cooking." He grinned. "Everything you make is amazing. But I'm finished, thanks." At least with food.

"Are you sure?" She stood up and started toward the coffeepot on the counter, but he grabbed her hand and pulled her into his lap.

"I'm positive. A brownie isn't what I want." He wanted her. All of her this time, and he aimed to have her.

"Oh, really?" She shifted until she was straddling him, then leaned forward and whispered in his ear, "What exactly do you want then?"

That was a loaded question if ever he'd heard one.

He wanted so many things he didn't even know where to start. Had wanted them from the minute he'd seen her raising hell in that biker bar. But right now what he wanted was a taste of her. To cover her mouth with his own, to slide his tongue deep, and to kiss her until her lips were swollen and her sex was wet.

So that's what he did. He cupped her face between his palms and lowered his mouth slowly, carefully, to hers. Like he had all the time in the world. Like he wasn't dying for a taste of her.

He was trying to be sweet, trying to take it slow. But he should have known slow and sweet wasn't Harmony's game. Instead, she tangled her hands in his hair and yanked, hard. Any thoughts he had of sweetness abandoned him as she delved in, delved deep.

It was hot and hard and so fucking sexy he could barely breathe. He opened his mouth wide and reveled in the way she took control. In the way she took what she wanted and gave so much pleasure in return.

Her hands were tugging at his hair, her tongue sliding along his teeth, his tongue, the roof of his mouth. Need coursed through him, made his dick hard and his hands shake. Made him want more of her. Want all of her.

And when she shifted, when she ground her sex against his cock, he knew that he was going to take control... and take whatever she would give him.

Sliding his hands under her shirt, he pulled it off. Then nearly died when he saw the teeny tiny bra she was wearing, and the clear outline of nipple rings through the lacy cups.

Leaning down, he licked his way along the edges of her bra, stopping only to swirl his tongue along the ivy vines that twisted and twined their way from her back to her shoulder. She moaned a little, arched her back to give him better access. Thank God.

With a groan of his own, he slid his tongue beneath the lace cups, getting closer and closer to her mouth with each circle of his tongue on her breast. She moaned again, then untangled her hands from his hair just long enough to reach behind her and unhook her bra.

Then she pulled it off and dropped it to the ground behind her.

And God, she was beautiful. So fucking beautiful that it nearly ripped him in two just to look at her. With the wild illustrations on her skin, the raspberry-pink nipples, and the scattering of freckles, she turned him on like no one ever had before.

Lowering his head, he traced his tongue along the colorful edges of her tattoos as they bled one into the next. From the time he was little more than a kid, he'd had a thing for tattoos on female skin. He didn't know what it was he found so sexy about a woman who decorated the most intimate and beautiful places on her body, but it revved him up like nothing else ever had.

And Harmony. Shit. With all her tattoos, she looked like a pretty birthday package just waiting to be unwrapped. And he was the lucky man who was getting to do the honors.

He moved lower, traced closer to her nipples. She shivered as he made patterns on her skin with his tongue, her hips arching against his while a low, keening cry came from between her lips. He nearly lost it at the sound, nearly reached between them, unzipped his pants and hers, then thrust into her, hard and fast.

But she tasted too good to rush, felt too amazing against him to end it just that quickly. Not when her mouth was cold and tantalizingly sweet from a combination of the strawberries and whipped cream.

Keeping his mouth on hers—like he had the fucking willpower to break away—he reached behind Harmony to the table and grabbed a handful of strawberries. Then stood up and balanced her perfect little ass on the edge of the table.

"Dalton?"

Her beautiful blue eyes blinked open in confusion, and he didn't do anything to reassure her, didn't say anything to put her at ease. He wanted her off balance, wanted her watching him with those wary, cat eyes that made him hotter and harder than anything ever had.

"Lie back," he said, exerting pressure on her shoulders with his empty hand.

"What, here?" she demanded breathlessly, even as she complied with the order he gave her.

"Of course here." He watched as she braced herself on her elbows, a move that had her pretty breasts jutting forward invitingly. "Haven't you ever done it on a table before?"

She smirked at him. "Wouldn't you like to know."

He would like to know, honestly, jealousy riding him hard at the thought of her with anyone else. But he didn't have the right to call her on it—didn't have the right to even be thinking like he was thinking. So instead of asking again, he murmured, "For once just relax and let me do all the work."

She didn't argue, so he chose to take her long, lingering sigh as acquiescence and lifted one of the berries across her lips. Her mouth opened up automatically and she bit the pretty red berry in half, then giggled as some of its sweet juice ran down her chin.

He licked it up with one long, slow swipe of his tongue, and she stopped laughing, her eyes darkening and her body growing tense. Good. He liked that she was a little on edge—it would make what came after all the sweeter.

He picked up another couple of berries, and her mouth opened invitingly, but he merely shook his head. Holding them above her body he squeezed hard, then watched as all their lovely juice leaked out of his fist and ran in rivulets down her beautiful torso.

###

Harmony gasped at the first touch of the cold juice on her breasts and her stomach. Gasped again as Dalton smeared the strawberry pulp around first one areole and then the second. Her nipples went pebble hard at the contact, though she wasn't sure if it was from the cold berries or Dalton's fingers or simply the anticipation of what was coming next.

She wasn't a virgin—she liked sex too much for that—but no other man had ever made her feel like this. No other man had made her so anxious and so excited all at the same time. That it was Dalton who did it—with his Armani suits and Rolex watches—only made it a bigger trip.

As did the wicked gleam in Dalton's eyes, the gleam that only seemed to come out when he was looking at her. It made him look even more handsome, even more dangerous. And knowing that she brought it out in him turned her on more than anything ever had.

He kept his gazes pinned to hers as he bent his head to her breast, and she nearly sighed in delight. Only the desire to mess with him a little, to make him sweat, kept her from sighing in delight.

But he didn't stop there, and he didn't ask for permission as he unzipped her jeans, then roughly yanked them—and her panties—down her legs and off. She didn't protest and she didn't cover herself, not when he was giving her exactly what she wanted. Exactly what she needed.

He groaned a little as he dropped the jeans to the floor, then he picked up more strawberries and once again crushed them in his palm, allowing the juice to drip over her abdomen, down to her mons and between her thighs. The contrast of the ice-cold strawberry juice and Dalton's warm mouth had her writhing in seconds, begging for him to finish the game.

He wasn't willing to be rushed, however, and he took his time teasing her with little flicks of his tongue over her breasts, down her belly, over her sex. He followed these with more demanding nips and with tugs on her nipple rings that had her blood boiling and her hands fisting in his hair.

"Come on," she whimpered as she tried to pull him over her. "Do it already."

His laugh was low and taunting. "Baby, I'm just getting started. There won't be anything *to do* for quite a while."

And then he set about teasing her, giving her no more time to talk or plead or even think. She could only feel, only revel in the sensations of unbelievable pleasure the feel of the strawberries and Dalton's tongue brought to her.

He leaned over her on the table, so that he was touching her in one long line from her shoulders to her toes. The roughness of his jeans scraped against the tender skin of her stomach and outer thigh, but she relished the contact. Embraced the burn that he was so carefully stoking inside of her.

Raising himself up on one elbow, he picked up the loaded spoon from the whipped cream bowl and held it suspended over her. He didn't move, didn't flick it over her, didn't do anything until he was sure he had her complete and total attention.

Pushing up on her elbows, she looked at him warily. "What are you going to do with that?" she asked.

He grinned and it was a scandalous, shameless thing. Her heart beat faster and then she was arching, her head falling back as he dropped the cool cream onto her lower abdomen.

"Dalton." It was a squeal. A protest. An invitation for him to do whatever he wanted. For him to do everything he wanted.

"Do you know," he whispered as he dipped one finger into the mound of whipped cream. "I always loved finger painting as a child."

"Finger painting?" She could barely form the words, all of her energy focused on the calloused finger currently drawing figure eights on her stomach.

"Yes. I loved to make designs with the paint, to create something beautiful where only chaos had been." His finger dipped lower, across her mons and down, until he was painting her pussy with the whipped cream. Circling her clit with it and then moving down to rub the sweet stuff over her labia.

"Of course, you're already so beautiful it makes my head spin," he murmured as he applied more and more cream to her aching sex. "But there's something to be said for making a little treat for myself, isn't there?"

She whimpered—the only sound she could make, as rationale speech was suddenly beyond her.

"Isn't there, Harmony?" His finger dipped inside of her, once, twice, and she nearly came from the contrast of hot and cold against the walls of her vagina. His burning-hot finger covered in the cold whipped cream was taking her higher than she'd ever been before. He was scrambling her brain, making her crazy, and she was loving every second of it.

"Harmony?" he murmured again, delving a little deeper with his cream-covered finger. "Yes or no?"

"Yes," she whispered through dry lips, not knowing—and not caring—what she was agreeing to. All that she had, all that she was, was focused on this man and the wicked, wonderful things he was doing to her body. Things she'd never been willing to let another man do to her. Things that made her vulnerable and more than a little weak.

And then he was leaning down, his tongue licking the cream from her stomach like she was a piece of fine china. He traced patterns on her quivering stomach, and whatever limited thoughts she'd managed to string together dried up and she could think no more. Only feel.

She moaned, a soft, breathless sigh that seemed to snap his control. And he was on her, his body covering hers, his shoulders flexing as he trailed hot, moist kisses down her body. He followed the trail he'd painted with the whipped cream, his talented tongue doing things to her that she had only read about before. He was everywhere, and as his tongue thrust inside of her, she lost the last remnants of control she'd been clinging to so desperately.

Her elbows went out from under her, and she sank back onto the table—collapsed really—and let him have his wicked, wicked way with her.

And what a way it was. He played her like a finely tuned instrument, loved her in those moments like she was the only woman he'd ever had. He was endlessly curious, unbelievably giving, and just a little bit kinky as his mouth brought her to one whipped cream orgasm after another. And through it all, he continued to explore her body, taking the time to learn what she liked, what she loved, and what drove her absolutely insane.

She was beginning to think everything about this man was going to drive her insane.

He licked her in long strokes, again and again, like she was the sweetest ice cream he'd ever tasted and he could never get enough. His tongue explored every crease, lingered for long minutes at her clit until she was clawing the table in search of relief.

But there was none, only more of the torturous pleasure that went on and on. His thumb pressed against her from behind, entering her at the same time his tongue thrust inside her pussy like a spear.

She screamed, bucked frantically against him, rode the orgasm out as wave after wave of pleasure crashed through her. And still he wasn't done—his face was buried between her thighs, his lips and tongue and breath coming at her again and again until sanity was only an abstract concept.

Until the world around her ceased to exist and Dalton was the only steady thing in it.

She was going beyond individual orgasms to a place where the overwhelming pleasure went on and on and on. She twisted desperately, tugged at his shoulders, begged for him to end the torture with the satisfaction of his thick cock within her. But he only laughed and continued to push her and push her until she was sobbing, mindless, an animal driven by the sweet, hot edge of pleasure-pain and the promise of completion.

Her body was no longer her own. It was under his complete control, enthralled, desperate, dying. In those moments she would have followed him anywhere, done anything, been anyone he wanted her to be. It was a scary thought, considering how she'd spent so much of her life hiding her true self, but the fear was mitigated by the fact that he only wanted to bring her joy—incredible, mind-boggling joy. And that was the biggest turn-on of them all.

Dalton spiked his tongue, boggled her brain, as he swirled it inside her before pulling out and going for her clit again. As he did, another wave snuck up on her, slammed through her, and she knew she couldn't take any more. She pushed him away and into the discarded breakfast chair. Then dropped to her knees in front of him, unzipped his pants, and took his glorious, incredibly hot cock in her mouth.

"Fuck, Harmony," he groaned, his hands fisting in her hair as she got her first taste of him. He was delicious, and it was her turn to tease, her turn to swirl her tongue down and around him until he was breathing in great shudders, his lower body arching off the chair, desperate for something more. Desperate for everything she had to give him and more. "Have mercy."

But there was no mercy in her, nothing but the driving need to take him as high as he had taken her. She slipped her mouth down over the hard length of him, lingered with her lips at the base for a moment, then pulled back with a long, lingering swipe of her tongue.

"Don't tease, baby." It was a gasp, sweat glistening on his body as he shuddered beneath her. "Please, just do it."

But she couldn't. She wasn't ready for it to end yet, wasn't ready to see his passion-glazed features go lax with completion. She wanted him as needy as she had been—and still was. She had to have him as desperate for her as she was for him.

And so she continued her ministrations, slipping and sliding her mouth over him. Relinquishing his cock for a moment, she slipped farther down his body to take his balls in her mouth, to lick the space behind them with hard strokes of her tongue that had him arching and pleading much as she had done only minutes before.

The power was a beautiful thing. The understanding that she could drive this beautiful specimen of manhood to insanity and beyond was a joy that she never wanted to give up.

"Do it." His voice was harsh, his hands tight and unyielding in her hair as he pulled her up. He was beyond gentleness, beyond thinking, and she loved him this way. As she licked her way back up to where he wanted her, she noticed the clear drop of fluid on the head of his cock and nearly whimpered in desire. Finally, she had driven him beyond control, to the brink of an orgasm he refused to take without her.

But the choice wasn't his anymore. *She* was in control now and his body *would* give her what she demanded.

Licking the pre-ejaculate off, she dawdled for a few long moments over the sexy length of him as he writhed beneath her, his hands in her hair a snare she had no wish to escape. "You have to... Harmony, please... I can't... baby—"

There it was, the note of surrender and desperation she had been waiting for—the same desperation that he had evoked in her time and again. Even as he'd done it, she'd wanted to give him the same thing, and she was thrilled she'd been able to. Thrilled that he'd let her.

With a secret grin, she swallowed him whole, sucking him all the way inside of her. She used her mouth and tongue and throat on him, lightly scraped her teeth across his great length. It was that moment of combined pleasure and pain that did it, that sent him careening over the edge he'd been clinging to with battered fingers.

With a hoarse shout he arched up, thrusting again and again against her seeking mouth. And then he was pouring into her with long, brutal jerks of his hips and she was loving every second of it.

His orgasm went on and on and on until nothing existed besides him and her and the fire that burned between them.

When it was over and Dalton finally pulled out, he was still semi-hard, his strong body trembling as wave after wave of sensation swept through him. She held him as he recovered, her head resting on his stomach, her arm around a powerful thigh.

They stayed that way for long moments, and a sense of peace she'd never felt before stole through her. Her body was content, her mind at rest. For a woman who'd spent so much of her time with her mind racing and her defenses up, it was an incredible feeling of peace.

Her eyes started to close, and then he was shifting, pulling her up and into his arms and walking her to her bedroom, where he tucked her under the covers before climbing into bed beside her.

She cuddled up to him until she was sheltered in the curve of his arm, then slid into sleep, perfectly happy for the first time in a very, very long time.

# Chapter 15

The next morning, Harmony shrugged into her T-shirt with a ridiculous, well-satisfied grin on her face. Dalton was one hell of a lover, no doubt about it. Not that she was about to tell him that. The last thing she wanted was for him to think she was going soft. Even if she might be—just a little.

"Getting dressed?" He sat up in bed, deliciously naked. "I'm not nearly done with you."

That's what she was afraid of. Even more, she was afraid that she wasn't done with him.

She grabbed the TV remote and leaned against the headboard. "I want to catch the news. See what Dallas–Fort Worth thinks about the little incident last night." It was six seventeen, so she turned on the TV, hit the DVR button, highlighted the news, and hit start over. From there, she only had a couple minutes to wait—just through the murders and other violent crimes.

Fortunately for her—and her reputation—last night had been a slow night on the murder front.

"Live and local, this is *Daily Fort Worth*, I'm Haley Lester." The platinum blonde sat on a green sofa and looked directly into the camera. "We come back from our break with a truly disheartening story. It looks like Dr. Lyric Wright-Montgomery, wife of our own Forth Worth Wranglers former quarterback and current offensive coordinator, Heath Montgomery, is quickly spiraling out of control. Her odd behavior was first noted two nights ago, when she caused, and participated in, a bar brawl at a local biker bar. But she's obviously been decompensating, because we have footage of her, from just last night, outside of the house she shares with her new husband. Despite being married to one of the sexiest, and richest, men to ever play in the NFL, she spent last night parading around in a bikini asking for a dinner date and wreaking general havoc in one of Fort Worth's quietest and most exclusive areas. Now we go to Tawny Shivley for more details."

The scene changed, and another platinum blonde nodded into the camera. She held a microphone and appeared to be standing outside the gated neighborhood. "That's right, Haley. Neighbors report that at approximately five twelve yesterday afternoon, Dr. Lyric Wright-Montgomery walked out the front door of her house in a gold-lamé bikini, carrying a sign asking for a date for dinner. Someone snapped a picture and hashtagged her as #HotGirlNeedsDate, and from there, things went viral—and out of control. Men rushed to get to the very street I'm standing on, and beneath me you can see remnants of broken glass, left over from the many car collisions that occurred due to the distraction. I'm told that in addition to multiple collisions, several fights broke out, resulting in thousands in property damage, and neighbors reported hearing gunshots fired. This occurred only days after Lyric and Heath were spotted in a biker bar fighting. I think it's safe to say that Heath and Lyric, America's sweetheart couple, might be calling it quits very soon."

Harmony's head was going to explode. It was going to explode or, at the very least, spin around on her shoulders as she spit pea soup everywhere.

Because this wasn't happening. This simply couldn't be happening. She'd been trying to ruin her own reputation, not destroy her sister's.

The camera switched back to the studio. "It does seem that they're headed for divorce," Haley agreed. "One can't help wondering if Lyric's strange behavior is a cry for help. Let's hope she gets that help before she hits Amanda Bynes territory. Some people just aren't cut out for life in the spotlight, no matter how dim it is." She shuffled her papers. "And now we turn to our special guest, a psychiatrist who specializes in mentally unstable celebrity marriages—"

Harm turned off the TV and barely resisted the urge to put her fist through the wall. What in the holy hell was happening here?

"Harmony, are you okay?" Before Dalton could say anything else, her cell phone rang. She picked it up off the nightstand, knowing who it was before she even glanced at the number. Of course, she was right. It was her mother. She thought about not answering, but she knew Livinia would just keep calling until she did. Her mother had the persistence—and the temperament—of a pissed-off porcupine on the best days. On days like today, well... Harmony slid her finger across the screen. "Hello, Momma."

"What on earth is going on up there in Fort Worth? Is your sister off her medication?"

"Lyric doesn't take any medication."

"Well, she should be taking some. Go get her and put her on the phone right now. I need to talk to her and she isn't picking up her phone. She's gone too far this time. Is she trying to give your father another heart attack? He's barely recovered from the last one." Livinia was in an even worse state than Harm had expected.

Seriously? No one believed it could be her. She'd been playing the good girl for so long that no one could imagine her behaving in a way that was anything less than perfect. It was now or never. "It wasn't Lyric. It was me. I was the one in the gold bikini strutting around the front yard."

There was a long silence, and then Livinia said, "You? Don't be ridiculous. And don't try to cover for your sister. Lyric needs help and I'm going to make sure she gets it. You can't let her lose Heath. He's the best thing that's ever happened to her, and now he's probably going to leave her." Her voice turned breathy, and the tears started. Harmony could hear it in her tone. Another mother might be crying because she feared for her daughter's mental health. But Harmony was pretty sure her mother was crying because she feared for her own social status. Lyric wasn't the only one Heath was the best thing to ever happen to. "You've got to get her under control."

"You're not listening to me. It was me, Momma. Not Lyric."

"You can lie all you want, Harmony Marie, but we both know you would never deface your body like that. How many tattoos does your sister have? Doesn't she know you can get AIDS that way? And hepatitis? It's a miracle Heath hasn't kicked her out already."

"Right. Whatever. I have to go." Then Harmony did something she'd never done before; she hung up on her mother.

"What am I going to do?" She threw the phone on the bed and started to pace. "If she doesn't believe it was me, how am I ever going to convince her to sell the bakery? And what about Lyric? At this rate I'm going to end up getting my sister committed, when all she's done is try to help me. This is hopeless."

She was a little shocked to realize tears were burning in the back of her eyes. She never cried.

"It's not hopeless. We just need to find another way." Dalton massaged her shoulders. "Maybe you and Lyric need to get caught on camera right next to each other so that everyone will know there's two of you. If you're both wearing clothes that show off your shoulders and midriffs, everyone will be able to see that you're the one with the fantastic tatts. And the personality disorder."

She chose to let the last comment go, because his idea was a pretty good one. And because he'd given her seven orgasms last night. A guy with a tongue as talented as Dalton's couldn't be overrated.

She sank down onto the bed next to him, and he reached for her, pulling her against him so he could slide his hands underneath her shirt to massage her lower back. As he did, his fingers kept tracing the lines of her tattoos like he couldn't get enough of them. "Your tatts are incredible," he said in between the soft kisses he was pressing into her neck and shoulders.

He really liked them, she realized. The last guy she'd dated hadn't liked them, which was why he'd only been the last guy she'd dated and not the last guy she'd slept with.

"I guess Lyric and I can take some photos together and post them on social media. If we make sure Heath is in them, right next to her, that should convince everyone that Lyric isn't one step away from the loony bin." It was so easy. Why hadn't she thought of it herself?

With that big worry off her mind, she was in the mood to reward Dalton for his suggestion—by letting him give her another orgasm or three. She lifted the hem of the T-shirt and yanked it over her head.

"Now that's what I'm talking about." Dalton pulled her on top of him.

"Don't you have to go to work? I know for a fact that there's at least one media circus for you to deal with this morning." Yet even as she said it, she relaxed into him for a second, relishing the heat and the strength of him against her.

God knew she hated to give him points for anything, but the fact that he was still here—giving her a massage and considering making love to her—when he should probably be running to the office to put out this latest fire she'd started had endeared him to her in a way she couldn't explain. All she knew was that she wasn't ready to let him go yet.

His hands slid up her rib cage to cup her breasts while his fingers toyed with her nipple rings. It was more than enough to have her reaching over to the nightstand and opening the drawer where she'd stashed a box of condoms when she'd decided two days ago that she was going to seduce Dalton. She pulled out the condom box. She shook it. Nothing rattled around. It was empty. "We're fresh out."

He grabbed the box and looked inside. "We went through an entire box. Wow, I'm amazing."

"A legend in your own mind." She sat back and reached for him. "It was a small box. Don't get too cocky."

"Too late," he said with a smirk.

She'd obviously let him get away with too much already, so she slid her hand around his very hard length and began to stroke.

"I can think of a few things we can do that don't require a condom."

"Hot damn. I do love a woman with imagination."

She'd just rolled over and started to kiss her way across his very built chest when a soft knock sounded at her closed door.

"In case my boss is in there, please remind him that we have a seven thirty breakfast meeting with the team owner. Also, you might want to mention that showing up in last night's clothes is only acceptable in college." Heath's signature drawl came through the door, loud and clear. "Also, I really hope all of that banging I heard earlier coming from your room has put the boss man in a good mood. Okay, I'm gonna go back to my room now and wait there for the next fifteen minutes so we can forgo that whole awkward bumping into each other over the coffepot thing. Oh, and Harm, can you bake some of those blueberry muffins that are so good they make me cry? I seem to have worked up an appetite of my own last night."

"You grew up with him. Was he always like this?" Dalton's grin had both his dimples popping out. She had the first inkling that she might be in trouble when it took way more willpower than it should have to resist leaning forward and kissing his dimples. Or licking them. Or—she cut herself off before she went too far around the bend. Especially since it looked like orgasm number eight was going to be a bust.

Dalton solved the problem by leaning forward and kissing her, hard, before reaching to grab his shirt off the floor.

"No. Usually he's much worse. We try not to hold it against him, though. Heath had it hard growing up. His mom ran out on them and his father dove inside a bottle of tequila and never made it back out." She rolled off the bed and shrugged back into last night's T-shirt.

"Why don't you go back to bed?" He stood and slid on his shirt. "You didn't get much sleep last night."

"Can't, I'm a morning person. I'm a baker, remember?" She smacked him on his very fine ass. "Sounds like I'm making blueberry muffins for breakfast. Are you staying?"

"I wish. Save me a couple." He picked up his suit pants and coat. "Have you seen my boxers?"

She stood and helped him search. "I thought I brought all the clothes in, but they might still be in the kitchen."

His face turned fifty shades of red. "Oh God."

"I'll go get them. I'd hate for you to leave with zero dignity left." She headed to the kitchen and yes, his shorts were next to the kitchen table, right where they'd left them.

Ten minutes later, she was at the front door kissing him good-bye. Normally, she was a love 'em and leave 'em gal, but something about Dalton made her want to stick around for a while.

"Dinner tonight?" He cupped her face. "My place, since it's my turn to cook for you. Say six?"

"Deal." She slid her arms up his chest and fisted his shirt, pulling him in for another kiss. "Should I bring a date? I am #HotGirlNeedsDate."

"Not if you want him to live." He waved as he walked to his car. "See you tonight."

She waved and waited for him to pull out of the driveway before she walked back inside and closed the door.

An hour later, she sat at the kitchen table beside Lyric eating blueberry muffins and drinking lattes.

"Mother called you too?" Lyric took a sip of her latte. "When she finally got through she screamed at me for a good ten minutes until Heath took the phone from me and hung it up. How come I always get the blame?"

"In case you haven't noticed, our mother is a bitch." Harmony studied her glow-in-the-dark-pink toenails. "But I am sorry you keep getting blamed. I've played the good girl for so long that no one believes me when I try to be myself."

Lyric studied her. "Why aren't you always yourself?"

Harm had never really thought about it before. "I don't know. You always had Daddy, so that left me with Momma. The only way she approved of me was if I was the good little girl, so that's what I became."

"That's not true, Daddy loves you just as much as me." But Lyric looked like she was sifting through memories looking for any evidence that Harmony had a point.

"Yes, Daddy loves me, but he worships you." Harm held up her hand like a traffic cop. "I'm not jealous, believe me. After everything Momma put you through when you were little, you deserve someone always on your side. I'm only saying that Daddy prefers you and you prefer him. The two of you are so alike. Don't get me wrong, I'm happy for you." She shrugged. "Only, that left me with no one but

Momma, which meant I had to be the good little girl …" At least, she did if she wanted any attention.

Lyric pondered it and sighed long and slow. "I see your point." She pulled Harm in for a one-armed hug. "I'm so sorry. I never looked at it from your perspective. Daddy was always my refuge, and you had, well... Momma." Her lips curled on the last word. "I was always jealous of you and Momma."

"I was always jealous of you and Daddy." It was hard to believe that they'd never talked about this before. Since they were being honest, Harmony felt like letting it all out. "I was always jealous of your brilliant mind. I'm not stupid or anything, but I'm not Lyric genius smart either."

"That's not true. Our IQs are exactly the same, only you have more street smarts. I wish I had more street smarts. And you are kind of a badass. I'd like to be a badass." Lyric took a bite of muffin.

"I'd love to believe that we have the same IQ, but I'm okay with what I have. It was hard growing up in the shadow of the famous Lyric Wright." She'd never said it out loud, but it was time.

"You think that was hard, try growing up with the perfect Harmony Wright. You always made friends so easily and also managed to keep them. I'd like more friends, but sometimes I get so wrapped up in my work that I forget I'm supposed to get together with them. After the third or fourth time, they stop calling me to ask to go out." Lyric had always been oblivious when it came to maintaining a social life.

"I still hate you for solving my Rubik's Cube in twenty seconds flat. I was so proud of myself for figuring out how to take it apart and put it back together like I'd solved it." Harmony had often thought that together they made the perfect person—with Lyric's brain and Harmony's canniness, they had most of the bases covered.

"I've always hated how you can walk into a room full of strangers, make friends instantly, and manage to remember everyone's name." Lyric shook her head. "Can't figure out how you do it."

"Simple, my brain isn't busy trying to figure out the mysteries of the universe like yours is." She tapped on her head. "Plenty of room to remember names and faces."

"I never thought of it that way." Lyric made it sound like she'd just figured out one of the science mysteries she spent way too much time working on. After a bit more thought, she shoulder-bumped Harmony. "So Dalton spent the night. I want details."

"Not much to tell. We had a lot of sex, ran out of condoms, and he left." Harm didn't like that her heart went all high school crush when she thought about Dalton. "But he did mention something interesting. He said we should take some pictures of you and me standing side by side and post them on social media. That way people will see my tattoos and know I'm not you."

Lyric shrugged. "Okay."

Thirty minutes later, Harmony posted several photos online with the #HotGirlNeedsDate tag. Now it was just a waiting game. All she needed was for her mother to disown her. But it was proving harder and harder to do.

Harm's phone buzzed, so she pulled it out of her pocket. She didn't recognize the number but answered anyway. "Hello."

"You gotta come back home, Harmony. We can't take it anymore."

"Is this Mr. McDonald? What's wrong?" She'd known Lucas MacDonald since she and her mother had opened the bakery, and she'd never heard him sound so panicked.

"Your Momma is insane."

"Tell me something I don't know."

"I'm serious. She's the meanest woman I've ever met. And she's ruining the coffee club."

"What did she do now?" Harm had been ignoring texts from the morning coffee club for a few days. It wasn't that she didn't want to help them, it was more like they were a bunch of whiney little girls, so it was hard to tell truth from exaggeration.

"She took our coffeepot away. She says if we're going to take up real estate in her bakery, we have to drink her coffee." He ground out a breath. "It tastes like *cinnamon*." He made cinnamon sound like toxic waste.

"Just do what I do and ignore her, then do what you want. If you want to drink your own coffee in the bakery, bring it in a thermos." Harmony picked up a bottle of black gel nail polish, shook it, and unscrewed the cap. Her toenails needed some black polish. The neon pink was getting on her nerves.

"We tried that. She put up a sign that says no outside food or drink can be brought in. She's vicious. I thought my late wife was mean... Compared to your mother, my wife was a saint." He was genuinely upset. She could hear it in his voice. "You know, your mother has been a thorn in my side for decades, and it's not fair that I have to spend what little time I have left on this earth being tormented by that woman."

Livinia had been Mr. McDonald's student way back when he was a history teacher. Thirty years later, he'd been Lyric and Harm's teacher too. Harmony didn't know what had happened between Livinia and Mr. McDonald, but whatever it was had had him crossing himself every time she or her sister walked into his classroom for the first two months of junior year.

"Now it's time for payback. Be a thorn in her side." She loved her little old men's coffee club. Most of them were widowed and lonely. If they didn't have the bakery, she didn't know what they would do with their time, and no way was she going to let her mother ruin it for them.

"She smacked me on the knuckles with a spatula just 'cause I put my elbows on the table. Can you believe that?" He was on his way from upset to full-on mad. "I survived the jungles of Vietnam and being married to the second meanest woman in Texas. If I want to eat with my elbows on the table, I should be able to do it. I'm an old man, and she hit hard enough to leave a bruise."

Harm brushed black polish on the tips of her toes, like a French manicure gone wild. "I won't be back for a couple of weeks, so y'all are going to have to sort this out yourselves. I think you should stand your ground. Don't let her push you around. If she comes near you with the Evil Spatula of Doom, you put your elbows on the table, look her directly in the eye, and tell her that it's bad manners not to respect her elders. Or better yet …" She finished her left foot and moved on to her right. "Out manners her. Wait for her to slouch or put her elbows on the table and make sure to point it out. Then start critiquing her baking and her clothes. She doles out criticism really well, but she can't take it at all."

"Okay, wait a minute, let me get my glasses so's I can take notes." There was shuffling on his end, like he was patting down pockets. "Oh no, be quiet for a minute. She's coming. I'll give you the okay when the coast is clear."

Harmony wasn't sure if he was talking to her or someone else in the room, so she stayed quiet.

A couple of minutes passed.

"Whew, that was a close one." It was another male voice in the background. "We almost got busted."

"Who's with you?" Harmony added a second coat to her toes.

"Stan Laramey and I are hiding out in the storeroom, waiting for her to leave for the day. We're gonna steal her cinnamon." Mr. McDonald was all covert ops.

"You do realize that without cinnamon, she can't make sticky buns, snickerdoodles, cinnamon twists, and several other things?" She loved their enthusiasm, but their plan could have been better.

"Oh." All of the wind went out of Mr. McDonald's sails.

"Now, what you *can* do is mix things up. Momma likes order, so if you want to mess with her head, go the spice rack and move everything around. Then go into the dining room and move the tables around. Last, take all of the pictures and plaques off of the walls and hide them behind the counter. Tomorrow morning, she'll be too busy baking and fixing things to care about your Folgers coffee or your elbows on the table." With any luck, Momma would also be so beside herself about how disgraceful her perfect little Harmony was acting that she wouldn't care about anything else.

"Good idea." It sounded like he really was taking notes. "What else?"

"You survived Vietnam and taught high school for a million years. I'm sure you can come up with some pretty creative ways to mess with Momma." Harm had faith in her little old men.

"Now that I put my mind to it, I've got a couple of ideas." His confidence and craftiness were back. "I'm gonna call you back tomorrow and tell you know how it went. I gotta go before we get busted back here."

"Good luck." Harmony screwed the cap back on the fingernail polish and then hung up.

It looked like Momma was about to have her hands full. And, God willing, Harmony was going to add to the chaos.

# Chapter 16

An hour later, Harmony not so patiently watched her phone for any new tweets. All of her social media accounts had been suspiciously silent. The twin pics had been out in the world for close to two hours and... nothing. Considering she had a hefty number of followers from her time on *Cupcake Cage Match*—and by virtue of being Heath Montgomery's sister-in-law—it made her nervous.

Before she could check Facebook for the fiftieth time in the last half an hour, the doorbell rang.

"I'll get it." Harm rushed to the door. Maybe it was a reporter coming to do a piece on Lyric's evil twin. She opened the door wearing her brightest smile in case they were rolling live.

No lights, no camera, no action. A short, thin man stood there wearing an American Airlines flight attendant's uniform, lots of attitude, and a name tag that read "Tre."

"Wonder Woman, I got here as fast as I could." Tre pushed past Harmony, pulling a black carry-on bag behind him. "I hope I'm not too late."

Harm fought the urge to look around for Wonder Woman. "I'm sorry, who are you?"

Tre analyzed her face like he was looking for signs of brain trauma. "Oh no, you really are on drugs." He pulled her into a tight hug. "Well, I'm here now." He patted her on the back and then let her go. "Let's get you cleaned up."

"Okay." She looked down at him. "I think you're here for my sister, Lyric."

"It's okay, you don't have to pretend, it's me. I've seen you at your... um ..." His eyes passed down her body and then moved back up again. "Actually, I think today's look is worse than the missing dress from the plane."

"Lyric, someone named Tre is here to see you." Harmony nodded for him to follow her. "Let's see if we can find her."

"What?" Lyric called from the kitchen. "Did you say Tre?"

Tre pushed passed Harmony again and rushed into the kitchen. He parked the bag by the pantry door and ran toward Lyric, who was sitting at the kitchen table working on her laptop.

"There's my Wonder Woman." He threw his arms around her and then pulled back. "Let me look at you." He took in her sister's baggy jeans and brown T-shirt with a wanted poster of Schrödinger's cat on the front. "It looks like I got here just in time."

Lyric smiled up at Tre. "Harm, this is the flight attendant I was telling you about. He saved me on the flight back from Hawaii when he duct-taped me into a dress."

"Baby doll, it was my pleasure." He pulled up the chair next to Lyric. "Now, what's this about you turning to prostitution to support your drug habit? Is there trouble in paradise?"

Lyric turned to Harmony for translation.

Harmony was surprised she didn't know. "The bar fight the other night. Somehow, the tabloids think you've turned to prostitution to pay for your drug habit."

Lyric looked like she was replaying the words in her head, trying to make sense out of them. "I don't understand."

"Then it's not true?" Tre fanned himself. "Thank Jesus."

Lyric smiled at him. "Sorry you came all of this way for nothing."

"It was no trouble. I live close to DFW." His phone buzzed. He pulled it out of his vest pocket and looked at the screen. "Did y'all just post some photos?"

Harm pulled out the chair next to him. "Yes. Why? Is there a post about them?"

Tre didn't seem to notice the urgency, so she grabbed the phone out of his hands.

"Now hold on, Little Miss Grabby Hands." He wrestled the phone from her. He was a lot stronger than he looked.

"That's an interesting selfie to take." Tre examined the picture she and Lyric had taken with them holding today's newspaper. "It looks like a proof-of-life pic kidnappers use when they send the ransom email."

"That's what I told her." Harmony pointed to her sister. "She insisted we needed today's newspaper. We had to borrow it from the neighbors."

"I just wanted to prove that we took the photo today." Lyric made it sound like the most logical thing in the world.

"What are people saying about it? Has anyone noticed that I'm not Lyric." Harmony tried to read over his shoulder. "I need credit for the mess last night."

"That was you?" Tre sounded so relieved. "I thought Wonder Woman had lost her mind." He crossed his legs. "Wait a minute, why on earth would you *want* credit for last night?"

She told him all about Momma, the bakery, Food Network, and winning *Cupcake Cage Match*.

"Hold the honey buns, that was you?" He looked her up and down. "It *was* you. Those chocolate pecan pie espresso cupcakes looked fantastic."

"Wait, you were at the finals in Las Vegas?" She'd never met anyone in real life who knew about *Cupcake*

*Cage Match*. It had only aired on TV once as an hour-long special.

"Of course. My ex was an underground baker. He wasn't very good so he didn't even make it to the state championships." Tre sighed dramatically. "He was so pretty to look at but so dumb. Perfect abs, though. I'm a sucker for a six-pack."

Harm threw out a fist. Tre was good people. "I hear ya."

Lyric nodded. "So do I."

His phone buzzed with a new notification.

"Uh oh." He pressed the phone to his chest so no one could read the screen. "I'm afraid I have some bad news." He tilted his head to the left and then shook it. "The media thinks the photos are faked. *TMZ* just reported that they're photoshopped."

Harmony threw her hands up. "This is crazy. How is this even possible? I can't catch a break."

"Calm down, Super Girl, I've got this." His eyes raked over her dirty T-shirt and comfy short-shorts. "First, we need to go shopping." He waved his hand up and down her body. "This, needs some coverage. I get the whole femme-fatale-meets-badass thing you're trying to pull off, but it most certainly is *not* working. Second, we're going to call a friend of mine who works for the morning news program, *Wake Up Fort Worth*. We need to get you on TV ASAP."

"Really?" Normally Harmony had a hard time accepting help from anyone, but there was just something about Tre that made her feel better already. And if he'd managed to fix Lyric's plane disaster, she was more than willing to give him a shot at fixing her mess too. "Lyric was right about you, you're just the right person at just the right time."

He put his arm around Lyric. "I do what I can."

"I can't go shopping. I have work to do." Lyric started typing again. Clearly, astrophysics involved lots of typing since that seemed to be all her sister freakin' did.

"Your family is in crisis." Tre looked down his nose at her. "Family first. Shopping second. Work third."

"I don't know if ruining my sister's reputation is actually a crisis, but I guess this can wait." Lyric closed her laptop.

"Good, now we need to think couture. I feel like we need to establish your different personalities through your clothes." He looked at Lyric and then Harmony and back to Lyric. "Correction, it looks like you've already done that. We need to establish the personalities I'm going to assign to you through your clothes." He put a hand on top of Lyric's. "I appreciate the Kat Von D meets Betty Crocker thing you've got going on, but I think we need to glam it up. There's a fine line between sexy and trashy." He patted her hand. "You're just south of sexy."

"That's harsh." Harm brushed some flour off of her T-shirt. "These clothes don't define me."

"Well, thank God for that. You look like a hobo hooker." Tre stood. "Now, someone point me in the direction of a guest room with a shower, because I just got off a red-eye I worked with Jolinda. She's a little heavy-handed with the perfume, so I smell like old lady." He pointed an index finger at Harm and then at Lyric. "You two need to get dressed."

"I am dressed." Lyric pointed to her T-shirt.

"Sure you are, Wonder Woman, but I meant in something that didn't come from T-shirts.com. Did your parents dress you like that and that's why y'all don't know any better?" He sounded like he was honestly trying to figure it out.

"You should meet our mother." Harm rolled her eyes. "She's just like you, only a little taller, a lot bitchier, and way meaner. And she only wears Chanel."

"So your wardrobes are some sort of rebellion, then." He thought about it for a second. "I admire rebellion, but this," he pointed to the T-shirts, "has moved into mutiny territory. And the only people you are hurting are yourselves."

"I take it back. Mom's not half as bitchy as you are." Harm stood and stretched. "I'll show you to the guest room across from mine."

"It will be good to get into some civilian clothes." He grabbed the handle of his rolling bag as they walked past it. "I feel like I've been wearing this uniform for a month."

"Just so you know, I have other clothes... different clothes." Harmony didn't know why she was so hell-bent on people-pleasing Tre.

"A gold-lamé bikini doesn't really count, Super Girl, but I'll give you points for trying." His rolling bag got caught on the lip of an area rug. She didn't feel the need to help him.

"No, I really do." She opened the door to her room and led him to the walk-in closet. "See."

He looked at the handful of dresses from Talbots, Ann Taylor, and Chico's that she'd brought with her. Then stared just as hard at the black leather mini and red catsuit.

He sighed dramatically. "I got here just in time. You have multiple wardrobe personality disorder. I know a cry for help when I see one." He one-arm-hugged her. "Don't worry, Sybil. I promise we're going to put all of your humpty-dumpty personality pieces back together again."

An hour later, they all walked into the garage. Lyric hit a button on the wall, and the garage door rolled up. Sunlight backlit Cherry Cherry.

Was it Harmony's imagination, or did Cherry Cherry have an ethereal glow? Then again, hellfire could give that same glow. Lyric would probably tell Harmony that she was glowing because Heath had had her waxed the other day, but Harmony wasn't so sure—even if she was parked to show off her shine, like she was staged for a car show.

"What in God's name is that?" Tre's nose was pinched up like he'd just drawn the short straw and had to change a stinky diaper.

"It's Cherry Cherry." Lyric opened the driver's-side door. "She's kind of temperamental, so you need to be nice to her."

Tre glanced at Harmony. "Is she for real?"

"Unfortunately. Cherry Cherry loves three things: Heath, a hand wax, and Neil Diamond. Not necessarily in that order. It's best if you flatter her." Harmony wasn't ready to acknowledge Cherry Cherry as a conscious being, but she'd stopped discounting her as one after she'd been locked out one time too many.

"You do know that cars aren't alive," Tre stage whispered.

"You've never met anything like Cherry Cherry." Lyric climbed in and closed the door. Harmony took the passenger's seat.

"Why can't we take the Porsche?" Tre looked longingly over at the Porsche Spyder.

"Are you planning on riding on the hood?" Harm pointed to the two-seater. "Two seats and no cargo space. Where would we put all of our shopping bags."

Tre wilted in defeat. "You have a point. Well, if I must." Reluctantly, he opened the back door and slid into the seat. "It's really roomy back here. His eyes darted around like he was looking for the spirit of Cherry Cherry. "I can respect another Diamond Head."

Cherry Cherry seemed to sigh in relief.

"Why does it smell like marijuana in here?" Tre relaxed back against the seat like he was a billionaire waiting to be driven around in his limousine.

"Her last owner could have given Bob Marley a run for his reefer." Harmony buckled her seat belt.

Lyric turned the key and nothing happened. She placed both hands on the dash. "Come on, Cherry Cherry. We have to go help Heath."

She glanced over at Harm like she needed some help convincing the car of the lie. Harmony nodded. "That's right. He needs our help."

Tre leaned forward between the seats. "I can't allow you to lie to another Diamond Head. It's just wrong. Cherry Cherry, we're going shopping. We need you to get us there."

Tre's door opened.

"I think she wants Tre to drive." Lyric looked back at him. "Is that okay?"

"I don't drive. I Ubered over. I like to be driven around. When I make my fortune as a designer, I'm going to hire a driver." He closed the door. "Cherry Cherry, please let Lyric drive. I'll buy you a brand-new air freshener."

The engine started right up.

"That's my girl." He blew her an air-kiss.

"It makes sense that you two would get along." Lyric rolled her eyes.

"Like-minded people should always stick together." Tre patted Harmony's headrest.

Harmony wasn't sure how long two divas could share the same space, but for now all seemed good.

"Where are we headed?" Lyric glanced in the rearview mirror before she backed out.

"Neiman's of course. It's my mecca." He checked his watch. "We have just enough time to make it there for lunch. Their café has the best club sandwich in the world."

Harmony wasn't sure whether Tre was going to make things better or worse, but at least he was interesting. And anyway, she was out of ideas.

# Chapter 17

Dalton had never had a longer day in his life. Minutes lasted for hours, and hours took days to pass. As he sat at his desk doodling on the ink blotter, he glanced at the clock on his computer monitor for the billionth time. It was only two seventeen. Was he in some sort of time loop like *Groundhog Day*?

He doodled some curly cues and a couple of music notes. He glanced at the clock. It was still only two seventeen. It wasn't like he didn't have a million things to do, but well, he missed Five-Alarm Harm. She was something special. He not only understood, but actually enjoyed, her brand of crazy.

And that was when it hit him—so hard that he dropped his Mont Blanc and sat up.

He was falling in love with Harmony.

Holy shit.

*He was falling in love with Five-Alarm Harm.*

He didn't know whether he should be terrified or elated. Probably both, now that he thought about it. Because one thing was for sure, if he could get her to love him back, his hopes for a sane, peaceful life would go right out the window.

As he sat here counting down the minutes until he could see her again, that didn't seem to matter. Just like it didn't matter that she wasn't wife material. All that mattered was that he was crazy about her, and he wanted her to be crazy about him too.

Which he thought she might be. How else could he have lived through handcuffing her in his office? But just because she cared about him too didn't mean that she was interested in trying this out for the long haul.

But he wasn't ready to let her go. Not even close. He just wished he knew how exactly this was going to play out.

Should he tell her tonight that he was falling in love with her? Or would that just scare her off? The last thing he wanted to do was put Five-Alarm Harm on the offensive... or to make her run in the other direction.

Nerves played Pac-Man with his insides. This was a nightmare. He wanted happily ever after just like the next guy, only Harmony wasn't a happily-ever-after kinda girl.

How stupid could he be?

He took a deep breath and let it out slowly, told himself he could do this.

He ran the reigning Super Bowl champion football team and negotiated multimillion-dollar deals for breakfast. He could handle one adrenaline-junkie baker with a short fuse, no matter what she decided to throw at him. It wasn't like he didn't deal with spoiled athletes every day of his life.

He'd just have to accept the fact that he wasn't going to be able to control her. She was too unpredictable. Of course, that was one of the things he loved most about her.

Life with her, he smiled to himself, would never be dull.

Three hours later, he was home and wishing for a little dull. He poured himself a tequila shot and chased it with a lime. Not that he was a big drinker, but right now he needed a shot. Or several shots.

All six burners of his stove had pots full of cooking food. He sniffed the air. Something was burning. He juggled pot lids trying to figure out what was wrong, but everything looked fine-ish. Why the hell had he volunteered to cook for Harm? He didn't cook. Well, besides microwave popcorn and the occasional egg. This morning it had seemed manly to prepare food for his woman, especially if he was going to ease around to a define-the-relationship discussion, but now he realized it was one of the worst ideas he'd ever had.

One more shot to steady his nerves—hell, he wasn't driving. Maybe he'd take two.

He was just reaching for the bottle when the smoke detector started screeching. The kitchen filled with smoke. And that was when it hit him. The oven. Crap, the turkey.

Goddammit. This was the worst idea he'd ever had.

But he'd wanted to do something special for Harmony, something to show her that he really cared. At his house, that thing had always been Thanksgiving dinner.

Growing up, it was the one time of the year his mother ever cooked. So to him, this was what a home-cooked meal should be. But now that he thought about it, that might have been a little ambitious to try for his first home-cooked meal.

As if to prove his point, when he yanked the oven door open, flames shot out. He grabbed the fire extinguisher from under the sink and doused Tom Turkey until he was swimming in white foam.

Was blackened turkey the same as charred turkey? Blackened sounded so much better than charred. And it looked better too. Surely, he couldn't serve this. It was burned all to hell and covered in—he looked down at the fire extinguisher—whatever was in there to put out fires.

To make matters worse, his whole place smelled like Five-Alarm Harm had already tried to burn it to the ground. He really hoped it wasn't a bad omen.

He jogged over to the giant floor-to-ceiling windows that served as the exterior wall of his kitchen and living room space in the old mill turned condos where he lived and opened the heavy multi-paned windows in an effort to get the smoke out before the fire department—or worse, Harm—showed up.

When the smoke detector finally stopped screeching and he could think again, he took stock of what he had left for dinner. There was the cornbread dressing... He slouched against the cabinets next to the kitchen sink. It had been baking on the rack under the turkey, so that was out.

There were French-cut green beans on the stove. He lifted their lid. They looked like black dried-out worms. He glanced at the chicken stock he'd been about to add to them when the turkey had broken out in flames. Too late now. Green beans were off the list.

He lifted the lid on the macaroni and cheese. Because it was a special occasion, he'd bought the deluxe box kind instead of just the plain old mac and cheese. Just to make sure the noodles were cooked through, he'd let them boil for almost an hour. Turned out that wasn't a great plan, since they'd fallen apart as soon as he added the cheese sauce. Now they kinda looked like bright-orange oatmeal.

The mashed potatoes didn't look that bad—he was kind of proud of them. As he didn't have a potato masher or a hand mixer, he'd ended up using a hammer to beat them into submission. Sure, they were kinda lumpy and—he peered closer—a little rust filled. But rust was okay, right? A little oxidized metal never hurt anyone. Or at least, had never killed anyone.

Shoulders slumped in defeat, he turned to look at the gravy. He lifted that lid and the smell was so bad it nearly knocked him over, so slammed the lid back down. When it cooled down, he was throwing that one away, pot and all.

Finally, there was the chocolate sauce he was making to put on the ice cream he'd bought for dessert. He'd also been hoping to pour it all over Harmony, but when he lifted that lid, all that was left of his beautiful sauce was a gritty, smoking blob. He obviously should have gone with the brown plastic bottled stuff from Hershey's.

Fuck. Just fuck. He'd ruined every damn thing he'd tried to make and nearly burned his loft down in the process. Five-Alarm Harm had nothing on him.

It was definitely time to order pizza.

Then again... He surveyed his kitchen. It looked like a bomb had gone off. Maybe they should go out for dinner and he should have a hazmat crew come in and hose everything down.

Resigned now, he grabbed a trash bag and was just starting to dump the mess—pans and all—when his buzzer rang.

He glanced down. Splotches of fire foam mixed with the other cooking muck splattered on his shirt and jeans. But if he took the time to change clothes, Harm might leave, thinking he wasn't home.

Fuck it. He'd made the mess. Might as well own it.

He headed to the door and pressed the buzzer to let Harmony up. He opened the front door, and in a moment the penthouse elevator door rolled open.

And there stood Harmony, wearing nothing but killer black high heels, tiny black lace panties, a black leather motorcycle jacket, and a sinful smile.

His brain shut down and all he could do was stare. He ran his hand across his mouth checking for drool. No drool.

"I'll take your slack-jawed expression as a sign that you like my new underwear." She tossed a black dress over her shoulder and strutted out of the elevator. If he thought the front view was nice, the back was even better. An itty-bitty string disappeared between her perfectly round ass cheeks.

"I hope you were wearing the dress when you walked through the lobby, or my doorman probably had a heart attack and is dead on the front sidewalk." He closed the door and leaned against it, just taking her in. Every square inch of her was perfect. Lucky, lucky him.

What a wonderful feeling it was to be in love with the person he was also lusting over.

She sniffed the air. "Is something on fire?"

"Besides me?" He looked around. Crap, one look at her and he'd forgotten all about dinner. "We're going to need to order in."

"I thought you were cooking?" She glanced at the kitchen and her eyes went so wide he could see the whites all around the iris. "Wow, that's a huge mess."

"You have no idea." He picked at the dried fire foam on his shirt. "It turns out, I can't cook."

She threw her head back and laughed. And laughed. And laughed. It sounded like the way rich, smoky bourbon tasted. Full and dark and absolutely delicious.

All of the stress of the last couple of hours melted away as he watched her. It might be the tequila finally kicking in, but it was probably the naked Harmony.

He grinned because he couldn't help himself. Then reached for her hand and dragged her through the living room to the kitchen. "You want a drink?" He nodded to the bottle of tequila on the counter.

She glanced at the discarded lime peels. "It looks like you've been drinking enough of that for both of us."

"Not even close." Then, because he couldn't keep his hands to himself for one second longer, he pulled her into his arms. "I'm glad you came."

"Me too."

He rested his chin on the top of her head for a minute and just breathed in the sweet honey scent of her.

She shoved against his chest, pushed him away. And for a brief moment he felt bereft, though for the life of him he couldn't figure out why.

Striving for control, needing to keep his hands busy with something other than her, he reached into the bar cabinet and pulled out a shot glass. "You ever tried Patrón?"

"You're talking to a Texan, baby. I was raised on Patrón."

"That's what I like to hear." He poured a shot and handed it to her, but he stopped her hand before the shot got to her mouth. "If you're going to do a shot, you've got to do it right."

Harmony lifted one cool brow, licked her full lower lip, and nearly had him coming in his fucking jeans. Goddamn, this woman had him wrapped around her little finger. "I didn't realize there was a wrong way to do this."

"Sweetheart, there's a wrong way to do everything." He was putting his hands on her waist and lifting her up so that her sweet ass was on the center island, her legs just a little bit open.

Stepping between them before she could change her mind, he slipped her leather jacket off her shoulders, letting his fingers linger on his favorite tattoo—a hibiscus flower blooming right over her rib cage. He wanted to ask her about it, wanted to ask her about the journeys behind all her tattoos, but then she moved against him and all he could think about was getting his mouth on her.

So he did, leaning down and licking a trail from the hollow of her throat to her breastbone. "Mmm, salty."

She blushed, then leaned back on her hands so that her breasts were thrust forward. "It's almost a hundred degrees outside. Hard not to sweat."

"And yet you're wearing leather."

She quirked a brow at him, those luscious lips of hers turning up in the wicked grin that haunted his dreams. "Leather is seasonless."

"It really isn't."

She reached a hand down and ran her fingers over the buckle of his leather belt. "It really is."

God, he was crazy in love with her. It was taking all his self-control to take things slowly when all he really wanted to do was to eat her alive.

"I wasn't complaining," he murmured as he trailed his tongue over the curve of first one breast and then the other. Then he slammed back the shot of tequila and finished it off by biting into a lime slice.

Her mouth was slightly open, her eyes wide as she stared at his lips. "*That's* the right way to do a tequila shot?"

He loved her voice. The husky sweetness was a turn-on even without the hard-ass tone she deliberately injected into it. With the hard-ass tone, it was irresistible. "It's the best way."

"I bet."

He poured another shot. Handed it to her. "Here. You try."

He shrugged out of his T-shirt. Her black leather jacket slid down her arms and landed in a heap on the floor.

Shit, he wanted her. Was dangerously close to becoming obsessed with her.

Her sexy pink tongue darted out, swiped across her top lip and then her bottom one, as if she couldn't quite decide where to lick. Every thought he had or might have had got lost in the wild need pumping through him.

Groaning, he tangled a hand in her hair and urged her closer. "Come on, sweetheart," he whispered. "Taste me."

Her mouth lowered to his chest so slowly that he wanted to howl. Then her tongue was on him, swirling in circles over his right pec, darting out to tease his nipple. Once, twice. Again and again, until it was all he could do to keep from ripping off her panties and sliding into her right there.

"You taste good." It was a whisper, but he heard it and his body reacted, his arousal ratcheting up another notch. Or twelve. Fuck—who would have thought it was possible to be this turned on and not come?

"So do you, baby. God, so do you." He reached over, put a lime slice in his mouth. Concentrated on the bitterness of it as her sweet mouth fastened onto his neck and began to suck. God damn but he wanted to do this with her for the rest of his life. His brain told him it was too soon to be thinking like that, but the rest of him didn't give a shit. She was his.

When she lifted her lips from his skin, he nearly shouted in disappointment. But it was so damn sexy to see her take the shot glass, to watch as she rubbed the cool glass over one cheek and then the other.

He felt himself grow harder, felt himself leak just a little as she dipped her tongue into the icy cold liquid. He clenched his fists, told himself not to rush her. That it would be sweeter if she took her time.

And was it ever. Her eyes met his, clung for long seconds before she tossed her head back and slid the tequila down her throat. Then she was reaching up, grabbing the back of his head, pulling his mouth down to hers, and biting the lime he still had between his lips.

He nearly came, had to grit his teeth against the orgasm that threatened to rise in him—sharp and clean and demanding. Fuck, this woman was turning him inside out.

He was loving every second of it.

"You want another one?" Was that his voice? So low and feral, as if all that was civilized had been stripped from him.

"I'd rather have you."

Her bold honesty went straight through him, turning up the raging inferno inside of him until he feared spontaneous combustion.

"The two aren't mutually exclusive, you know." He tipped the tequila bottle slightly, let a few drops dribble onto her breasts and down her stomach.

She gasped as the cold liquid hit her, arched her back so that her nipples—and the little barbells she had inserted through them—were front and center. Because he was dying for another taste of her, he bent down, followed the trail the alcohol had made with delicate flicks of his tongue.

Then, because he couldn't resist, he tilted the bottle so that the tequila coated his index finger. He swirled it first over one of her nipples and then the other before bending his head and circling the barbells with his tongue. Then he sucked them between his teeth and tugged a little, loving the way she went pliant at the first pull.

He sucked until all the alcohol was gone, savoring its rich burn as it slid down his throat. Then he brought his hands to Harmony's shoulders and pressed her back slowly until she was fully open to him.

Her cheeks were flushed, her eyes heavy with desire, her lips slick from the shot she'd taken. Laid out on his counter like a dessert more delectable than anything she'd ever made, her legs open and dangling over the edge, she was gorgeous. Sexy. Completely overwhelming.

"I may never take a shot any other way." He lifted the bottle, poured a steady stream of the liquor over her stomach.

She gasped as it ran down her sides, pooled in her navel, and he bent forward, sipping from her slowly. Savoring the spicy-sweet taste of her that mingled with the smooth heat of the aged tequila.

She moaned, a low, sexy sound that had him glancing up, wanting to see her face. Needing to know that she was as into this as he was.

She had a slice of lime clenched between her front teeth, and he groaned as he swooped down, bit it, taking it into his mouth as he longed to take her.

"My turn," she whispered, grabbing his hand and sucking his tequila-coated finger into her mouth.

His knees actually shook as she twirled her tongue around his finger, stroking it up and down in the same rhythm she'd used on his dick the other night. His heart was pounding out of control, the need to fuck her an all-consuming ache inside of him.

"Harmony, baby." He tried to retrieve his hand—along with his sanity—but she lifted her arms and curled her body around his arm, holding him like he was a prize she had won. And then, just when he didn't think he could get any more turned on, just when his knees were locking and his dick throbbing, she bit down hard on the tip of his finger and shot his lust-crazed body into overdrive.

He ripped his finger out of her mouth, slid out of her embrace as he strived to get himself under some kind of control. Taking a deep breath, he reached over and grabbed the bottle with a hand that shook so badly it was all he could do to get the tequila in the glass. He handed it to her, but she set it aside. Hooked her fingers in the front belt loops of his jeans and tugged until he was nestled right up against her sex. "I'm more interested in the salt."

And then she leaned forward and pressed her mouth to his chest and he knew he was done for. Her tongue—her wicked, wild, wonderful tongue—was everywhere at once. Flicking over his collarbone, sliding up his neck to toy with his earlobe. Moving lower to press into his chest.

"Harmony, baby, stop." He moved his hands to her head, clenched his fists in her hair. Tried to pull her off.

But she was having none of it, her hands slipping around his waist as her nails dug into the muscles of his back. The flickers of pain were exquisite, the feel of her clawing him unbelievably sexy.

"Stop," he gasped again, but even he didn't know if he meant it anymore. All he knew was that he would die if he wasn't inside of her soon, would come in his pants like a teenager with his first girlfriend. The humiliation was almost more than he could take, even as the incredible desire, the unbelievable experience of wanting her this much, only pushed him higher.

She lifted her head, looked at him with passion-dazed eyes. Smiled wickedly and murmured, "Oh, I don't think so," right before she unbuttoned his fly.

Her hand slipped inside, closing around him firmly enough to have him seeing stars. Eyes crossing, hips thrusting, he pumped against her for a few seconds before reaching down and disentangling himself.

"You don't want this to be over before it begins, do you?" he muttered in response to her quizzical look.

"I don't care. I just want to watch you come again."

He groaned, yanked her off the counter so he could strip her of the little black thong that revealed more than it covered. "I like this," he said as he sunk to his knees in front of her, twirling the panties around his index finger.

She grinned down at him. "So do I.

"I'll say." He stood, shoved his jeans down and off so that he was standing there—in the middle of his kitchen—as naked as Harmony. And she was taking her time looking him over, her eyes eating him up as if he were one of her chocolate cannoli. For a moment he felt oddly vulnerable, totally exposed, but then she was pressing her body against his, and everything fled but the need to make her feel as good as he did.

Sinking into the nearest chair, he pulled her onto his lap, had her straddle him so that her hot, wet sex rested directly over his dick. She gasped at the first slide of him against her, then wiggled even closer.

It was his turn to gasp, to shudder as her warm heat enfolded him in a new way. And then she was moving, her slick, hot body sliding against him, and he almost forgot how to breathe.

"You feel amazing," he muttered, his hands curving around her ass.

"I think it's you." She moved forward and backward slowly, so goddamned slowly he wanted to shout, but it was the most incredible feeling he'd ever had—this being in her without being in her, being cradled by her body without the heavy thrusting that would take him all the way inside. "Everything about you amazes me."

Her words humbled him even as he arched off the chair, desperate to get more of her. "Harmony." His voice broke as he called out her name.

She slid back until the tip of his cock was poised at her entrance, rising on her tiptoes to torment him for a minute with her incredible heat.

"You're killing me, sweetheart." He stroked his hands up her back, tangled them in her wild blonde hair.

God, there really was miles of the stuff—soft and sweet-smelling and so sexy it had him arching against her even as he tangled his fists in it and tugged.

"Dalton." Her voice was low, startled, and incredibly excited—so excited that he did it again as he rolled his hips against her.

She whimpered, arched, her eyes closing as the pleasure went through her and he couldn't resist a grin. Or doing it a third time as he realized just how much Harmony got off on the little licks of pain.

Shifting his hands so that they were at the nape of her neck, he pulled down hard enough to have her tilting her head to the side and opening her eyes. Then he lowered his mouth to hers, sucked her lower lip between his teeth, and bit softly.

She cried out, her body shuddering reflexively against his. And she felt so good he wanted to slam inside of her and pound away until orgasm swept through them both.

She opened to him, parted her lips so he could slip inside and explore her. His tongue stroked inside, licked the top of her mouth before stroking down one cheek and then the other. Curling his tongue around hers, he sucked until she was inside him. Relinquishing control for just a moment, he relaxed as she took him as he had taken her.

# Chapter 18

Harmony moaned, her tongue tangling with Dalton's as she took her time exploring every part of his mouth. She wanted to go on kissing him forever, never wanted this moment to end as she savored the incredible taste of him. Tequila and lime and the deepest, darkest chocolate.

For a moment, just a moment, she was distracted wondering what dessert she could make to capture his exact flavor. A dark-chocolate cake with lime curd and tequila icing maybe. Or a chocolate Napoleon with—

Dalton must have noticed her wandering attention, because he fisted his hand in her hair and yanked. Not hard enough to hurt, but definitely hard enough to get her attention.

Impatience rolled off of him. She could feel it in the muscles bunching under her hands, sense it in the restless movements of his hips beneath her own. Even so, she took one more minute to taste him, one more minute to savor the dark and complex flavors of him.

Before she could prepare herself, long before she was ready for her exploration to

end, Dalton grabbed his jeans from the floor and yanked out a condom. Harmony watched as he opened the package and rolled it down his long, hard length. And then he was plunging upward, entering her with an urgency that had her trembling on the edge of orgasm.

"Take me," he muttered, plunging deep again and again. "Take all of me."

"God, yes." She twisted her hands in his hair and she smoothed them over his powerful chest. Clutched at the strong muscles of his back. She wanted to touch him everywhere, wanted to feel every part of him against her as he took her higher than she'd ever gone before.

She jerked against him, desperate to get closer. Desperate to take all of him. He growled low in his throat, brought his powerful hands to her hips and held her still as he slammed inside of her with what felt like every ounce of strength he had.

She screamed. She couldn't help it, couldn't control it. He was so strong. So hard. So powerful as he took her over and over again. Turning her on, driving her crazy, making her want more and more of him when he was already giving her everything.

"Dalton," she sobbed, her body spinning wildly out of control. "Please, let me come. Let me—"

He reached down and stroked his thumb over her clit. Once, twice, again and again as he continued to thrust furiously inside of her.

Then he was leaning down, pulling one of her nipples into his mouth.

She bucked against him, tried to rush him, but he used one hand to hold her hips still, then used the other to grab her wrists and hold them behind her back.

"I want to touch you," she gasped, yanking against the tight hold he had on her wrists. With her arms pinned behind her she was completely at his mercy, able to take only whatever it was he chose to give her.

"Not now, sweetheart. I'm too close." He buried his face in the curve of her neck, bit her shoulder in an effort to establish dominance—as if she didn't already know who was in control. At another time, with another guy, it would have bothered her. Would have had her bucking against him and what he was trying to do with her body. But this was Dalton, the man who had seen all the crazy she could throw out and who wanted her anyway. The man who—despite the tatts and the body piercings—kissed and touched and held her like she was the sexiest, most important, most precious thing in his world.

Still, he wasn't the only one with tricks up his sleeve. He drove her crazy, took her higher than she'd ever dreamed possible, but that wasn't enough for her. She wanted, needed, to do the same for him.

With that thought in mind, she pushed her knees into his sides and slowly—oh, so slowly—clenched the muscles of her sex around him. She felt his response in the jerk of his cock, saw it in the clenching of his jaw as he fought to maintain control.

She did it again, squeezing a little bit harder, a little bit longer, before she released him.

"Stop it," he growled, his free hand coming down hard on her ass.

She threw her head back and laughed, even as she tightened the muscles again and again. "Make me."

"Harmony." His voice was low, a warning more animal than human as she continued to caress him with her body. He was getting ready to lose it—she could feel it in the thighs that trembled beneath her own and the hand that clenched more firmly around her wrists.

But she didn't care. She wanted him to lose it, wanted him to plunge inside of her with all the darkness and passion and emotion he had inside of him. She wanted him as crazy and out of control as she was.

She wanted him every way she could have him.

"Come on, Dalton," she whispered tauntingly. "Fuck me like you mean it."

He released her hands with a roar, his fingers clenching on her ass to keep her in place as he stood. He took two long strides, slammed her back—hard—against the kitchen wall.

"You asked for it," he growled, as his hips began to piston against her. Harder, deeper than before, he pounded into her. Again and again he slammed inside her, until she was overwhelmed. Surrounded. Completely taken over by him. More, she was completely in his thrall. This man who was so strong and smart. This man who made her want to cede control for the first time in her life.

And still he surged inside of her. Desperately. Furiously. Each quick, hard stroke of his dick a branding that told her exactly who owned her body.

Harmony moaned as she wrapped her arms around him and held his shaking, furious body against her own. She'd wanted to push him, to see him without his infernal control. To show him that she could take whatever he dished out. And she was taking it, but God, she'd never felt anything this intense before, not even the last time he'd made love to her.

Her orgasm slammed through her. Heat radiated along her every nerve ending, radiant incandescent flames that she couldn't control. That she could only experience. She called his name then, her hands tangling in his hair, her legs clenching tightly around his waist.

"I love you, Harmony." Dalton's voice was low, hoarse, his body jerking spasmodically against hers as he emptied himself inside of her in long, jetting streams. His shudders—and his words—set off another explosion inside of her, and then she was crying out his name, whimpering, wailing, burying her face against the heavy muscles of his chest as her body spun onto a whole different plane, one where the pleasure went on and on and on.

When it was over, when the pleasure had finally receded and she was left limp and lazy and utterly exhausted, she kept waiting for him to say it again. Kept waiting for him to whisper that he loved her, that he wanted her—just the way she was.

But he didn't say anything and neither did she. How could she, when he was wrapped around her, filling up an empty space inside of her that no one else had ever been able to reach?

# Chapter 19

"Wakey, wakey." Someone slapped Harmony on the ass a couple of times. She knew that saccharine-sweet voice... it was the only reason he wasn't dead. Tre.

"I just crawled in bed." She cracked one eye open. It was 4:06 a.m. No hangover, so that was good. "Go away, I'm tired."

"Get your ass up, young lady, we have hair and makeup. Remember *Wake Up Fort Worth*?" Tre pinched her on the bottom. "It's not my fault you had a close-to-overnighter with Mr. Tall, Dark, and You Didn't Let Me Meet Him."

"Ouch." She rubbed her bottom. "I'm up."

She had to be on set for *Wake Up Fort Wor*th by six, and according to Tre, it would take close to thirty minutes to get there. They only had an hour and a half for makeup, hair, and clothes for both her and Lyric. In Harm's opinion, that was about an hour and twenty-five minutes too much, but what did she know? Tre had stolen her gold-lamé bikini and refused to give it back.

"Don't make me carry you into that shower, because I will and you won't like the cold water I turn on for you." Tre was downright snotty. "Your sister's already up and in the shower."

"Good for her." Slowly, Harmony rolled out of bed. Usually she was up way before now, but considering she'd only gone to bed two hours ago, she was running on fumes. "Lyric's always been an overachiever."

"Yep, that's what I love most about her." Heath popped his head in and jumped back. "Damn, you look rough." His face was all shock and horror. He glanced at Tre. "Got your work cut out for you there."

Harmony grabbed a pillow and fired it off in Heath's direction.

Heath dodged it. "That's not very nice. And to think, I made you breakfast."

He popped a blueberry mini-muffin in his mouth.

"Aren't those the muffins I made yesterday?" She yawned and stretched.

"Yes, but I warmed this one up," he said around the muffin in his mouth.

"You also ate it." She headed to the en suite bathroom.

"All your negativity made me hungry," he called after her.

"Bite me," she fired back.

"I love you too, little sister—"

She slammed the bathroom door and turned on the shower so the water could heat up.

Fifteen minutes later, she was showered, shampooed, and wrapped in a yummy-soft terry cloth robe.

Several dresses were laid out on her made bed. She was learning that Tre was a neat freak. She looked around. He'd picked up her clothes from the night before, folded them, and set them on a chair by the bay window.

He hovered, impeccably dressed in gray slacks and a pale-pink dress shirt. Who was impeccably dressed at four in the morning?

"What do you think of the outfits I've laid out?" Tre waved his arm like a game show hostess showing off prizes.

They all showed a lot of skin. True, she'd picked everything out with Tre, but before she'd left Dalton's last night, Dalton had suggested she tone it down for the interview. While normally she wouldn't pay any attention to what he said, he'd been on TV a lot more than she had. Plus, she didn't want to embarrass him or Lyric anymore than she already had. She'd been causing damage ever since she got here, and she couldn't help wondering if maybe it was time for her to cool it, just a little.

It hurt that Dalton didn't like the way she dressed, but since she was pretty sure she was falling in love with him, she wanted to make him happy. Harmony knew she was falling into the same old trap she was trying to escape with her mother—being who everyone else wanted her to be instead of being herself—but maybe Dalton had a point. Was curbing her fashion sense really that bad? After all, she'd let Tre do the same thing and had never questioned his choices.

"I'm leaning towards the black crop top and matching skater skirt. It's edgy without being trashy." He shook his head. "I don't know about the shoes though."

"Pick something from the closet," she told him. "I never go anywhere without a pair for every occasion."

He whistled when he saw her collection, but it didn't take long for him to come back with a pair of wicked-looking Louboutins. When he put them next to the outfit he'd chosen, it was all she could do to blink away the tears.

Which was stupid. She wasn't a crier, and yet twice in the last few days she'd had to struggle to hold back her emotions.

She tried to hide it, but Tre must have seen because he pulled her in for a hug. "Now, come on, Super Girl, there's no crying before a large-market TV appearance. Think about the Food Network exec who will be watching. We can't have you with puffy red eyes."

Tre was the Tim Burton version of a fairy godmother—dark, well-meaning, and a little angry. He had a good heart and impeccable talent.

"I feel like the clothes we bought yesterday are the first ones I've ever had that feel like me. Thank you for that." She didn't know how to explain the closet filled with Junior League on the right and Roller Derby on the left.

"You're too young to be drowning in so much Talbots," he said. "But I'm all for the Loubies."

"I bought them all on eBay. I'm pretty sure they're either fake or stolen, but since I paid less than three hundred dollars for each pair, I don't care." She might compromise on her clothes, but the shoes were all Harmony. "My mother wants me to be Ann Taylor and I thought I was Harley Quinn, but I don't know anymore. I like lace short shorts, but I'm not sure they're who I am. I don't know what to do. Dalton told me that he loved me, but then he told me to tone it down for the interview today." She honestly didn't know what to do.

"Do you love him?" Tre led her to the bed, carefully moved a blood-red dress over, and sat her down.

"I think so. Unfortunately." With the sleeve of her robe, she wiped her face.

"Listen, sweet cheeks, I know a little something about not fitting in. I'm a gay man who grew up in Gilmer, Texas, population five thousand. I played the straight guy until I didn't recognize myself. I hated everything about me. My senior year in high school, I met a man."

"Your first lover?" Harmony knew how it felt to look in the mirror and not see the person you really were.

"No, far from it. He was gay though." Tre turned sad and serious. "He had end-stage lung cancer. I volunteered at the hospital …" He laughed. "I had this crazy idea that because my father was a doctor, I needed to be one too." He wiped the tears from his own eyes. "Anyway, Charles had been a loving husband to his wife of more than twenty years. They had four daughters. But, he was gay. He said, 'I always thought there was time to be true to myself. I always said one day I would do this or one day I would do that. One day... one day... but I'm out of one days, and I don't think I've ever been truly happy. Don't let life pass you by because you're waiting for one day.' He was right. I went home, told my parents I was gay, and I haven't looked back since. Has it been easy? No, but I'm living my truth. You need to be true to yourself." He smiled sadly up at her. "To thine own self be true. The real you is fantastic and funny and fabulous. Don't get confused."

He was right—she knew he was right—but she'd been wearing a mask so that people would love her for so long that it was frightening to take it off. "You're right, I know it."

"You don't have to decide about the rest of your life right now. All I need you to do is pick out something to wear. We're running out of time, and I need at least forty-five minutes to turn you from a pumpkin into Cinderella." He snapped his fingers. "Let's get a move on."

It wasn't what she wanted to hear, but it was exactly what she needed to hear. Tre was just the right amount of bitchy to get her moving.

"I'm wearing the black crop top and skater skirt," she said firmly. It felt the most like who she was inside, and she would start living her truth one outfit at a time. "But I think the black lace-up Loubies are too much for prime-time TV. Let's go with the floral ones. The black background ties everything together, but the neon flowers are the right pop of color. What do you think?"

"I think we're finally dressing for your inner Harmony. I love it. Now for hair and makeup." He headed for the bathroom.

Five hours later, she was seriously rethinking her inner Harmony as the *Wake Up Fort Worth* executive producer continued to yell at her in the greenroom—which was a sickly eggshell and not green at all, much to her disappointment.

"We are a family-friendly TV show. Do you know what you've done?" His name might have been Les or Brett. Harmony couldn't remember.

"Don't be an ass." Tre stepped between her and Les/Brett. "All she did was uncross and cross her legs."

"I didn't realize that when I sat down, my skirt would be so short." The outfit was cute and totally her, but there was no way around it. She'd had a serious wardrobe malfunction on live TV.

"Are you going to claim you didn't know you weren't wearing any underwear? Putting on underwear is a choice. One you should make every single day of your life." Les/Brett's face was turning a deep shade of purple. That couldn't be good.

"I did have underwear on, but right before the last segment, one of the straps holding it on broke. It's not like I could sew it back together." If she hadn't taken them off, they would have ended up around her knees. She'd made it through most of the segments with underwear on. Didn't that count for something?

"Back off." Lyric stepped into Les/Brett's personal space. "She didn't do it on purpose. I don't see what's so wrong. So what if she showed her vagina? Every second person in the world has one. Get over it."

Harmony took a step back. Usually she was the one standing up for Lyric, not the other way around. But she'd be lying if she said it didn't feel good to have Lyric in her corner. Plus, defiance looked good on her. Clearly, being married to Heath was doing her some good—and not just in the sex-life department. Not that Harmony had any intention of ever telling *him* that.

"What's *wrong*?" The producer's voice was at a screechy level that only dogs should be able to hear. "We can't even say the word vagina on morning TV, much less show one to our viewing public. This is a disaster. The network is talking about pulling our show."

Tre shot Les/Brett a glare that should have singed the producer's hair plugs. "That's it. We're going." He stabbed an index finger at the producer's chest. "You're no longer invited to my monthly dinner party, and you're off my Christmas card list. You are dead to me."

Tre put his arms around Harmony's and Lyric's waists and walked them out.

Once they were back in Cherry Cherry, Harmony sighed in relief. "Well, that sorta went well."

"At least the world at large now knows there are two of you." Tre closed the passenger's-side door. "Mission accomplished."

"How can you say that?" Harmony didn't know what to do next. What if her wardrobe issue cost her the Food Network show? Dalton had been right; she should have toned it down. At least then she wouldn't have pulled a Sharon Stone in *Basic Instinct* on live TV.

"Didn't Food Network want a badass baker? Hello, they just got what will become national and possibly international free publicity." Tre sounded very satisfied with himself.

"Did you sabotage my panties?" Harmony knew Tre meant well, but his methods were another thing entirely.

"Trust me, Super Girl, I've never done anything with a woman's panties in my life, except admire them on a shelf from afar." Tre poked his head between the seats. "I'm a glass-is-overflowing kinda guy. The bright side is free publicity, which I'm afraid is also a downside."

"No, no... I think he has a point." Lyric turned over the engine and for once, Cherry Cherry didn't protest having Harmony in the car. "You're getting your name out there."

Chopin's Funeral March played on Harmony's phone, and Lyric shot her a look of sympathy. It was Momma and she wouldn't be happy. Come to think of it, she was never happy.

Harm slid her finger across the screen and held the phone to her ear.

"Harmony Marie Wright, you are a disgrace and a disappointment. I expect this of Lyric, but not you. What on earth—"

Tre grabbed the phone from Harmony. "I don't know who this is, but you will never address Harmony or Lyric in that tone of voice or spew such vile words at them ever again. When you regain some composure and common decency, feel free call back. Until then, don't call this number." He hit end.

Silence cut through the car.

Lyric leaned over and kissed Tre on the cheek. "That was our mother. I doubt anyone has ever spoken to her like that before in her life. You really are our fairy godmother."

Harmony didn't know what to say. She knew she'd have to talk to her mother at some point, but for now, she didn't have to take the verbal abuse. It was safe to say that Harm's reputation was finally tarnished beyond repair. The fact that she'd done it unintentionally was neither here nor there.

Harmony's phone rang again, and Tre turned the screen so she could see it.

"It's not Momma this time." She didn't recognize the number. She slid her finger across the screen. "Hello?"

"It's Holly Braeburn from Food Network. Please tell me you didn't do it on purpose." She didn't sound happy.

Talk about kicking Harmony when she was down.

"I really didn't do it on purpose." Harmony could feel her dream slipping away.

"It's not a total loss. We can find a way to spin it, just don't ever do it again." Holly sounded like she was swigging something. Was it Jack Daniels or Pepto-Bismol? Or some weird mix of both?

"I won't."

"What was with the gold-lamé bikini? I said badass baker, not badass streetwalker."

"I know. Sorry." She wasn't one for apologies, but if it kept her dream alive, she'd say sorry a hundred times. After the last few days, she knew what she wanted, and it wasn't to run back to San Angelo in shame with her tail tucked between her legs.

"Why don't you lay low for a few days. Stay out of the media while I do some damage control on this end." Holly sounded like she'd aged ten years.

"I thought we were going to tape a practice show before the pilot?" Considering what had just happened and Holly's current level of anxiety, she didn't want to bring up any more bad news, but she really didn't have a choice. "We can't film at the bakery in San Angelo, but I have a better idea. My twin sister Lyric is married to the Fort Worth Wranglers' own Heath Montgomery. They've invited me to tape the show in their kitchen."

She sent Lyric a pleading look.

Lyric gave her a double thumbs-up.

"Fort Worth is a much bigger market, and we have the tie-in with the Fort Worth Wranglers we can exploit." Now Harm was practically begging.

"It's not a bad idea. I guess we could tape the pilot there." Holly didn't sound convinced. "Since we're scheduled for next week, it's kind of short notice to change the location, but it can be done. As long as you swear that you'll keep all of your clothes on."

"The pilot? I thought we were shooting a test show before the pilot." Harmony wasn't sure what the difference was, but from Holly's tone, there was a huge one.

"Plans change. The higher-ups at the network have decided all you get is one shot." Holly paused like she was collecting her words. "I'm not going to sugarcoat this for you. Everything is riding on the pilot—for you and for me."

No pressure there at all.

"I understand." Harmony wanted to crawl back in bed and hit rewind on the whole morning. "I won't let you down."

"I hope so. Talk to you soon." Holly hung up.

"So?" Tre asked, eyes wide and handkerchief at the ready. "What's the verdict?"

"The verdict is I better not mess up again or I'll be stuck hocking brownies out of the back of Cherry Cherry."

The car backfired, as if to say no way in hell.

Damn it. She'd been trying to be herself, trying to live her life on her terms. Instead, she'd nearly lost her dream job, she'd embarrassed herself and her sister on live TV, and she could only imagine what Dalton was going to say when she finally talked to him.

Tre might think it was time to put the Talbots dresses to rest once and for all, but all of a sudden Harmony wasn't so sure. Things sure as hell went smoother when she was pretending to be someone else.

# Chapter 20

Two days later, Harmony was ready to quit everything and join a cult. In a cult, she wouldn't have to think about anything. She'd just mindlessly take orders from some guy on a power trip. How hard could that be?

Now that she thought about it, it would probably be really freaking hard. She'd have to take orders from a man, and that really went against everything she believed in. Plus, all the cult members she'd ever seen on TV wore really bad shoes, and there was no way in hell she was giving up her Louboutins.

Were there any female cult leaders? She figured they'd be more understanding of her little shoe obsession. Then again, cult leader didn't seem like a job that a woman would want. After all, womankind didn't need to twist the truth or use the Bible to brainwash men—all it took was a bikini wax and some spiked heels.

She put the finishing touches on some creole cream cheese tarts. For the next few days, she was trying out new recipes and watching back seasons of *Food Network Star*. Being in front of the camera was more about personality than cooking. Yes, she needed to know how to bake, but she also needed to know how to schmooze the audience.

The front door opened, and she heard the now familiar footsteps followed by rumbling that heralded the arrival of Tre and his rolling suitcase. His apartment was being renovated, so he was staying with them for a while. Plus, he was helping get Harmony ready for her one and only shot at TV fame. Which she really hoped was going to be better than the last day of TV infamy had been. There was nothing quite like logging onto Twitter only to realize that her vagina was trending …

Surprisingly, Dalton had taken it pretty well, but she kept waiting for the other shoe to drop. And she still hadn't told him she loved him. Then again, he hadn't said anything about his feelings for her either, except that one time. A girl was only prepared to suffer so many tragedies in the space of two days before she lost her mind completely.

Her phone rang. She checked the screen. She couldn't help the smile. "I was just thinking about you."

"I'm always thinking about you." Dalton shuffled some papers on the other end. "Sorry about tonight. I'm swamped. The contractor just informed me that his head electrician just quit, which somehow translates to more work for me. The hotel rooms aren't ready, so now I need to find a place for a hundred and fifty-two people to stay." He shuffled more papers. "Sorry, I don't mean to dump on you."

"Poor baby. You can dump on me anytime." She missed him. It had been all of one day, but she still missed him. "Too bad you're so busy. I have some really effective relaxation techniques. They involved whipped cream and my tongue."

"Wow." He took a couple of deep breaths. "I am definitely going to take you up on that later."

"Work faster. I want to see you." Being with him was so easy.

"Okay, I'll be right there." Dalton's voice was muffled, like he was partially covering the phone. "Sorry, babe, I have to go. But I wanted you to know I was thinking about you, so I got you a present. It should be there soon."

"I love presents." Every girl did. But that wasn't why she was with him. She wanted him and not what he could buy for her.

"I miss you." He hung up.

Her phone buzzed with a text. It was from Dalton. "Love you."

She smiled to herself. She loved him too. Only she really should tell him in person first instead of via text.

Tre came into the room followed by his suitcase. "Whew, I've had a day. It's so good to be off of work. Can I tell you how much I hate rude people?" He parked his bag by the sofa and melted onto a barstool.

"I'll fix you a latte and you can tell me all about it." She put two tarts on a napkin and set it in front of him. "Tell me what you think."

"I think my ass is going to be the size of a billboard if I don't stop eating all of these carbs." He picked up a tart, sniffed it, and then bit into it. "Yum. These are really good... only, they need a little something like fresh raspberry or blackberry. The cream cheese is tart, ha ha, but it needs something just a bit acidic to push it over the edge into world's greatest."

Tre was a foodie, which totally worked in her favor.

"Good to know." Harmony made notes on her iPad.

He put the tart down. "Before I forget, the blackout brownies were a hit in first class, but the pear sandies received mixed reviews. Most people liked the flavor but thought they were a little dry."

Tre had used today's first-class cabin to taste test her recipes.

Harmony pulled up the pear sandies recipe and made some notes to add more moisture to the dough.

Her phone played the Funeral March, and Tre plucked it up and answered it. "Hello, Livinia, are you ready to apologize to your daughters yet?"

Even from across the four-foot-wide granite counter, Harmony could hear her mother screaming.

"We talked about this. You're welcome to call back when you're prepared to be civil and act like an adult instead of a spoiled child." Tre hung up the phone and looked at Harmony. "Is Lyric keeping her promise to not answer your mother's phone calls? Heath and I have let Livinia know in no uncertain terms that if she wants to yell at someone, she's welcome to call the two of us, but that all contact with her daughters must come through us or not at all."

"Have I told you lately that I love you?" Harmony had just about resigned herself to never having a loving relationship with her mother. It was okay... sort of. She fixed Tre a latte and placed it in front of him.

"Yes, but I can stand to hear it again." Tre sipped his latte and smiled at her over the rim. "Family is complicated. God knows mine is."

It broke Harmony's heart that Tre was estranged from his family. When he'd come out to them, they'd kicked him out with only the clothes on his back. They were Southern Baptist and ready to throw away their son just because he was gay. She wanted to run his parents over with her bakery delivery van.

In the last few days, Harmony had learned that family was made rather than born.

The doorbell rang.

"I'll get it." Tre stood and stretched.

"No, sit. You've been on your feet all day. I'll get it." Harmony had been on her feet all day too, but she hadn't spent the last ten hours dealing with the public. She opened the door to find a delivery man holding a black garment bag. "Can I help you?"

"I have a delivery for," the man looked down at the tag on the outside of the garment bag, "Harmony Wright."

"I'm Harmony. Thanks." She reached for the garment bag. She hadn't ordered anything. Roberto Modesto was written on the side. She couldn't afford Roberto Modesto—maybe resale, but they were few and far to come by.

"Can I get you to sign for it?" He held out a smartphone.

With her finger, she signed her name. "Thanks again."

"Have a good day, and enjoy." He waved as he turned and walked back to the nondescript white delivery van parked next to the mailbox.

She closed the door and walked into the kitchen. "Someone sent me something from Roberto Modesto. Was it you?"

"I love you more than my own sister, but if I scraped together enough money to buy something from Roberto Modesto, it would be for me." Tre clapped in excitement. "Open it. I can't wait to see it."

She pulled the zipper down, and a small white envelope fell to the floor. She leaned down and picked it up. After gently laying the bag on the back of a kitchen chair, she opened the card.

She read the card out loud. "I know you've been busy, so I took the liberty of picking out a dress for you to wear to the cocktail party. I hope it fits. I love you. Dalton."

"Ohhhh." She and Tre squealed like little girls—Tre because of the dress, and her because Dalton had just said that he loved her. In three words. For the first time. In a *card*. Well, the first time had been at his apartment when they were having sex, but she didn't know if that counted. Men said all kinds of things when they were inside a woman, and it wasn't like he'd repeated it since then. Before now. She wasn't sure the "love you" text counted, since it was only two words.

"Mr. Tall, Dark, and Yummy is so thoughtful." Tre's eyebrows bobbled up and down. "I want one." Harmony wasn't sure if he meant a Dalton or a Modesto. Maybe both.

He picked up the garment bag and pulled the dress out.

They both stood there speechless. It was royal-blue chiffon with a high collar, five rows of ruffles, and no discernable waist. It reminded Harmony of a ruffle-y bedsheet with two armholes. And not in a good way, if there even was a good way …

She looked at Tre and he looked at her.

"Maybe it's one of those dresses that looks better on." Tre sounded like he was trying to convince himself as much as her.

They walked to her bedroom, where she slipped out of her clothes and into the dress.

She turned around and Tre just stood there with his mouth hanging open.

"Say something." She pulled at the dress, trying to see what the designer and Dalton had both seen in this dress. Had Dalton really picked this out for her? Was this who he thought she should be? He'd wanted her to tone things down, but this was a little over-the-top toned down. It covered her from neck to toe, and if it had any shape at all, it would have been toga-esque.

Maybe Dalton hadn't picked it out at all. Maybe he'd just called the store and told them to pick out something for his girlfriend. But he didn't seem the type to have someone else pick out something so personal and important to him. And she felt like she was important to him—the man had told her he loved her.

Tre closed his mouth and then opened and then closed it again. "I've lost all respect for Roberto Modesto. And for your man." He stepped behind her and tugged on the back of the dress. "Maybe it's a knockoff."

"Does it really matter? It's terrible." Being conservatively dressed was one thing, but this went beyond anything Ann Taylor or Talbots could have dreamed up.

Tre pulled at the waist. "Maybe there's a belt or something." From behind, he pulled at the material, trying to give the dress some shape. That actually made it worse. "It's maternity meets matronly meets kitchen curtains. But hey, the color's really nice—it's perfect for your skin tone, and it makes your eyes even darker blue."

He tilted his head to the left and then to the right. "Maybe you have it on wrong?"

"I've been getting dressed for years. I'm pretty sure I know how to put on a gown."

"This isn't the week to be touting your dressing prowess." Tre shot her a one-eyebrow-up look.

He had a point. Harmony undid the single button at the back that was holding the dress closed and stepped out of it.

They spent the next five minutes looking for another way to put it on, but the armholes made it pretty clear how the dress was supposed to be worn.

"Could it be inside out?" Harm checked to make sure the tag was on the inside.

"Put it back on." Tre steepled his fingers in front of his mouth. "Maybe it got all discombobulated in transit. Put it on again, and maybe the ruffles will lie down. That's it. Too much handling made it extra poufy."

She slipped the dress back over her head.

Lyric walked into the room and looked Harmony up and down. "Why are you wearing a blue chiffon trash bag with ruffles?"

Wow, if Lyric—who thought high fashion was wearing her glittery red Converse court shoes—thought it was bad, the dress must be even worse than she'd thought.

"It looks like the dress Momma picked out for Great Aunt Lucille to be buried in. Except hers was prettier." Lyric sat down on the bed. "Great color, though."

"Yes, that blue is beautiful." Tre's nose screwed up. "I don't know about the dress." He sat down next to Lyric. "Dalton sent it over for her to wear at the cocktail party. It's Roberto Modesto."

"Is he a clothing designer?" Lyric asked.

Considering the dress, it was a fair question. Harmony looked down at the dress that had swallowed her whole. "He claims to be."

Lyric drew her knees up to her chest. "What if it's just a starting point? You know, like Dalton is having it completely custom made for you. This is like the foundation that they build from—or in this case take away." She sounded so hopeful. "Like when men have a suit custom made. It starts out as just fabric, and then there's a man with a tape measure around his neck who pins stuff and makes it into a suit."

Tre sighed like the weight of the world had been lifted from his shoulders. "That must be it. This is just the material and there's a dressmaker on their way here right now."

Everyone froze, waiting for the doorbell to ring. Nothing but dead air.

"They're probably stuck in traffic." Tre didn't sound convinced. "You have three days until the party. Plenty of time."

"You're right. No one in their right mind would take this for a dress." Harmony slipped out of it and back into her jeans and T-shirt. Carefully, she hung it up. The dressmaker would probably contact her soon. Until then, it would stay in her closet. There were a million and one other things she needed to worry about right now.

Tomorrow, a production team contracted by Food Network was headed over to measure the kitchen, take light readings, and do several other things Holly's assistant Max had mentioned but Harm couldn't remember. It was hard to believe that in five days, she would be Food Network's newest and hopefully brightest star.

"When's Dalton coming over tonight?" Tre yawned.

"He's not. He's working late into the night, and I need to pick out three recipes I'm planning on using in the pilot."

She couldn't decide what three items best showcased her talent.

"So exciting." Tre's grin morphed into another yawn. "I'm going to bed. I've been up for thirty-six hours straight. The life of a flight attendant isn't as glamorous as you've been led to believe." He stifled another yawn. "See y'all in the morning."

"Night, Tre." Lyric blew him a kiss.

Harmony gave him a brief hug. "Get some sleep."Harmony waited until he'd left the room to share the news about Momma. "He hung up on Momma again today." Harmony had been tempted to answer the phone one of the dozen times Momma had called today, but she'd made a promise to let Heath and Tre handle things. "I'm surprised she hasn't driven up here to yell at me in person."

"Don't you mean us?" Lyric raised her hand like she was volunteering for something. "She blames me for your downfall. I moved all the way to Hawaii to get away from her... remind me why I came back?"

"To be with the love of your life," Heath said from the doorway. "What did I miss?"

"Not much. Momma called to yell at Harm, but Tre took care of it. Dalton sent her a really ugly dress that we hope is just stage one in the dressmaking process, and Harm is force-feeding me baked goods." In three sentences, Lyric had just summed up Harm's entire day.

It felt like it should have taken at least a couple of paragraphs.

"Here's the big question, what's Harm making us for dinner?" Heath slid in behind his wife on the bed and massaged the muscles at her neck.

Seeing up close and personal how much Lyric and Heath truly cared for each other was nice. They were affectionate and considerate and laughed at themselves and each other. Momma and Daddy never laughed at all, or at least Daddy never laughed when Momma was around. It was good to see different versions of love.

She liked to think that she and Dalton might end up like Health and Lyric—with a loving relationship, and not the suck-the-fun-out-of-life marriage that Momma and Daddy seemed to have. She pulled the card out again and looked at the three little words at the bottom. *I love you.*

He loved her.

She was going to hold on to that for a very long time.

"Ever wonder why Daddy wanted to marry Momma in the first place?" She'd never really questioned her parents' marriage until she'd seen how different marriage was in the Montgomery house. True, they were newlyweds, but knowing Heath and Lyric, she didn't see them ever evolving into Momma and Daddy.

Lyric shook her head. "No."

She was too busy trying to figure out the origins of the universe to worry about personal relationships.

"I have. Who puts up with that? Was she always so horrible?" Heath continued to massage his wife's shoulders. He seemed to like touching Lyric, and he always found a way to have her close to him.

"I know they met in high school, but other than that, they don't really talk about how they met or what it was like dating." Harmony had always found it strange that other people's parents talked about how they met and had inside jokes about when they were dating, but her parents never joked around about anything.

Heath's hands stilled. "Wait a minute. When's their wedding anniversary?"

"April twentieth. This year they celebrated their thirty-third wedding anniversary." Harmony knew that because she'd made the cake.

"Interesting. Don't y'all turn thirty-three this year?" Heath beamed.

"Yes." Lyric nodded absently. No doubt her brain was already working on some mystery of the universe.

"Don't you see? They had to get married." Heath looked from Lyric to Harm and back again. "That explains so much."

"Wow, I never did the math." Harmony sat on the end of the bed. "Okay, I get why he married her, and I can see why he stayed, but what about after we left? Surely he isn't still putting up with Momma for us?"

If that was the case, her father was just plain crazy.

"I feel like I should feel sorry for him, but he's free to leave. Why doesn't he?" Harmony had always wondered.

"Growing up, that was one of my biggest fears. I was so scared that he'd leave me and you alone with Momma." Lyric was paying attention, even though she didn't look like it.

"Me too." It had been Harm's job to step between Momma and Lyric and keep her sister safe. Looking back on it now, she'd lost part of herself in taking the path of least resistance when it came to their mother. Well, no more. She'd love to have both of her parents in her life, but only on her terms.

Heath resumed the massage. "You know I adore you, Lyric, but if you suddenly morphed into Livinia, I'd have to think long and hard about running for the hills."

"If I suddenly morph into Livinia, I'm running for the hills. Or the nearest shotgun." Lyric shivered at the thought, or maybe at the movement of Heath's creative hands.

"That makes two of us," Harmony said. She'd spent more than enough of her life pretending to be a mini-Livinia. It was past time she started worrying about pleasing herself. She wanted a life with no regrets.

# Chapter 21

Harmony stared at herself in the full-length mirror on the back of her bathroom door. The Roberto Modesto dress was still huge and shapeless and terrible. No one had called about it or shown up to alter it in any way. The color was gorgeous, but everything else was a mess.

She wanted to ask Dalton about it, but at the same time, she didn't want to hurt his feelings. Even though he'd kind of hurt hers by putting her in this monstrosity. Obviously, he didn't trust her enough to dress herself for the Wranglers' cocktail party, so he'd sent this instead. While she admitted he might have a right to be afraid—the gold-lamé bikini would live on in the worst kind of infamy—she still felt like he could have talked to her about it instead of sending her the most ridiculous dress on the planet.

Then again, it wasn't like she'd seen much of him these last couple of days. She might have been super offended, thinking he'd told her he loved her and then bailed, but Heath hadn't been around much either. The Wranglers were gearing up for an exhibition game at Lasso Stadium, and it was all football, all the time over there. Or so she'd been told by both Dalton and Heath.

He had sent her flowers today, though, along with a super sweet card that once again ended with the words "I love you." Which had made the score 3-0 in the whole I love you game, and she was 0.

Considering she was pathologically allergic to losing, she figured it was past time for her to remedy the score. Tonight. Even if she looked like a giant blueberry wedding cake when she did it.

"It looks like we're on our own, Super Girl." Tre stood behind Harmony, pulling at the dress and trying to make something not-so-terrible out of something truly hideous. "I can't let you leave the house in that."

"Dalton obviously sees something that we don't. I have to wear it." She glanced at the clock on her phone, which was on the bathroom counter. "In less than an hour."

"Don't panic. I've got this." He pulled one hand out from behind his back and waggled a fresh roll of silver duct tape. "It worked for your sister."

"I can't imagine that I'm going to like this, but this dress can't get any worse." Her other choice was the blue chiffon trash bag swallowing her from neck to ankle.

"Take it off and let me see what I can do with it." He ripped off a long strip of duct tape. "God, I love that sound."

She slipped the dress off and grabbed a robe and slid it on over her bra and panties. For the evening, Lyric had bought her a way too expensive but beyond sexy Agent Provocateur bra and panty set.

Lyric had a thing for lingerie like Harmony had a thing for shoes. And hey, at least she'd look good when Dalton finally peeled that monstrosity off of her.

"Just try not to make it too sexy. Dalton wanted me to tone it down. I'm pretty sure that's why he sent me this dress." She ignored the anger that simmered under the hurt, then shoved the hurt down deep inside. Between the #HotGirlNeedsDate free-for-all and the vagina gone viral, she was willing to admit that maybe she really did need to chill. But it sucked that the man she was head over heels for was the one who had to tell her that.

And she got it. She did. He was worried that she would embarrass him tonight. Given her track record and her outrageous campaign to sully her reputation, she understood where he was coming from. But still, didn't he trust her enough to know that she wouldn't deliberately embarrass him? Especially now that they were a thing and this was his job. She knew how seriously he took his job. Of course she did. How could he not know that she'd never do anything to jeopardize that?

Clearly, he thought the real Harmony wasn't good enough. He wanted her to wear this dress, tone it down, and not embarrass him. It seemed that her only two choices in life were to be the good girl or to raise hell. Tonight, she would be the good girl because she loved him. And then the two of them were going to have a talk. One that settled the weird feeling inside of her once and for all. Because she hated second guessing him and hated even more that she was second guessing herself.

Tre turned the dress inside out and laid it down on the bed. "I have an idea, but I need you to trust me."

Harm shrugged. "It can't get any worse. I say go for it." She hugged him. "Besides, I do trust you."

"Go take a long bath and soak your cares away. I've got this." Tre gathered fabric here and there, coming up with a design. "I mixed you up a batch of margaritas. They're on the table next to the tub."

"I'll take you up on the dress and the margaritas." She closed the bathroom door, turned on the tub faucet, added a gardenia bath bomb, pinned up her hair, shrugged out of her clothes, and waded into warm bliss.

Reaching over, she turned on some heavy metal, poured herself a margarita, and let the world fall away.

Thirty minutes and two margaritas later, she emerged from the bathroom. The tequila had definitely taken the edge off. That must be why Momma drank so much Southern Comfort. Being perfect all of the time—especially when it mattered and wasn't a joke—was a huge weight to bear.

Tre looked up. "Almost finished." He ripped off more tape and smoothed it down over a gather he'd made with the fabric. Carefully, he turned the dress inside out and gently laid it on the bed.

Her hand came to her mouth. "Oh my God. How did you do that? It's beautiful."

The dress now had a V-neck that had the appearance of being a wrap dress, but only to the cinched waist. He'd gathered some of the extra material and fixed it to the left hip. The ruffles had been replaced by an asymmetrical hemline. It was very 1940s glam.

The floor was scattered with fabric scraps.

"I had to cut it, but beauty always comes at a cost." Tre watched her very carefully. "Are you mad?"

"Are you kidding? Now I can wear it and actually make eye contact with people. I can't wait to put it on. Not something I thought I'd ever say about that dress." She hugged him. "Why aren't you a designer?"

"You're sweet." He smoothed out a wrinkle in the fabric. "Don't be silly. I could never design clothes for a living."

"That's what everyone said about me and baking." Especially Momma, but Harmony had finally worn her down, and now Momma acted like she was the one who had encouraged Harm to open the bakery. And she lorded it over her with a Chanel-gloved fist. "I heard a lot of 'oh, it's a great hobby and you're so good at it, but there's no money in it.'" She shrugged. "They were partly right. I'm not going to make millions, but I make a decent living doing what I love."

"Correction, you haven't made millions yet, but Food Network wants you to. That's a really big deal." Tre inspected the dress for flaws. He brushed some stray threads away. "Besides, I haven't had an art class since elementary school. My parents didn't believe in frivolous things like art and music, or anything that was any fun."

"Can I just say that they sound like terrible people? I think we should give Cherry Cherry their address and have her run them over." Tre was such a fantastic person but his parents had thrown him away.

"I call shotgun." He raised his hand.

"You know you're our family now. All holidays will be spent under this roof. No exceptions." She pulled him in for a hug.

"Now, Super Girl, don't make me cry. I don't have time for a breakdown. I've got to get you ready for the ball." He tugged the clip out of her hair. "What were you thinking, up or down?"

"Before you Tre-ed the dress, I was going to wear it down so I could cover at least some of that blue balloon. Now I want it up so everyone can see an original Tre in all of its glory."

He hip-bumped her. "You're just flattering me so I'll make you a matching purse." He pointed to something on the bed. "Oops, already made one."

"Oh my God." She picked it up. The delicate fabric had been shaped into a drawstring bag. The silver duct tape behind it deepened the color. "How do you know how to do this?"

He was truly gifted.

"Just comes to me. Kinda like baking for you and math to Lyric. It's just in us." He beamed. He was so proud.

###

Twenty minutes before the party started, Dalton parked his Maserati in his reserved parking space and helped Harmony out of the car. "You are so beautiful. I knew that dress would flatter you."

She glanced away, which was so un-Harmony-like that it gave him pause. She wasn't exactly the shrinking violet type, so there had to be something else going on for her to be acting so weird.

He just wished he knew what it was.

He'd complimented her numerous times since he'd picked her up, and while she'd always responded to the compliment, something hadn't felt right. She'd been quiet, off, and he wasn't sure what the problem was. He only knew that he didn't like it.

Where was his Harmony? The woman with the big attitude and even bigger mouth? The one who teased him, who challenged him, who gave a million times better than she got? He missed her.

"You doing okay?" he asked as he escorted her toward the front door of the complex. "You're awfully quiet."

"I'm good. Just trying to tone things down a bit." Her eyes met his for the first time all night, and he felt the sizzle all the way to his bones. At least, until he caught the wariness behind her smile.

It hit him down low and had him pulling her aside only a few yards from the center's entrance.

"What's wrong?" she asked, nodding toward the lights sparkling right in front of them.

"That's what I want to ask you. Is everything okay?"

"Yeah, of course. Why?"

"I don't know. Something is telling me I'm missing something." He cupped her cheek, ran his thumb along the seam of her lips. "I know I've been busy these last few days and I'm sorry about that. Now that the opening is done, things should go back to normal."

"I know what it is to be wrapped up in a project, Dalton. I don't mind that you had to work."

"Are you sure about that?" He didn't know what else could be making her look so... reticent, for lack of a better word.

"Of course I'm sure."

She wrapped her arms around his neck and then pulled his head down to give him a kiss. For a few seconds, he let himself luxuriate in the feel of her mouth under his. In the fantasy of pulling her into the building and up to his office, where he could bury himself inside of her so deeply, so completely, that she could never get him out.

But duty called, and as he heard voices coming up the walkway behind him, he forced himself to pull away. The last thing the Wranglers' GM should be doing was all but devouring a woman on the front steps of the Lasso Center. No matter how much he wanted to do just that.

And reporters were going to be here tonight, along with a bunch of high-society types, and the last thing he wanted to do was make Harmony feel uncomfortable. Especially when he knew how guilty she still felt about everything that had happened with Lyric these last few days.

Reluctantly, he pulled away, disengaging himself one agonizing piece at a time. "Sorry, baby." He smoothed a hand over his hair to try to smooth out the furrows Harmony's fingers had caused . "We should probably tone it—"

"Down," she interrupted. "Yeah, I know. We don't want anyone watching to get the wrong idea."

She gave him a smile that didn't quite reach her eyes and then turned and marched into the building, leaving him no choice but to follow her.

He started to tell her that wasn't what he'd meant—he was proud as hell to have her on his arm, and he didn't give a shit if all of Fort Worth knew about it. Actually, he wanted them to know about it. But he didn't want to cause any more problems for Harmony either, and he knew she was trying to walk the straight and narrow until Food Network signed on definitively for *Badass Baker*.

Before he could say any of that, or so much as catch up to her, the team owner swooped down on him. Followed by one of the team's biggest donors. Followed by someone from ESPN. And no matter how much he wanted to talk to Harmony about whatever was going on in her head, he was there because he had a job to do. He'd never shirked his responsibilities in his life, and he wasn't about to start now. No matter how much he wanted to play hooky with a certain gorgeous blonde.

As Barry Lamont started to pull Dalton away for a little shoptalk, Dalton reached out, grabbed onto her hand. His eyes made a plea for understanding, and she must have gotten it, because she smiled—for real this time—and nodded for him to go.

"I won't be long," he promised her, dropping one last, quick kiss on her lips before she could turn away. "If I haven't told you this already tonight—"

"I know, I know. I'll be on my best behavior."

He frowned, unsure of where all this best-behavior and tone-it-down stuff was coming from. Surely she knew how much he loved it when Five-Alarm Harm came out to play? "That wasn't what I was going to say," he told her, dropping another kiss on her lips.

"No?" There was just a hint of a challenge in her lifted brow.

"No." He shook his head. "I was going to tell you that you're the most beautiful woman in the room."

She laughed, and it was the first genuine emotion she'd shown all night. "That might be more believable if my identical twin wasn't standing on the other side of the room."

"Is she?" he asked, going for old-school corny. "I hadn't noticed."

"Really? You hadn't noticed your former quarterback holding court over there with his wife?"

Dalton just grinned. "Why would I waste my time looking for Heath's ugly mug when I could spend my time looking at you?"

It was a corny line—totally embarrassing, really—and he waited for Harmony to call him on it. But when all she did was grin, a slight flush lighting up her cheeks, he couldn't help bending his head and kissing her one more time. To hell with being a modern man. He wanted the whole damn place to know that Five-Alarm Harm belonged to him.

# Chapter 22

Harm didn't get Dalton. She really didn't. While he'd spent half the night playing host at the most exclusive party of the year, he'd spent the other half at her side, introducing her to anyone and everyone who was important to the Wranglers' organization.

While she stood at his side he kept his arm around her waist, his body pressed to hers, as if he couldn't get enough of her. As if he wanted them to be as close as two people could get.

It would have gone a long way toward easing her mind about the two of them if he didn't dig his fingers into her side whenever anyone talked to them, like he was warning her to keep things on a steady keel. The argument could be made that Dalton just wanted to touch her, or that he had his arm around her as a way to claim her.

It didn't feel like that. It didn't feel like that at all, no matter how many times he complimented her that night. And he complimented her a lot—told her how beautiful she was, how much he thought the dress suited her, how much he appreciated all she was doing in her hostess duties. But somehow, it wasn't enough. Somehow, every word he said only made her feel more like he was using his comments as positive reinforcement as opposed to them actually being genuine.

Yes, she knew she was being paranoid and was probably assigning blame to him where there was none. But if he told her that he wanted her to tone it down, she was going to lose her shit completely.

And since that was the last thing either of them needed or wanted, she figured she'd better disentangle herself from him pretty damn quickly.

Of course, she should have known it wouldn't be that easy. The second she shrugged him off, he turned to her with a frown. "What's wrong? Are you okay?"

"I'm fine."

She knew she didn't sound fine, even before his eyes narrowed. "Are you sure?"

"Absolutely. I'm just going to mingle."

"We are mingling." He stopped her with a hand around her wrist.

"Yeah, well, I need some air. Is that all right with you?"

His eyes widened at her tone—and damn it, she really had used a tone, even though she hadn't meant to—and he dropped her hand like she had suddenly turned radioactive.

She started to apologize, but then the quick glance he darted around the room—like he wanted to make sure no one had heard her snap at him—set her off all over again. Suddenly, it took every ounce of willpower she had not to put her arm around the nearest man who wasn't Dalton—a man who she was pretty sure was the NFL commissioner—and proposition him just to piss Dalton off. Just to show him that he couldn't keep her tied down forever.

But this was the new Harm, the one who actually thought about the consequences of her actions. The one who was trying to get her own cooking show and knew she couldn't afford any bad press. The one who wanted Dalton to be proud to have her on his arm.

It was that last thing that had her slipping away without causing a scene, even as she cursed herself as a fool.

She spent the next hour dodging Dalton. She helped the servers clear dirty dishes, helped the caterer load trays, even opened a few bottles of champagne when the bartenders came under fire for being too slow.

Through it all, she was conscious of Dalton watching her, and conscious of the clock ticking down between them. She'd figured she had until the end of the party to get her shit together, but somewhere around eleven thirty, Dalton lost his patience. And his cool.

She'd turned her back on him for a just a minute to chat with a couple of the players—men so big they had tree trunks for necks. They were talking about why instant grits should be outlawed in every state south of the Mason-Dixon line, then suddenly he was there, his hand on the center of her back as he guided her toward the closest bank of elevators.

"Where are we going?" she asked, trying to pull away from him. "People are going to notice—"

"Fuck people. They can notice whatever the hell they want."

The anger in his voice annoyed her, considering she'd spent the last for hours doing her level best to be the best hostess he could possibly ask for. She'd been pleasant, helpful, and as nice as she could possibly be... even when several men made innuendoes to her. Even when one of the defensive linemen got grabby with her ass.

The elevator doors slid closed behind them, and Dalton turned on her. "What the hell is going on?"

"I don't know what you're talking about." She took a page out of her mother's book called ignore what you don't want to talk about. Now wasn't the time to have this out—she just wanted to get through the party and go home.

"Bullshit," he growled. When the elevator dinged at the top floor, he grabbed her elbow and started dragging her down the hallway to his office.

That kicked her anger up another notch. And even though she bit her tongue, even though she told herself to keep her shit dialed down, the second he all but pushed her into his office, she lost her shit completely.

"What the hell is wrong with me?" She was so damn tired of toning it down. "What the hell is wrong with you?"

She expected him to fire back—he was so pissed, his green eyes were blazing—but the second she snapped, he seemed to calm down, at least a little. He didn't fire back. Instead, he leaned against the nearest wall, crossed his arms over his mountain of a chest, and said, "I don't know. Why don't you enlighten me?"

"Oh, don't pull that smug male bullshit on me. Tonight isn't my fault."

"I never said it was."

"I've been on my best behavior."

"I know you have."

"I've put up with so much shit from so many men who thought it would be funny to ask if they could see my vagina in real life since they'd already seen it on TV, when all I really wanted to do was deck them."

"Why didn't you?"

Of all the things he could have said, that one hadn't occurred to her. "Excuse me?"

"I said, why didn't you deck them? I'd be pissed that you didn't get me to take care of it, since most of these guys are people I work with, but I know you don't need me for that shit. Five-Alarm Harm is more than capable of taking care of herself."

"Don't stand there and pretend you'd be okay if I shoved my foot up some guy's ass in the middle of your cocktail party." Because that was definitely *not* toning it down.

"If that guy was being an asshole to you, damn straight I would. If I'd heard someone talking to you like that I would have put my fist through his face, party be damned."

That gave her pause, but not for long. Because the double standard was such bullshit. "So I have to tone it down and be a good girl while you get to go all Neanderthal? In what world is that fair?"

"First off, you can go Neanderthal too, you know. I totally believe in equal opportunity for knuckle dragging. Second of all, when have I ever told you you had to be a good girl? I would never say that to you—I value my balls way too much to ever make that mistake."

"You've been telling me some variation of that all night. All week, really. 'Tone it down, Harmony. Maybe not so much, Harmony. Maybe if you just showed them a little less, Harmony.' And don't even get me started on the hideous dress you sent me."

"What the hell are you talking about?" Any trace of amusement was gone, and Dalton was in full-on defense mode. "I've never said any of those things to you, ever. I don't give a shit how wild you are—I like you wild, in case you haven't figured that out by now. I thought you liked the dress. It's fucking gorgeous on you."

"Now it is. After a friend of mine deconstructed the whole thing and came up with this out of that high-necked, overly frilly potato sack you sent me. Why would you do that, anyway? If you weren't interested in changing me, why the hell would you send me the ugliest, most modest, most ridiculous dress on the fucking planet?"

"I never saw the dress." He blurted the words out in a rush.

"What do you mean you never saw the dress?"

"When we were having dinner at Heath's house, you told me that shade of purplish blue was your favorite. So when I called Roberto Modesto and asked them to send you over a dress, I told them I wanted it to be that color. I never saw it." He paused, his eyes narrowing. "If you didn't like the damn thing, why the hell didn't you pick up the phone and tell me? We could have gotten you something else."

"Yeah, because that's what any normal woman does after her boyfriend sends her a present. She calls him up to complain about it. Especially after he's just asked her to tone down her personality to make life easier for him."

Dalton shoved his hands into his hair and pulled so hard she was afraid he was actually going to yank some hair out. "Since when have you been normal, Harm? I met you when you were standing in the middle of a bar wielding a pool stick like a weapon, and nothing in my life has been normal since then. So why the hell are you hiding behind what is right and normal when you never seemed to give a shit about either before?"

"Since you asked me to be someone I'm not." This was on him. Why was he mad at her?

"I never asked you for that. I *would* never ask you for that."

"You did ask me for that." She wanted to punch someone—namely him. "Otherwise, what was with all the tone-it-downs and the warnings about the press and the implication that you didn't want me to embarrass you?"

"Is that what you thought? That I was worried about you embarrassing me? Harmony, you're the one who said you really wanted to do this cooking show. I was just warning you about the press or whatever because I figured you'd want to know they were around. The last thing I want is to put you in some kind of awkward position where you end up losing the cooking show you've been dreaming about."

"Bullshit." The last of her defenses dropped. "You can't tell me you're okay with a woman who flashes her vagina on TV—even accidentally. You can't tell me you want a girlfriend who's first instinct it is to destroy your office when you lock her in for her own good. You sure as hell can't tell me that you want someone who starts brawls wherever she goes. I know you, Dalton. I know how much you value peace. I know how hard you've worked to make a normal life for yourself away from that ridiculous biker gang."

"Really? Because it seems to me that you don't know shit, Harmony." His anger had turned to a sad resignation.

"What's that supposed to mean?" She still couldn't figure out what he was upset about. She'd done everything he'd asked and more.

"It means that you're the one who's worried about all that stuff, not me."

"No—"

His eyes narrowed dangerously. "I let you talk, now you are damn well going to do the same for me. I love who you are. I love everything about you, including your ability to get into the most ridiculous situations. I also love how you brazen your way out of those situations. And how you have this great big heart that you hide behind a tough-girl bitchiness. And I absolutely adore the need you have to take care of everyone in your life, especially me. Thank God."

He raked his hands through his hair again. "So if you can't see that, if you can't see all of the wonderful things that make you who you are, then that's not on me. That's on you."

"You're just saying that because—"

"Why? Why would I just be saying anything like this if it wasn't true?" He wanted to touch her but shoved his hands in his pockets. "I love you, Harmony. I've told you that numerous times over the last few days, but you don't seem to believe me, and I can't quite figure out why that is." He thought about it for a second. "It occurs to me that you've never said it back. Not once have you given me any indication that you are actually in love with me."

"Don't you dare change the subject here—"

Dalton looked like he'd just lost a battle with himself. He moved closer, looping an arm around her waist and pulling her into the circle of his arms. "I'm not changing the subject. I'm broadening it, trying to get the big picture of what exactly is going on in your head."

"I do …"

"What?"

"I do, I …" She froze, unable to get the words out that she'd been planning on saying to him just that morning. It wasn't because she didn't love him—because she did. So much. Even more so after he'd just said all those things about her.

Something was holding her back. Something was making it impossible to say the three little words she could see he was so clearly dying to hear. The three little words she'd never said to a man that wasn't her father.

When they didn't come, he stepped back, the devastation on his face heartbreaking. "Is this going to be my fault too?" he wondered. "The fact that you don't love me? Or the fact that you can't trust me enough to say that you love me even though we both know it already?"

"I don't know."

"You don't... know?" Clearly, it wasn't the answer he'd been expecting to hear.

"I don't know why I can't say it. I just know that I can't." Even as she said the words, she could feel adrenaline hitting her system, and not in a good way. It was panic because this was the end. This whole conversation sounded final, when that was the last thing she'd expected—or wanted—it to be.

"Harmony." Dalton's voice dropped, became the low, soothing murmur that she loved so much. But it was too late. She was already freaking out. Already backpedaling across the carpet as fast as her Louboutins would carry her.

"I have to go." The walls were closing in on her. She had to get out... she had to get away.

"You have to go," he repeated blindly.

"I do. I have to—" She didn't have it in her to make up an excuse. All she knew was that she couldn't be there.

She couldn't look him in the eye when her heart was breaking wide open and her whole world was collapsing in on itself.

He went to take her hand, made a gesture like he was going to pull her into his arms. But she yanked back as hard as she could, and then she was running out of his office, running down the corridor, running as far from Dalton Mane as she could get.

Not because she didn't love him, but because she did. No matter what he'd said about loving her for who she was, he deserved so much more than a woman who was going to constantly put him—and his job—right in the middle of one disaster after another.

# Chapter 23

Harmony's big TV show day was finally here. And somehow, it didn't seem to matter to her at all.

It had been two days since she and Dalton had had their fight. Two days since he had sent her reeling by saying she didn't trust him. And two days since she hadn't been able to tell him she loved him.

She felt like shit. Her head hurt, her body ached, and her heart—her heart felt like it had gone fifteen rounds in *Cupcake Cage Match* and had lost every single one. And she didn't have a clue what to do about it.

She was about to do a television pilot—one that would make or break her professional dream—and she was so broken up, she could barely remember her own name let alone her famous brownie recipe.

But the show must go on. If she couldn't have Dalton, then maybe she could have this. It was a poor second place, but her life couldn't just stop because she had messed up the best thing that had ever happened to her.

Or at least, that was what she told herself as she sat in a makeup chair while Tre oversaw her hair and makeup. She'd chosen classic desserts with a twist, like carrot bread, cheesecake brownies, and coconut cream pie. She knew the recipes inside and out. She was ready for this. She could do this.

Tre leaned over and whispered, "Which of the outfits do you want to wear?"

She glanced at the bed and her heart sank. Nothing he'd chosen would work. She'd taken risks time after time since getting to Fort Worth, and what had it gotten her? Not a damn thing. In fact, it had cost her everything, had even paralyzed her when she needed to be most able to take a risk.

No, this was it. She was done trying to be herself, done trying to be anyone or anything but the woman her mother had raised. She needed to play it safe, take the path of least resistance. Dalton was wrong about that. The times she hadn't taken the path of least resistance were the only times when she'd screwed up. She was Ann Taylor and Talbots and pearl chokers. Hiding from it didn't change that fact. Admitting it to herself burned a hole in her soul, but if she'd learned anything in the last couple of days, it was that she couldn't run from who she was, because it always caught up to her.

"I'd like to go with the black Chanel suit." It had been her mother's and it cost her to admit that Livinia was right. Tasteful beat stylish every single day.

"Are you sure?" Tre glanced at the closet. "I thought you only kept that around to remind you of why you hate your mother."

As if she needed a reminder.

"Yes, I'm going with the suit." If she weren't all cried out, she'd weep for the stiff, hollow suit she was about to wear to make the world fall in love with her. That was all she had left. "The recipes I've decided on are all classics with a twist. I was hoping to do the same with the suit."

"Okay." Tre drew out the last syllable like he really didn't believe there was any twist that could make that suit anything but awful.

She could make this work. She had to.

Ten minutes later, she was dressed in the suit, her hair and makeup were flawless, and she couldn't have felt more empty.

Walking into the kitchen was like walking into a whole new world. Six giant Clegg lights spotlit the stove with its side-by-side double ovens. They also raised the temperature in the room a good five degrees. What seemed like miles and miles of black electrical wiring snaked over the floor. She barely made it into the kitchen on her floral Loubies without tripping. Even those, with their cheery neon flowers, couldn't cheer her up.

A production assistant named Annie had explained the process. It was much like *Cupcake Cage Match.* They would set up the shot, give her the five count, and click the clapperboard. After that it was go time. She was prepared to take several shots.

"There's our star." Holly picked her way over the wires to Harmony. She eyed the black suit and pearl choker but didn't say a word. "We're almost ready to start. You look like you're ready to take on the world."

Harmony faked a smile and nodded a little too manically. "I can't wait."

If only Dalton was here, but she knew better than to look around for him. It was over. He'd been very clear on that.

"Break a leg." Holly clapped her on the shoulder and then moved out of the shot.

"All quiet on set please," someone called.

Annie stepped in front of the camera. "In five, four, three …" She used her fingers for the two and one.

Harmony's mind went completely blank. She stood there for a full minute just staring into the camera. Finally, her voice came back to her. "Are we rolling?"

"Yes," the director bit out.

Harmony plastered a smile on her face and announced in an overly loud and sticky-sweet voice, "I'm Harmony Wright and welcome to *Badass Baker*."

She felt anything but badass.

She swept her arms out in front of her like she was revealing a new car to the audience on *The Price is Right*. "This is my kitchen."

After glancing down at her note cards, she grinned back at the camera. "Today I'm making Caribbean carrot bread, cheesecake brownies, and coconut cream pie."

She stood there grinning into the camera for what seemed like an eternity.

"Okay, let's begin."

Six hours later, her cheeks hurt from smiling, her feet hurt from wearing shoes no one could see, the pearl choker at her neck was choking the life out of her, and she'd only just noticed that she'd grated two fingernails in with the carrots, which explained why no one would touch the carrot bread. Deep in her soul, she knew she'd blown her shot at Food Network stardom.

As she sat at the kitchen table and watched the crew packing up, she couldn't help but notice the tension and defeat in the air. This wasn't merely a disaster, it was the death of her dream.

Heath put a hand on her shoulder, leaned down, and whispered, "What the hell was that?"

He'd been at work most of the day and had only caught the last thirty minutes.

"I don't know what you mean." Did she have to spell it out for him? She wasn't Food Network material.

"Yes, you do. I need to see you in my office... now." The look on his face told her he wasn't going to take no for an answer.

Normally, she'd fight him just for the sheer joy of fighting him, but today... today she just got up and followed him.

Like a gentleman, Heath waited for her to enter his office, and then he followed her in and slammed the door. "What in the holy hell just happened out there?"

"I'm done. I suck at this." She hated being pitiful, but that was exactly what she was.

"Stop feeling sorry for yourself, go change into something that doesn't look like Livinia, get your shit together, and go out there and do it again." He pointed in the general direction of the kitchen.

"I can't. They're almost gone." Harmony had never been this low in her life. If she went back to San Angelo, she'd have to deal with Momma, and she couldn't stay here forever. Especially now that Dalton had written her off. She didn't fit in anywhere, and she didn't have anywhere to go.

Heath took a knee in front of her. "You've been fighting your whole life, so what's changed in the last three days? I don't get it. You're Harmony freakin' Wright. You're always up for a challenge, and if you get to kick some ass then more's the better. Dalton dumped you. I get it, it sucks. But trust me, he's going to pay. No one screws with *my* family."

Good to know that Heath was going to make Dalton feel as low as she did now. If she were a better person, she'd tell Heath that Dalton wasn't at fault for their breakup. But she'd never claimed to be a good girl. That was half her problem.

"Right now, you need to decide who you are and what you want. Are you a quitter who mopes around looking like a beaten puppy? Or are you a badass baker who kicks ass and takes names? You're a fighter—hell, you fight not only your fights, but everyone else's too. You may drive me crazy, but the way you always stick up for the people you care about, no matter the odds, is one of the bravest things I've ever seen."

"Not anymore. I'm done and I'm tired." What was the point of fighting if it was never going to get her anywhere?

"Since when are you such a pussy?" He stood and threw his arms skyward. "Hell, you just took on an entire biker gang and an Okinawan hooker, and you're going to let a little cooking show bring you down?"

She opened her mouth to tell him that that had been different, but he had a point. Acting the whipped puppy wasn't making her any happier than being the total badass had.

Middle ground, Tre had told her. Find the middle ground, and she would be okay. With her clothes and with her life. But could she do that? She'd been one extreme or another her entire life—always trying to be who she thought she had to be on either end of the spectrum.

Was there a way to just stop trying so hard? A way to just be her, to just live her life the way she wanted to live it?

"You only get one life. Don't waste it pretending that you're happy. Freakin' go out there and be happy. Be the best Harmony I know you can be." Heath opened the door and yelled, "Tre!"

Tre appeared in the doorway with shot glasses in both hands. He thrust them at Harm. "Drink them both. You need them."

"She's going to go out there and badass bake something, so get her out of that funeral suit." Heath nodded at the suit. "We'll burn it later. Right now, I want to see some tattoos, some clothes that make a statement other than 'I'm a Livinia clone,' and I want to see some of that badass attitude that makes Lyric's and my life so crazy." His voice was iron-hard. "I'm going to stall the crew and charm them into unpacking everything again—I have a special smile reserved just for occasions like this, and it never fails. You go change. And when you walk into that kitchen again, I want your head in the game. I don't care if all you do is boil water, you better boil the best damn water of your life. Now move. You have fifteen minutes."

"Great motivational speech, Coach. No wonder you're the best offensive coordinator in the NFL." Lyric's look as she leaned against the open door said that it didn't matter that he hadn't yet coached a winning game. "I couldn't have said it better myself." She winked at him, then turned to Harmony. "Remember your favorite red sweater from tenth grade?"

"The one you donated to the orphanage in Mexico?" Harm didn't know what that had to do with badass baking.

"Yep, I spilled grape jelly all over it and threw it away." Lyric grinned. "Wanna know what I did to your favorite UGGs?"

"You little bitch. I knew you were lying about the orphanage. Who mails a single sweater to a mysterious orphanage? Lying about orphans—you're going to hell for that." Harmony could feel the adrenaline she thrived on seep into her bloodstream. "You were the one who stole my UGGs out of my locker during the homecoming dance?"

Lyric just grinned.

"What about the bleach on my brand-new black ballet flats in eighth grade?" Harm was starting to feel like herself.

"You stole all of the chocolate out of my Halloween candy." Lyric crossed her arms. "I really like Reese's Peanut Butter Cups."

Heath stepped in between the two sisters before things got ugly. "It's the quiet ones you need to worry about."

Tre grabbed Harm's arm and pulled her out of the room.

An hour later, Harmony lay on the kitchen island like a chanteuse on a grand piano, her fitted black leather pencil shirt outlining her hips and her clingy red lace crop top showing lots of ink.

She pointed a double-dark-chocolate-filled nine-millimeter cannoli directly at the camera and said, "That's how you take the gun and eat the cannoli. Until next time on *Badass Baker*, remember that a bad attitude is a beautiful thing."

"Cut." The director, Chaz, just stood there stunned.

The whole crew stared at her.

Harmony climbed down off the counter. They didn't like it. Disappointment should have had her questioning everything about herself, but she wasn't. She knew she'd nailed it. It didn't matter that Food Network wouldn't be producing *Badass Baker*. Harmony Wright had finally figured out who she was, and she wasn't about to change things now. Just like she wasn't going home to San Angelo with her tail between her legs and she wasn't moving in here permanently. She was going to open the Badass Bakery in downtown Fort Worth and give the whole world baking with attitude.

"Now that's what I'm talking about." Holly started clapping. One by one the entire crew put their hands together.

Chaz hugged her. "I hope you're ready for fame and fortune, because sweetheart, you're the best I've ever seen."

Relief swept through her, but as the whole room crowded around to congratulate her, she couldn't help looking for the one person that was missing. The one person that really mattered.

# Chapter 24

Dalton was miserable. Abso-freaking-lutely miserable. He'd been this way since Harmony had walked all over his heart in her silver Louboutins on Saturday night, and he had the sick feeling he was going to be like this for a long, long time.

It was a depressing thought, but he couldn't bring himself to care. Not when he'd finally got everything—and nothing—that he'd ever wanted and it had been perfect. And not when it had all been snatched away from him just as quickly.

Why the hell hadn't he checked on the dress? Why the hell hadn't he made sure it wasn't some ridiculous monstrosity that would send Harmony careening over an edge he hadn't even known she was close to? After their breakup fight—no, their nuclear implosion—the other night, he'd checked with Roberto Modesto to see what they'd delivered to her. The second he'd seen it, he'd known he'd screwed up, big time. Because if ever there was a dress designed to bring out Harmony's insecurities, that disaster had been it. The fact that it was the only dress in the entire store in the color he'd requested was neither here nor there.

He should have followed through, should have made sure it was okay. Maybe then she wouldn't have stomped all over his heart when he'd begged her to tell him that she loved him. Maybe then the two of them would still be together.

Shutting his computer off, he grabbed his briefcase and began the lonely trek to his car. Which would lead to the lonely trek home. Which would lead to a lonely night spent staring at the walls of his condo.

Goddammit, he missed Harmony.

She was a hurricane. A five-alarm fire. A disaster waiting to happen. He loved that about her. Sure, he'd promised himself that when he finally found the right woman, she would be normal and steady and ready to settle down. That had been total bullshit.

Harmony wasn't normal, and he was pretty sure she wouldn't settle down even when she was ninety. But she was steady as a rock. Loyal to a fault. And one hell of a fighter. Why the hell would he want someone normal when he could have her?

Except that was the kicker, wasn't it? He couldn't have her. Because underneath that balls-to-the-walls exterior, she was more insecure than he'd ever given her credit for. So insecure that she couldn't even risk telling him that she loved him.

Or at least, that was his story and he was sticking to it. Because the other alternative, the idea that she really didn't love him... that was hurl-himself-off-a-cliff territory.

So what if she couldn't say it? He knew she loved him. He saw it in her eyes when they made love, felt it in the way she always knew exactly what he needed and worked so hard to give it to him.

But that hadn't kept her from walking away Saturday night. Hadn't kept her from giving up on them like they were nothing. It had blown his mind as she'd walked away in the middle of the fight. Sure, he'd hit below the belt, but so had she. And Harmony had never quit on anything important in her life. So why the hell had she quit on them?

It blew his mind.

Maybe he should ask her. Maybe he should just drive over to Lyric and Heath's house and demand to see her. If he begged enough, surely Heath would relent. Plus, the man was his employee. If nothing else, he could threaten to saddle him with locker-room inspections and a mountain of paperwork if he wouldn't let Dalton see Harmony. She wasn't the only diabolical one in this relationship.

As he approached his car, he realized right away that he wasn't going to be driving it anywhere. At least not for a while. Harmony was draped across his hood like a model at a car show. She was lying on her side dressed in nothing but a red lace shirt and a tiny black miniskirt. she had one hand propped on her waist and the other handcuffed to the driver's side mirror.

Hot fucking damn. She hadn't given up on them. She was here. Whatever terms she dictated he might even agree to... maybe.

The world became bright and wonderful again.

He all but ran the rest of the way to the car.

How long she'd been out here like this? It was in the nineties. He'd told her it was too hot for leather.

Hopefully she hadn't been out here long, because he really hated the idea of any of the men he worked with seeing her like this. Not because he was embarrassed by her but because there was no way he wanted sexual fantasies of his woman going on in their heads. Anyone who saw Harmony like this would definitely have a fantasy or two.

She looked like a bondage wet dream come to life. If only she'd been posing on a motorcycle... maybe he could talk her into that later.

He smiled to himself.

She was his, all his. Even if she didn't know it yet.

He forced himself to slow down as he covered the last few feet between them. Harmony Wright was a badass, and any man who hoped to keep up with her needed to be just as big of a badass. Lucky for her, he'd had a lot of practice growing up.

"I gotta say," he said as he stepped up to the bumper of his Maserati, "you make one hell of a pretty hood ornament."

"A girl's gotta do what a girl's gotta do."

"That she does, though your John Wayne impression needs some work."

"Does the fact that I'm not wearing any underwear make up for the fact that I can't impersonate the Duke?" Her eyes licked up and down his body, and he knew she was imagining him minus the suit.

"I don't know. Why don't you spread your legs a little and let me take a look? Then I'll decide." He wanted to do so much more than take a look.

She narrowed her eyes. "I'm not that easy."

"Really? Because you're currently handcuffed to the roof of my car. I'm pretty sure that's the definition of easy." He loved that she didn't take things lying down—even though she was currently lying down.

"Yeah, well, maybe I'm sick of things being hard." The challenge in her eyes kicked his heart into overdrive.

He closed his eyes and said a prayer of thanksgiving to the universe for bringing this beautiful woman into his life. He hadn't even known he'd needed her, but now that she was here—now that she was his—he couldn't imagine his life without her. And he was going to make sure he never had to.

"Are you? Tired of hard things?" He stepped closer to the car—and to her. He still didn't touch her, though. He knew Harmony well enough to know that he'd lose a hand if he touched her before she was ready. While he would normally have been willing to take that risk, right now he had too much riding on this to risk screwing it up.

"I don't know." She gave him a sultry look. "Do you have anything hard to offer me?"

"How about the rest of my life? I'm sure it will have its hard moments." He'd never wanted anything or anyone this badly.

She inch-wormed her way into a sitting position. He had to give it to her. That leather kept sticking to the paint. If only he'd known she'd be handcuffing herself to his car, he'd have had the damn thing waxed.

Her eyes filled with tears.

"Shit, I'm sorry. I didn't mean to rush you—"

She shook her head. "I'm sorry. I was an idiot, too afraid—"

They both stuttered to a stop as their words ran over each other.

"You go first," he said, after pausing to take a shaky breath. He had so much riding on this—they had so much riding on it—that he was terrified of screwing up again.

She stared at him for long seconds, her beautiful blue eyes swimming with tears that broke his heart. He tried to keep his hands to himself, but he couldn't stand to see her look like that, so he reached out and cupped her cheek. Then stroked his thumb across the stray tear rolling silently down her face.

"Hey, it's okay," he told her. "I promise, it's all going to be okay."

"I'm an idiot," she said. "A stupid, insecure idiot, and I let old wounds ruin the best thing that ever happened to me."

"The baking show?"

"You, Dalton. You're the best thing that has ever happened to me in my life—the best thing that will ever happen—and I'm sorry. I'm so, so sorry I hurt you. So, so sorry I didn't trust you or myself enough to tell you the truth."

He'd never been anyone's best thing before, and he'd be lying if he said it didn't make him feel about ten feet tall. "So what is the truth?"

She looked away.

"Oh no, none of that." He put two fingers under her chin and pushed until she was once again looking into his eyes. "Don't hide from me."

"I won't. Not now and never again." She took a deep, shuddering breath. "I love you, Dalton. I love the way you don't let me get away with anything and the way you let me get away with everything. I love the way you think things through and the way you let me convince you to leap without looking. I love the way you love my cooking, and I love that you made the biggest disaster I've ever seen when you tried to cook for me. I love the way you hold me and I love the way you make love to me—"

"Don't you mean the way I fuck you?" he asked.

"No." She shook her head and all that shiny blonde hair of hers went everywhere. "I mean make love. Because that's what we do. That's what you taught me to do, and I would do anything to take back hurting you. I love you. I love you so, so—"

He slammed his mouth down onto hers before she could finish, but it didn't matter. He didn't need to hear any more. Because Harmony Wright loved him and he loved her right back. Nothing else mattered.

Her lips parted under his, and she kissed him back like he was the most important thing in the universe. Or maybe that was how he was kissing her, because God knew it was the truth.

He was breathless by the time he finally pulled back.

Harmony moaned a little, tried to follow him with her lips. He let her, for a second, then pulled away again.

"Why do you keep doing that?" Exasperation radiated off of her. "I want to kiss you."

"I want to do much more than kiss you."

She grinned. "Do tell."

"But first, I have a question to ask you."

Her eyes grew wide, and she looked like she was about to be hit by a truck. She smoothed down her skirt and then her hair. "Okay, I'm ready." Her swallow was audible.

He was a bastard for stringing her along like this, but that was what he and Harmony did. The fact that he would pay for it later only made it more exciting.

"Harmony Marie Wright?"

She put her free hand to her heart. "Yes?"

Gently, he took her free hand and got down on one knee. "Would you do me the honor of... telling me where the key to the handcuffs is?"

Her breath left her in a rush, and she lightly kicked him in the shoulder. "Bastard."

He grinned. "I'm sorry, but I really want to get laid and that handcuff seriously limits my options."

"You're pretty confident about getting laid. Who says this whole scenario is about sex? Can't a girl just handcuff herself to her boyfriend's car? Maybe I'm working on my tan." Harmony was the only girl in the world who could pull off nonchalance while handcuffed to the hood of a car.

"Oh, I'm so getting laid." He slid his hand up the inside of her thigh, stroked his fingers along her wet, bare sex. "You wouldn't have shown up here without underwear if I wasn't going to get laid."

"I don't know about that. It's hot and I'm wearing leather." She spread her legs a little, then moaned when he slipped a finger inside of her. "Get me off, and I'll tell you."

"Tell me, and I'll get you off."

"You don't really think I'm going to give in that easily, do you?"

He grinned. "I think you already have." He slipped a second finger inside of her, just to prove his point.

Harmony was no pushover, and it wasn't long before he was frantic to be inside of her. He circled her clit once, twice, a third time, then nearly came in his pants as she flew over the edge right there on the hood of his Maserati.

As he watched her fly, her beautiful face alight with pleasure and love and more joy than he'd ever seen, he promised himself that he was going to get the whole damn car bronzed.

Later, after she'd whispered the location of the key to the handcuffs into his ear and they were finally at home and tucked up safe in his bed, he rolled over and opened the drawer to his nightstand.

"Harmony, I've got another question to ask you." It was time to make an honest woman out of her.

"No."

"You mean no, you don't want to hear the question?" He wasn't taking no for an answer.

"I mean the answer to your question is no." She knitted her fingers behind her head and lay back like she didn't have a care in the world.

"You don't even know what I'm going to ask you." His hand trembled a little as he reached for the small, light-blue box that had been sitting in this drawer since the day after they first made love.

"It doesn't matter. After that stunt you pulled earlier, you'll be lucky if I ever say yes to anything you ask ever again."

"But I really want you to say yes to this question."

She snorted. "And I really want to ride a rocket ship to the moon, but I'm pretty sure that shit's not happening either."

Figuring they'd be there all day if he didn't take matters into his own hands, Dalton rolled over on top of her and kissed her until she didn't have enough breath left to form sounds, let alone actual sentences. And then he pressed the box into her hand.

Her eyes widened. "You better not be fucking with me again."

"I'm not."

"I mean it, Dalton. If you're messing with me, I will make your miserable for the rest of your life."

"I would expect nothing less." He kissed her again, this time soft and sweet and so, so perfect. "I'm not messing you," he whispered against her lips. "I swear."

She nodded and only then did she bring her hand up to see the small Tiffany's box he'd handed her. "Is this—"

"I love you, Harmony Marie Wright. I think I've loved you since the moment I laid eyes on you, and I know I'll love you until the last breath I take. Marry me."

Her eyes narrowed and she shoved against his chest until she could hitch up on her elbows. "That didn't sound like a question."

"What?"

"I said, that didn't sound like a question. And If you don't have a question, then I don't have an answer."

He laughed. He couldn't help himself. Harmony really was one of a kind. "I'm sorry, baby. Let me try this again. I love you, Harmony, and I want to spend the rest of my life making you the happiest woman alive. Please, please, please, will you marry me?"

She studied him for long seconds and then she raised one eyebrow. "I'll think about it." She rolled over and pulled the covers up to her chin.

He waited for her to say something else, to admit that she was just messing with him. But minutes ticked by, and she said nothing at all.

When he couldn't take it anymore, he rolled her back onto her back and demanded, "Seriously? That's all you're going to say?"

"Payback's a bitch." She busted out laughing.

"Harmony." The most important moment of his life, and she was messing with him. God, that's why he loved her so much.

"Dalton." She returned his staunch tone.

"You're going to marry me." He wasn't taking no for an answer.

"Am I?"

"Damn straight you are." There was only one thing left to do. He tickled her until she was writhing beneath him.

She laughed. "Okay."

"Okay what?"

"Okay, I'll marry you. What the hell else have I got to do?" She grinned up at him. "Besides, I hear you can get me fifty-yard-line seats to all of the Wranglers games."

He grabbed her hand and shoved his ring on her finger, where it belonged. Where he was determined it would stay for the rest of their lives.

And what do you know, it looked absolutely perfect.

# About the Authors

New York Times and USA Today Bestselling author **Tracy Wolff** collects books, English degrees and lipsticks and has been known to forget where—and sometimes who—she is when immersed in a great novel. At six she wrote her first short story—something with a rainbow and a prince—and at seven she forayed into the wonderful world of girls lit with her first Judy Blume novel. By ten she'd read everything in the young adult and classics sections of her local bookstore, so in desperation her mom started her on romance novels. And from the first page of the first book, Tracy knew she'd found her life-long love. Now an English professor at her local community college, she writes contemporary romance and erotic romance as Tracy Wolff, paranormal romance and urban fantasy as Tessa Adams and young adult novels as Tracy Deebs.

**Katie Graykowski** is an award winning author who likes sassy heroines, Mexican food, movies where lots of stuff gets blown up, and glitter nail polish. She lives on a hilltop outside of Austin, Texas where her home office has an excellent view of the Texas Hill Country. When she's not writing, she's scuba diving. Drop by her website www.katiegraykowski.com.